EARLY PRAISE FOR
HOW WE WERE BEFORE

"In an innovative and daring reimagining of the literary crime novel, author Jonathan Kravetz has created a killer novel-in-stories that explores the impact of a brutal home invasion upon the lives of the victims' surviving relatives and friends. Told with distinctive wit and wisdom, and caulked with flickers of the dead couple's romance, *How We Were Before* is the rare work that glides with grace, both forward and backward, through time and emotion. The murdered Blythes might easily be our own neighbors. They might easily be ourselves. Kravetz has created a world that is panoramic and yet touches all too close to home. A brilliant debut."

— JACOB M. APPEL, AUTHOR OF
*MILLARD SALTER'S LAST DAY* AND MANY
OTHER BOOKS OF FICTION AND NON-
FICTION

"Death, any death, has a profound ripple effect, but none more than murder. If it takes a village to raise a child, it takes much more than that to process violent, senseless murders. *How We Were Before,* Jonathan Kravetz's beautifully crafted collection of interconnected stories focusing on the citizens of a small town where just such murders occur, illustrates how far-reaching and profound such a violent act can be. It is the proverbial butterfly flapping its wings, changing the world continents away."

— CHARLES SALZBERG, TWICE NOMINATED SHAMUS AWARD AUTHOR OF *DEVIL IN THE HOLE* AND *SECOND STORY MAN*

"*How We Were Before* is a beautiful collection of connected stories about well-drawn characters who are living in the aftermath of a horrific town event that affects all their lives. Jonathan Kravetz writes beautifully about themes and realities that transcend class and political barriers, [reminding] us of what we all have in common, what we have to lose, and what can keep us going. This is a wise and poignant book."

— ALICE ELLIOTT DARK, AUTHOR OF *FELLOWSHIP POINT* AND *IN THE GLOAMING* ASSOCIATE PROFESSOR, RUTGERS-NEWARK HTTPS:// ALICEELLIOTTDARK.COM HTTPS:// LINKTREE/ALICEELLIOTTDARK

"Every murder is a sudden, violent tear in the fabric of humanity with ripple effects that never end. With subtle virtuosity, Kravetz traces these effects in the immediate aftermath of a murder in a small town. *How We Were Before* is, therefore, only incidentally a murder story. It is a story, first and foremost, about the human condition."

— MARK GOLDBLATT, AUTHOR OF THE
BESTSELLING CHILDREN'S BOOKS,
*TWERP* AND *FINDING THE WORM* AS
WELL AS MANY BOOKS OF NON-
FICTION INCLUDING *RIGHT TOOL FOR
THE JOB: A MEMOIR OF MANLY
CONCERNS*

"Jonathan Kravetz reveals the emotional damage left in the aftermath of violence to show how it changes — magnifies — every passion and thought."

— BENJAMIN B. WHITE, AUTHOR OF
*CONLEY BOTTOM: A POEMOIR, THE
RECON TRILOGY +1,* AND *ALWAYS READY:
POEMS FROM A LIFE IN THE U.S. COAST
GUARD*

"Jonathan Kravetz's *How We Were Before* is a novel that explores the aftermath and aftershocks of an act of senseless violence. Moving back and forth in time over a span of nearly fifty years and offering the perspectives of a wide range of characters, this book is both immersive and deeply felt. And it pays tribute to the griefs, small and large, that define and shape our lives."

— NICOLE COOLEY, AUTHOR OF *GIRL AFTER GIRL AFTER GIRL* AND *OF MARRIAGE*

# HOW WE WERE BEFORE

JONATHAN KRAVETZ

RUNNING WILD

RUNNING WILD PRESS

# CONTENTS

"Conch" first appeared in *Cardinal Sins*, Fall 2017.
"Black and White" first appeared in *Narrative Northeast*,
Winter 2019 under the title, "The Garbage Man."
"Diva" first appeared in *The Opiate Magazine*, Winter 2019.
"Weekly" first appeared in *The Furious Gazelle*, May 2020.

*For Claire.*

# PROLOGUE

## JANUARY 3, 1966

P ete rolled down the window, tossed a half-smoked cigarette onto the highway, and then took a deep breath. The winter wind chafed his cheeks and the rushing air deafened him. For the first time in his life, at twenty-one years old, he felt free. No drunken father to avoid. No mother to console. No boss telling him to sell more policies. No New Haven. His life was now the humming sound of tires racing over the highway. He'd drive on to Boston, find a place to sleep before midnight, and decide where to go the next day. Back on the road most likely. He'd heard there were jobs on fishing boats in Maine, but he wasn't worried about money. Not yet. He patted the envelope full of cash he'd lifted from the bottom drawer of his father's bureau—a small victory.

A worn billboard caught his attention: "BENFIELD DINER. FINE LOCAL DINING. NEXT EXIT." There was a picture of a large plate of sliced turkey with gravy and potatoes. His stomach growled. He hadn't thought much about food, but he liked knowing there was someplace he could stop, flip open a menu, and have anything he wanted.

*He rolled the window up and rubbed his hands together for warmth. The other cars on the highway sped past him as he slowed down and aimed his Pontiac Grand Prix for the off-ramp.*

# JANUARY 2014

## WEEKLY

**M**att pushes open the rear door to the office and creeps across the floor in torn jeans and a flannel shirt. He wipes his nose on his sleeve and peers through the square hole separating the front office from editorial. He clenches his teeth against the bitter air but can't discern any sounds except the light tapping of a keyboard and the radiator clicking. Then a woman's voice and then another buzz like a radio going in and out of tune. Leaning closer, he attempts to translate the sounds into language, but can only make out hard K's and soft S's. One of them is Carol, his editor, and the other is Mary Ellen, the twenty-five-year-old receptionist. His girlfriend. Maybe they're talking about the weather or the details of an important delivery, but Matt doubts it; when he'd seen them through the window a few moments before, Mary Ellen's grave expression had suggested a more personal conversation. A chair scrapes against wood and Matt abruptly steps backwards, careens over Carol's desk, and crashes into her chair, spilling it on its side. He rushes to his own desk and turns on his computer. It's coming to life when he feels a tap on his shoulder.

"When'd you get in?" Carol comes around to the front of his desk.

"A few minutes ago."

"You came in the back?" He shrugs and presses his palms into his desk to stand up, trying to think of an excuse.

Carol says, "It's okay, I'm just checking in."

"Everything's fine with me," he says. "How are you?"

"Tony snored again last night so I'm pretty tired."

She doesn't look tired, Matt thinks. At forty-four she could easily pass for thirty-four.

"Otherwise, I'm fine," she adds.

"Good, good." He smiles and it feels fake. He stops smiling and that feels worse. "Where were you a second ago?" He says just to break the silence.

"Out front."

"Chatting with Mary Ellen?"

"You know. Getting the day started."

"How's she doing?"

Carol smiles knowingly. She's always been able to read his mind. It's one of many qualities that makes her an ideal editor for him. "Why don't you ask her yourself?"

"I will in a sec." He points to his smartphone. "Gotta prep for the Lawson interview first."

"You saw the crime scene photos?" She points to a folder on his desk.

"Yes."

"And you're still up for doing the story? It's pretty grim." Matt shuffles through the pictures, then presses them face-down on his desk. Carol puts a hand on his shoulder and says, "I can always give it to Jake if you want."

Matt has worked at the weekly for five years, which is longer than any reporter has lasted by nearly eighteen months, and the Lawson murder trial is a chance to write a front-page story that could catch the attention of a bigger paper; it's a juicy bit of news that for once isn't coverage of the latest school committee meeting or a profile of the new pizza joint on Marlboro Street. "No. I want this one."

"Good boy." Carol taps the top of his computer monitor. "Any luck with the daughters?"

"Samantha politely declined." Matt smiles slyly. "Shelby told me where I can stick it."

Carol sighs. "Lovely."

"But I'm calling Mrs. Lawson right now."

"Good. Very good."

An unused moment passes, but they're never uncomfortable with each other. She says, "Speaking of Jake. You see him?"

"Not yet." He's the only other reporter at the paper, a twenty-three-year-old Bowdoin grad.

"Well, that's par for the course." He's been coming in later every day for about two weeks. "I'll finish up a few things and wait to have a little chat with him."

"You do that," he says and watches Carol stroll back to her desk. She pauses a moment to examine her overturned chair and looks back at Matt—hers are the only eyes he's ever seen twinkle.

Matt rests his fingers on his desk phone, steels himself, and punches the numbers.

"Hello. My name is Matt Foster from the Benfield News. I have an appointment to speak with Mrs. Lawson this morning."

There's a puff of air on the other end, as though someone is about to speak, but then the line goes dead. He stares at the phone as if this will revive it, and then calls again. This time it goes directly to voicemail. This is bad.

Carol is on a call herself and hasn't noticed. Matt takes a

cleansing breath and makes a decision. He walks casually around the sports and proofreading desks and past his editor.

Mary Ellen is the only one in the front office. Her blonde hair tumbles over her white wool sweater.

*Casual. Be casual.* "Hi, hon."

"Hi, Matt."

"I'm off for the Lawson interview."

"In person?"

"Yep."

She flicks her eyes up at him. "Are you sure you can handle this, Matty?"

"Of course!"

She hesitates for a brief but palpable moment, and then smiles a bit too enthusiastically. "Well, great!" Another smile. "If you think you're ready, then I'm excited for you."

Why does she have to doubt him? "Yeah, well, I have to learn to deal with this kind of story if I'm gonna move up the ladder." A week ago, he had asked her if she ever thought of marriage. It was a roundabout way of proposing; the direct approach never worked with Mary Ellen. Ideas had to work their way into her mind slowly, like acorns that grow into sturdy oaks. Now, he searches her face for evidence that the prospect of him succeeding had inched her closer to saying yes.

"Good for you," she says. "I'm sure it'll be an amazing interview."

"I don't think *amazing* is exactly the right word." Mrs. Lawson's son had been arrested for murdering an elderly couple in their sleep. He'd broken into their home and grabbed a bunch of jewelry but was too tweaked out to notice the wedding ring on the dead woman—the only piece of any value.

"Of course not 'amazing.' Christ. You know what I mean."

"Sorry," Matt says. Mary Ellen is sensitive to criticism, and he shouldn't have corrected her. "I gotta learn to keep the editor brain in my back pocket." He drops his eyes to avoid her glare and notices the framed photo of the two of them over Christmas. They're grinning in front of the tree at Rockefeller Center in New York City. "Anyway, I should get back to work," he says.

"Yeah. I should too."

He mutters to himself as he walks across Main Street to his Toyota Camry.

He thinks about the New York trip as he winds the car through narrow roads. They'd been dating a year at that point and Matt had researched the best places to eat and drink and all the sites worth seeing. On the bus trip back Mary Ellen had leaned over to him and said, "You really know a lot about New York." She idealized the city and had vivid dreams of the successes she would have on Broadway, often talking to Matt about her favorite musicals. But in reality, Mary Ellen wasn't sure she could risk her life on such a tenuous career. Her mother wanted her to pursue marketing, which she'd majored in at Stonehill College. Matt had resisted the urge to reply with a self-deprecating comment about how it didn't take a genius to Google "New York City." Instead, he tried to shift his focus to the flowery smell of her hair as she rested her head on his shoulder. They must have looked like the perfect couple. Mary Ellen took Matt's hand. "We could move there together," she'd whispered. "You're the only one who really believes in me."

Mrs. Lawson lives alone in a black–and–white painted ranch-style house on North Street. Matt parks on Forest Drive, just down the way because there's an old Dodge Journey occupying her driveway. A January breeze kicks up and the barren branches shiver. The lawn and shrubs, even the white pine trees, are well maintained. It could be anyone's house in normal suburbia.

How had a murderer grown up inside these walls? As Matt reaches out for the doorbell, a rustling sound coming from the bushes to his right startles him. A thin raccoon limps out and makes eye contact with him.

"Get away from here! Scoot."

The animal scampers as best it can across the lawn toward the road. Matt holds his breath, but the raccoon makes it across safely and then hobbles into the woods. Matt is annoyed by the distraction. He'd already psyched himself up for the confrontation with Mrs. Lawson, imagining her at the door, angry. He feels off balance now when the door swings open and she stands there, hands on her hips, wearing a white terry cloth bathrobe. In the photos Matt had seen of Mrs. Lawson, she had looked pale and tired. The dark circles under her eyes and her slumped posture had left Matt expecting someone in her fifties, so he's thrown when he's greeted by an olive-skinned woman who couldn't be a day over forty. He can't help noticing the shape of her body under the snug-fitting robe.

"You're that reporter from the Benfield News, right?" She looks him up and down. "You're cute."

"I'm Matt Foster." *Cute?*

"I'm sorry about this morning. My phone died and, well, I disconnected my landline."

"No problem. I figured it was something like that."

"Do you want to come in?"

"Thank you." He notices her slender arm as she motions him forward. She scratches her throat and leads him into the kitchen.

He sits on a stool as she crosses to the sink to fill a glass with water for him. He'd expected to find chaos, but everything is in its place: the island in the center with wooden placemats and silver salt and pepper shakers, the fireplace in the adjacent living room, the large LCD TV attached to the wall next to a shelf of books. Even the ceramic tile countertops shimmer.

He pulls out his digital tape recorder. "You don't mind if I get this on the record, do you?"

"How old are you?" She hands him the glass.

"What does that have to do with anything?" The water tastes rusty.

"I'm curious, kiddo. No need to get defensive."

"I'm not defensive." He knows he *is* defensive about this subject, however. "I'm twenty-nine."

She takes a hard swallow from a drink that is definitely not water, pursing her lips together to force it down. "Sure, you can record this. But tell me what you want exactly. How can I help you?"

He clicks the recorder on. "I was hoping you could tell your side of the story."

"That's a funny way to put it."

"What do you mean?"

"That my son killing Pete and Tara is a story. Like it's entertaining, like a TV show."

"So you think he's guilty?"

"Of course he's guilty. He shot them with that pistol his father bought him last year."

This isn't an interview. It's a damned headline. *Lawson Mom: He Did It!* "Did Billy tell you all this?"

"He sure did."

He can't believe what she's saying. "Gosh, that's terrible. I'm really sorry, Mrs. Lawson." He downs the rest of his rusty water.

"You're sorry?"

"Yes."

She takes another sip of her drink and then turns to him.

Her eyes are bloodshot and slightly unfocused. "You mean you feel bad for me?"

"I shouldn't have said anything."

"It's okay. Really." She rises and leans over to take his glass. Her bathrobe opens and Matt catches a flash of appealing thigh and the curve of her calf. "Do you want something stronger to drink?"

"It would be a little unprofessional."

But she hands him a glass of some brown liquid anyway. It burns going down.

"Now you're a real reporter," she says.

He takes another sip and coughs. "Why do you think he did it, Mrs. Lawson?"

"Money. Everyone knows he was a junkie."

Another one for the headlines: *Mother Calls Son a Junkie.* "But why *kill* them?"

"I don't know."

"He didn't say?"

"No."

"But why do you think?"

She considers him. "You might be the last innocent man on planet Earth." Before he can explain that she's wrong about him she says, "Why do people do anything?" She leans closer, only an inch, but the room suddenly feels hotter.

He fidgets nervously. "I should get some background information from you if that's okay."

"Sure, like what?" Another inch closer.

He buries his gaze in his notebook. "Where were you born?"

"Lansing. That's in Michigan."

"How'd you end up in Massachusetts?"

"Billy's father. We got married and he got a job in Boston.

Selling pharmaceuticals, which, when you think about it, is ironic. He lives in Tennessee now."

"What happened?"

She shrugs. "After a few years, we didn't talk anymore. Except when we were fighting."

"I'm sorry."

"It is what it is. I was born to be a statistic."

"I'm really sorry."

"You apologize a lot for a reporter. Are you supposed to do that?"

"No, you're right. I'm—" He stops the phrase before it passes his lips, but the thought rings in his head.

Matt watches as her face softens. "How do you feel, Mrs. Lawson, about what happened?"

"How do I feel?" She sighs languorously. "What do you think? I feel like shit." She puts her drink down and wipes a damp stain from under her eye.

Matt isn't sure how to respond. He pulls a tissue from the box on the island countertop and hands it to her. "The world is crazy."

She dabs her eyes. "It sure is."

He looks around the room, notices the bland green and yellow wallpaper, the photographs of her son wearing his Little League uniform. "I should leave you alone."

"No, wait." She takes a soft step toward him. "Don't go."

"I don't want to be any more trouble."

She touches his arm. Her fingers are long and thin, but her fingernails are bitten down to the nub. "Stay," she says. "Stay with me."

Her perfume is not as sweet as Mary Ellen's; it's almost bitter. In fact, everything about Mrs. Lawson seems different from his girlfriend: straight dark hair; black, intense eyes; faint laugh lines that have just begun to show. He wants to put his lips over her small mouth. But he's a reporter. He shouldn't. He's here for the story. "Mrs. Lawson—"

"I like talking to you," she says. "You're sweet."

He pulls away.

"I'm sorry," he says. "But I really should get going."

Her eyes narrow, but otherwise her expression doesn't change. "Fine. Whatever."

As he steps outside, he notices a pile of wadded up wrappers and scraps of food behind the shrubs.

"You shouldn't throw food away like that. You're creating a real pest problem."

From behind the screen door she replies, "That thing would starve to death without me."

"The raccoon? You're throwing that stuff there on purpose?"

"I'm not a monster." She cinches her bathrobe closed at the top. "I care about things."

"I know. I'm very sorry." There's nothing wrong with saying it when he really feels it. "Thanks for your time."

"Wait," she says sharply just as he begins to turn away. "You can't print anything I've told you today, Matt Foster of the Benfield News."

"What are you talking about? We agreed this was on the record. This interview will be part of a larger story that's going to appear in this week's—"

"I was drunk and didn't mean to suggest that my son—" She tilts her head so they make eye contact and something inside him rips in half. "Please," she begs him. "Please don't print any of this."


Mary Ellen hops up when he returns to the office. "How'd the interview go?"

"It went well."

"Really?" She tugs anxiously at a strand of hair.

"It couldn't have gone better."

"Great!" She seems to relax. "We should celebrate tonight!"

"Definitely," he says. "We definitely should."

He rushes past her before she can lean in for a kiss. He turns his computer on at his desk, taps a few stray keys, and then rests his head on the keyboard. Heavy footsteps approach, but he doesn't budge.

"Tough interview?" Carol is tapping a pencil against her head. "You doing all right?"

He's bursting to tell her that he has a scoop, but part of him wishes Mrs. Lawson hadn't admitted she believed her son was guilty. He pictures the desperation in the woman's eyes. Why does his job come down to these difficult ethical problems? He surprises himself when he says, "She didn't have anything new to say, I'm afraid." He jams his fist into his thigh and lifts his head. "But I'm fine, trust me."

"Okay." Carol uses the pencil to search for what must be a ferocious itch somewhere on her back. "It's a little disappointing, but it was always a Hail Mary that she'd offer you more than she's been giving. Write what you have; it's still page one."

Matt rotates himself in his chair to look up at his boss. "Do you think I'm naïve?"

"What?"

"You can tell me if I'm an idiot or whatever."

"I'm not sure what you want me to say here, Matt."

"How else am I going to know if I'm cut out to be a reporter?"

She shrugs. "You're a good person, Matt."

Matt isn't sure what that means. He gestures to his computer. "I should really get back to work."

"Great. I won't keep you."


He goes home early, takes a nap, and dreams he's a train engineer. He wakes and thinks about the Freudian implications —all that plunging into train tunnels—and an image of Mrs. Lawson's thigh and calf flickers repeatedly in his mind. He gets up and begins preparing hamburgers and mashed potatoes for dinner. He wants to cry but won't let himself.

Mary Ellen comes over at seven and they sit across the table from each other. She's wearing a green sweater with a knitted bouquet of flowers over her heart.

She considers the hamburger. "There's no pepper in here, right?"

"No pepper."

"Because my acid reflux—"

"There's no pepper, Mary Ellen."

The sound of their chewing fills the room for several minutes.

Matt is the first to speak. "I've been thinking a lot this week." He pushes the potatoes around his plate. "Is it okay if we talk?"

"If this is about getting married, then please don't. I still need some time."

If she keeps putting him off like this, she'll eventually decide she doesn't want him. "But are you really thinking about this? Because—"

She's holding her fork inches above her plate as if she's trying to bend it with her mind. "What do you mean? Of course, I'm *really* thinking about it. I think about it constantly. It's eating my guts away."

*You can't put the genie back in the bottle.* It's the first time he's ever really understood that expression. "Maybe that's true, but I'm afraid you're going to end up moving to New York to pursue acting and that will be that. You'll date a hundred guys and end up marrying some edgy hipster with a beard and leather jacket and we won't talk anymore."

"A beard? What does that have to do with anything? What's wrong with you?"

"Ever since I popped the question, you seem miles away."

She hesitates. "I'm not sure what I want with my life. New York maybe. I don't know." She's still staring at the fork. He wouldn't be surprised if it begins to melt.

"Why," he starts and stops. "Why are you even with me?"

"What kind of question is that?"

"We used to have fun, right?

"Of course." He waits. Finally, she says, "I felt like we were going somewhere together. It was exciting. Now, I don't know. You seem stuck." She stares at the utensil. "And maybe I'm stuck too."

"I'm not stuck. I don't want to jump at the wrong opportunity."

"Something happened with that interview, didn't it? You couldn't deal with Mrs. Lawson. She scared you or something."

"What?" He rests his fist on the table. "Jesus, Mary Ellen. I just want a teammate. Someone who'll be on my side no matter what."

"No matter what?" Her eyes meet his.

"Yes."

She glowers. "That's not fair."

"It's fair," he replies. "It's very fucking fair."

She puts the fork down and clamps both hands around the edge of the table. "Maybe this isn't working anymore. I don't want to be sad all the time." She swivels, shoulders back, and walks to the door. She gathers her coat and leaves his apartment without looking back.

Matt can't sleep that night. He gets out of bed at five-thirty and drives around town, finally stopping at a Dunkin' Donuts for a coffee and bagel. He naps in the back seat of his Camry, running the engine to keep the car warm, and then drives to North Street. He parks on the side of the road, gets out, and looks up at Mrs. Lawson's house. It's dark except for a dim night light illuminating the front foyer. He sits on the hood of the car, clutches a chocolate candy bar with gloved hands, and begins slowly pecking away at it.

He is glad to see Mary Ellen's chair empty when he skulks into the office at 10 a.m., late for the first time since he started working at the paper. Jake isn't in either—the fucker—but before Matt can pass by Carol's desk, she stops him.

"I have something to discuss with you."

"What?"

"Jake is leaving the paper."

"Really?"

"He got another gig. Somewhere in Rhode Island."

He bites down on his upper lip. "Jesus. That didn't take long."

"The kid is hungry. What can you say?"

"Right." He unzips his parka. "What *can* you say?"

He spends the day polishing the Lawson murder trial story, but he's restless and the words on the screen seem feeble to his ear: *murder investigators...crept into the house...motives for murder unknown...*

At three o'clock he goes across the street to Center Bar and Grill. The TV is showing highlights from the Celtics game the prior night. After two beers, he drives with the window down to Mrs. Lawson's. The freezing air whips through the car and bites at his ears.

Standing on her front stoop, he notices for the first time the paint peeling from the shutters, the greasy stains on the window. He looks into the shrubs, but either the raccoon is hiding or it's rummaging somewhere else. He pictures Mrs. Lawson sitting out in the morning eating breakfast burritos and tossing away tomatoes and peppers and wrappers.

She answers the door before he knocks. "Hi there, Matt. You look nice."

"Do I?" He looks himself over and can't see anything appealing.

She exhales a cold puff of air, which he takes to mean she's exasperated with him. "Come inside."

They stand in her kitchen. She's wearing jeans and a white blouse this time.

"How are you doing, Mrs. Lawson?"

"Will you call me Peggy?"

"Okay." On the drive over he knew what he was going to say, but now feels unsure. He wanders into the living room. "You have a lot of records." He picks one up. It's *This One's for You* by Barry Manilow.

"I guess I do."

"Not many people have records anymore."

"Do you like them?"

"I've heard the quality is better."

"Oh, it is." She puts the record on, and it sounds as if there's a live band playing somewhere inside the room.

"That's incredible."

"New technology doesn't always mean progress."

"I see what you mean."

They stand side by side, listening.

"Can I get you a glass of water or something?"

"Sure," he says.

"Or wine?"

"That'd be great."

She pours. "Cheers," she says, and they drink.

He sits at the kitchen island running his hand along the edge of his glass. "Do you ever think about moving someplace exciting? New York, for example."

"I used to. Not so much anymore. Now I just try to get through the fucking day."

"Are you happy you stayed all these years in one place?"

"What do you think?"

"Right." He puts his drink down. "I apologize for running out of here last time."

"Oh yeah?"

"Yeah."

She circles over to him. "Are you going to publish any of my interview, Matt? I really didn't mean to go on the way I did."

Without a word he touches her hand. "You have a wonderful sadness, Mrs. Lawson. Do you know that?"

"I have no idea what that means."

"There's something about you. I can't describe it."

"Thank you, Matt."

"You have amazing skin, too. You could pass for thirty." It's true.

"I get that a lot. It's not easy. Eating healthy, working out."

"What kind of working out?"

"Lots of Spin classes. And free weights. Keeps me toned."

"You look great."

She stands. "Do you want to come upstairs?"

"It would be unprofessional of me." His voice trembles.

She moves her fingers to the back of his head and caresses the small hairs there. "Yes, it would be very unprofessional."

Mary Ellen has lately seemed distracted during sex, like she's constantly remembering she's late for an appointment, but Mrs. Lawson's intensity makes him aware of everything: the winter air swirling around them from the open window, the creaky mattress, her intermittent, guttural, quiet moans.

Later, when they're lying together, she rests her arm across his bare stomach. "You're such a nice kid," she says.

*Nice.* What a terrible word, used to describe people without ambition. Losers. She doesn't know him at all, he thinks. "Do you know Jake Becker, Mrs. Lawson? He's the other reporter at the paper."

"I can't say I've had the pleasure."

"It's not really that much of a pleasure."

"Ha. Tell me what you really think." She brushes his hair with the tips of her fingers.

He ducks his head away from her. "He got a better job. I found out today. After only six months at the paper."

"Good for him." She brushes his hair again.

He rolls over to look at her. "He's an asshole, Mrs. Lawson. A real dick."

"Well, it takes a certain charm to do what you guys do."

"I've got charm," he says. "Don't you think?"

She rests her arm over his side. "You've got something better than charm."

"What's that?"

"Sincerity."

He pushes her arm off his stomach and onto the bed, then stands up. "I should go."

"Why? Stay a while."

"Why do you want me to stay?"

"I don't know."

"Because I'm a nice kid? A good person"

"I don't know. Why does it matter?"

"Do you think I'm a good reporter?"

She sits up, looking scared. "Of course."

"Then why do you want me to stay? I mean, that doesn't

make any sense. If I were a good reporter, I would—" He stops himself from finishing the sentence, but his chest feels heavy. He wants to explode.

She covers her face with her hands. "I'm lonely, Matt. Fuck. That's why I want you to stay. Don't read anything into it, okay?"

Matt walks to the window, still naked, and gazes out at the back yard. Tangled branches lean over a short chain-link fence. There's a rectangular sandbox, a rusting swing-set with only one white seat still suspended from the top, and a ping pong table bubbling up and warped from wear and weather.

"Why don't we get a bite to eat?" she says. "Have dinner like regular people and talk about your future."

Maybe this is what he wants. Someone to listen to old records with. Someone sad who understands life.

He tugs on his pants and shirt and finally his shoes. Mrs. Lawson sits on her knees waiting for him to speak. Her skin looks pale and vulnerable in the dying light.

"I'm going to sell the interview," he says. "You said he's guilty."

"What?" Her hands drop to the bed like anchors.

"To the *Boston Herald,* I think."

"You can't do that. I'll say it's a lie."

"I have the recording, Mrs. Lawson. Or did you forget?"

She shakes her head. "Matt, please. You said you wouldn't." She expels air like she's been punched in the gut. "Why are you doing this?"

"It's my job. Gathering news."

"Oh." She flops back onto the bed. "It's your job. Well, then, of course. Sell your damn story."

He stands. "I'm sorry, Mrs. Lawson."

"You really should stop saying that." She tucks her chin into her chest. "Real reporters don't fucking apologize."

He walks down the stairs and through the front door. It's dusk. The wind rustles the trees. In the distance a white Corvette speeds down the street, the roar of its engine growing louder as it gets closer. Matt digs in his pocket for his car keys. The gimpy raccoon emerges suddenly from the shrubs, clutching a bag of chips with both paws. The creature scurries in the direction of the house, then stops short when it sees Matt. Its eyes are wide and dark. The young reporter takes a step. The raccoon drops the chips, rises on its hind legs, and darts toward the road. Matt closes his eyes as the tires of the oncoming car screech.

Tara adjusted her veil and dug her fingernails into her hand. Her footsteps echoed throughout the near-empty church on Windflower Way in Benfield as she walked down the aisle. She ran her hands over the barely visible bump of her belly. The minister stood at the pulpit. Pete and Tara exchanged vows they'd written themselves. After they kissed, he lifted her off her feet and squeezed her, and the few who'd gathered for the ceremony applauded. They kissed again and ran back down the aisle.

At the reception, Pete—his long hair hanging loose, brushing up against the five o'clock shadow of his jaw line—held her small hand in his own damp palm. As the band played popular covers like "You Can't Hurry Love" and "Help Me Rhonda," he leaned over to his bride. "I'm glad we did this."

She twirled a strand of her dark brown hair around one finger. "I'm happy too."

They danced a waltz they'd learned by taking lessons with a local teacher. They were stiff and it was easy to see that Pete was counting as they moved, but they were earnest and that's all that *mattered. After that, they walked together from table to table, greeting their family members. Pete's mother was there, but his father was supposedly too ill to make the trip from New Haven. Pete suspected he was just on a drinking binge. Tara wept when both her parents hugged her. "No need to cry," her mother said. "You'll ruin your make-up."*

*After the best man's toast, Pete stood up to say a few words. He thanked everyone for coming and quoted a few philosophers on the nature of love—how it comes when you least expect it. "I was just driving that day, sure my destiny was out there, not a worry in the world. I stopped for a quick bite and there she was. The most gorgeous creature I'd ever seen sitting over at the counter by herself. The Lovin' Spoonful's "Daydream" was playing overhead and I sat next to her and she looked at me with those brown eyes and everything stopped. I bet you get to feel something like that two times in your entire life. Once, when you fall in love. The second time is when your heart quits for good, so you better take advantage of that first one. And man, I tell you, I did. Today is the second greatest day of my life. To Tara Blythe." He raised his glass; everyone drank and then cheered.*

*Minutes later, Tara cried in the bathroom. The maid of honor, her best friend Evelyn, patted her on the back. "What is it, hon? Aren't you happy?"*

*"Did you hear that toast?"*

*"It was lovely."*

*Tara stopped crying. "It was, wasn't it?"*

*"I wish I felt things as deeply as you."*

*"Thanks for saying that." Tara wiped her eyes. "I'm really scared. I feel like everything is out of control."*

*"Look there, hon. In the mirror." Tara did. "That's real. It's solid." Tara made eye contact with herself. What Pete had said was true; she was beautiful, even though she wasn't used to the*

changes in her body yet. This gave her comfort. "You don't have to worry so much."

"Maybe you're right." She tried to stand, but the tears slid down her cheek in rivulets and she collapsed back to the floor.

"Oh, honey."

"What if this is a terrible mistake?"

"It isn't dear. But if it is, you can always get out of it. Okay?"

Tara shrugged and then sat up and looked at her crumpled dress sagging around her. "Help me up."

\* \* \*

That evening in the hotel room, Pete ran his rough fingers along her thin arm. She rolled over and they made love. Afterwards, they lay side by side on the soft mattress, smoking cigarettes and eating pastries.

Tara shivered and slid closer to Pete.

"Are you cold?" He put his arm around her shoulders. "I've got you. You're mine now." A clock on the mantle ticked.

Tara's shoulders angled into his chest, her head nodded, and she began to relax. "This feels so good."

Pete waited for her to fall asleep, but the sound of the rain ticking against the roof and the wind whistling kept waking her. He felt a tension in his legs, like if he didn't get up soon he would have to leap to his feet and crash through the window.

"You know something? I'm gonna shoot down to the bar and get us something to drink." He rolled athletically off the side of the bed.

"Don't leave me." She clutched at him.

"Leave you?"

Her eyes were wide. "Please, stay with me."

"I'm going downstairs for three seconds."

"Please."

His legs felt itchy and hot. "What the hell is wrong with you?"

She couldn't control her breathing. "It's our wedding night. I want us to be together."

"I said I'd be back. Don't be dumb." He backed up to the door, pulled on his pants and shirt. He put his hand on the knob.

"Please, Pete."

He moved back to the bed swiftly, like a cat, angry, his eyes, smoldering embers.

She retreated. "Pete?"

He bent over her. The fire left his eyes. "Everything is going to be okay. You don't have to panic, okay?" He lit another cigarette.

She turned over and buried her face in the pillow.

He left the room.

When he returned at three in the morning, she pretended to be asleep.

# FEBRUARY 2014

## UNICORN

Vice-Principal Zachary Rivers picks up Lucy, his eighteen-pound Carne Terrier, and carries her from his front door to his Lincoln MKZ. She pants in his arms and then, when she's settled into the passenger seat, begins barking again —a high pitched, clipped "arf." Her barks are not directed at Zachary or, as far as he can tell, anything in particular. She's angry at the world, he thinks; she was meant to be a Pit Bull or a Great Dane, but instead she's trapped inside an adorable ball of fur. Traffic is backed up—construction workers are repaving one side of the road—and Lucy takes this personally. She clamps her jaws onto the arm rest, digs her paws in and almost manages to rip out a chunk of leather before Zachary can dislodge her.

"No, Lucy!" The dog tilts her head at Zachary, then resumes barking. "Bad girl!" But who is he kidding? He loves the dog more than his precious car. Or any human being. People are mean and selfish. Little Lu is his sweet muffin. "Never mind, Lucy. You bark all you want. They deserve it." Lucy isn't a bad girl; she just sees the world for what it is.

When the traffic clears, he zips past a construction worker holding a sign that says "Slow." He restrains himself from giving the guy the finger, but do they really need to do this work during rush hour?

As he steps through the front office, Lucy, tucked under his arm, growls and barks at Keith, one of the administrative assistants.

"I think she's having some problems with her teeth," he says. Zachary is struck instantly with déjà vu; didn't he use that excuse for Lucy's cranky demeanor last week? No matter. He doesn't care what the admins think. They're a pathetic lot.

"That's okay, I don't mind," Keith says with a mysterious emphasis on the word "I." His already thin lips squeeze tightly against his teeth, then suddenly peel back and unleash what Zachary interprets to be a rancorous smile. "But Principal Miner is waiting in your office."

"Thank you, Keith. And make sure those attendance reports are on my desk by the end of the day." That wipes the smile off his cocky face.

"But it's Friday."

"I am aware of that."

Zachary, pleased with himself, struts into his office. The principal is standing, looking out at the patch of worn grass that passes for a lawn in front of Benfield High. In the sprawling woods beyond school grounds, daggers of ice hang from leafless tree branches.

Zachary takes his seat at his desk, still holding Lucy. "Hello Toby," he says. "How are you?"

Principal Miner turns away from the window. He wears a blue Brooks Brothers button-down shirt and black Bonobos Stretch Weekday Warrior Dress Pants that cling to his bulging stomach.

"I'm pretty good." Toby strokes his thick, well-groomed Magnum P.I. mustache. "How about you?"

"I'm doing fine."

"Good, good." That pompous caterpillar on his lip seems to be crawling right off his face.

"Hold on a second while I tie up Lucy."

"Sure." Toby rolls up his sleeve and looks past Zachary, admiring his white Corvette in the parking lot. Zachary squeezes his eyes closed. How did someone like Toby become principal? Principals don't have to be suave. All they have to do is give a shit. And here's Toby, a chubby con-artist getting by on sham charm, going through life without helping a single kid.

Zachary ties his dog's leash to the radiator next to her water dish and gourmet, grain-free dog food.

"You're looking good, Zachary," Toby says. "I'm glad you're over all that unpleasantness."

Zachary grimaces. Toby is referring to Billy Lawson, the kid who murdered the Blythes back in December. Zachary had suspended the boy a few months before the incident for bringing drugs into school. It was an appropriate punishment, but Zachary hadn't been kind to him. He'd raised his voice and pounded his fist on his desk. And Billy never came back. Zachary knew what happened wasn't his fault, but he still felt terrible; he'd taken a leave of absence through December and the first two weeks of January, hoping a break from school would help him put the whole mess behind him.

He doesn't know how to respond to the principal. After all, not much has changed: he's the same old Zachary with the same old house, the same old job, and the same old routine. During his time off he'd considered trying one more time to find a girlfriend, but he'd had two failed engage-ments in his thirties and couldn't bring himself to re-enter the fray. The only good thing to come out of the "unpleasantness" was adopting Lucy. Zachary reflects for a moment. "Well, I guess I lost some weight," he says. "Thanks for noticing."

"You'll have to teach me your secret."

Zachary restrains himself from staring at Toby's fat stomach. There is no secret; just stop popping blueberry muffins down your gullet like raisins. "Any time."

Meanwhile, Lucy is napping. Her little barks and yips sound out in the real world as she chases dream squirrels through a dream field. Zachary quietly chuckles, but then snaps back to reality. He knows Toby isn't in his office to check on his well-being. "So," he says. "What's up?"

"Actually, Zach, it's your dog. That's what I've come to chat with you about."

He despises being called "Zach;" it's the name of a twenty-something college bro with a crew cut. "Zachary" is a respectable name: a man who works his entire life in education, who keeps children on track, away from drugs and violence. A man who believes in cleanliness and discipline.

"You want to talk to me about Lucy?"

The principal sits down and peels back the paper lining of what appears to be a jelly donut. "I'm afraid people have been complaining."

With a raised eyebrow. "Who's been complaining?"

"Oh, you know. Students. Teachers." He takes a sloppy bite of his donut. "A lot of folks have complained." Probably Keith, that passive-aggressive snot.

Zachary knows what's coming and although Toby never changes his mind once it's made up, he wouldn't forgive himself if he didn't make a case. "She's not hurting anyone," Zachary says. "She brings a sweetness to the workplace, and she keeps me calm. What are people complaining about?"

"She barks incessantly, Zach. It's getting difficult to get

work done around here. Now, I know I gave you permission to bring her into the office—"

"Yes, you did."

Toby's mouth hangs open mid-sentence and Zachary prays for a fly to vanish down the moist, coffee-stained tunnel. "That was before we knew she'd be such trouble. Surely, you can understand."

"I understand that eventually she'll grow out of this phase."

"Of course, of course, we can only hope, but for now I'm afraid it has become too much of a disturbance." He swallows the last of his sticky donut.

"I really don't want to leave her home without supervision."

Toby eyes Zachary. "Get a dog walker. I'll have Viki send you a list." He strokes the furry caterpillar on his lip. "Believe me, this doesn't bring me any pleasure. Things must be hard since...well, you know." His voice trails off. "Anyway, you know how it is." Toby stands and a cluster of muffin crumbs tumble from his shirt to the floor. Zachary clamps his eyes shut again and squeezes the top of his nose with his thumb and forefinger. Toby couldn't relate to another human being if his life depended on it. How did he get to run a school? "She can stay the rest of today, but beginning Monday you'll have to make other accommodations."

"I understand." He rubs the back of his jaw where it aches from clenching it shut every day at work. Lucy was his only source of joy. "Thanks for letting me know."

"It's my job around here to have difficult conversations. I'm so glad this one went well." The asshole ambles toward the door.

Zachary kneels next to Lucy, who yaps at the trail of cologne left by the principal. "That's right, baby. You tell him what you really think." He rubs the scruff under her chin. "You're a good dog." Wishing he had a modicum of her fight, he imagines the two of them back in the Lincoln MKZ, racing west toward adventure. It would be an incredible relief to be away from all this bureaucracy. No one really makes a dent with these kids anyway. But he needs the job. Only seven years until he can retire and collect his pension.

He rubs Lucy's belly and doesn't hear Keith enter.

"Mr. Rivers?"

Zachary shoots up, but something catches in his lower back and he grimaces. "Don't you ever knock? I've told you a thousand times."

"I'm sorry, Mr. Rivers. It's only, there's a kid waiting to see you."

"Already? Which kid?"

Keith unleashes another nasty sneer; the two of them have engaged in a schadenfreude war for the last four years, and Keith is about to win their latest skirmish. "It's Barry Epstein."

The knot in Zachary's back tightens. Barry Epstein: "Bad Barry," "The Epicenter," and, most cringeworthy, "Epstein Barry," like the kid was some kind of virus. And to be fair, Barry *was* trouble. Into smoking, drinking, taking and selling whatever drugs kids did these days, skipping class on the regular. He was the kid who'd gone with Billy to the Blythe's house the night of the murders. At least he'd had the sense to back out, even if it was at the last minute.

The vice-principal shudders. He doesn't want to think of Barry ending up like Billy.

"What did he do this time?" Zachary says, hoping it isn't anything too terrible.

"Spray-painted the side of the building."

"Oh yeah?" At least it was something creative.

Keith pulls out a smartphone and shows him a picture of the graffiti. It is unmistakably a well-executed depiction of an anus. Zachary looks up and, seeing a huge grin on Keith's stupid face, rolls his eyes. Keith was just as immature as the students. Why, Zachary thinks, is he surrounded by so many dolts? "All right. Send him in."

"Okee doke."

Once Keith's back is turned, Zachary allows himself a small smile. "And send me that photo!" After all, the art is pretty good.

Lucy yaps when the kid enters. His worn jeans hang off his narrow hips and what must have been a band name on his slate-gray T-shirt has mostly peeled off. The laces on his high-tops trail behind him like slithering worms. Bad Barry pushes a strand of thick hair out of his eyes and plops into the seat in front of Zachary's desk. He has always been catnip to girls, but now his chest and arms have begun to fill out and he looks a little like a boyish matinee idol.

The kid scratches at a cut on the top of his hand. "Howdy, chief."

"Good afternoon, Barry." Zachary fiddles with his phone and then opens the picture Keith emailed, holds it up, and narrows his eyes sternly. "Take a look at this."

Barry bobs his head up and down as if he's listening to smooth jazz. "Good photo. Did you take it?"

Zachary resists the urge to slam the phone on his desk. "I gotta say, I don't like the path that you're heading down, young man." He had sworn when he'd been promoted to this job six years before he would never use that phrase; calling a teenage boy "young man" meant you had surrendered to the impossibility of ever making a human connection with a student.

"What path is that, Mr. Rivers?"

"I think you know exactly what path I mean. You'll be in prison or dead before you're thirty. You don't want to end up like Billy Lawson."

"Because tagging a wall is definitely the gateway drug to murder. You're a wise man, Mr. Rivers."

Zachary wishes he could slap the smirk off the kid's face. "Education is very important to your future. Don't you know that?"

"I look forward to the day I graduate from Harvard Law School."

"Mocking me won't help you."

"I see your point—you've reformed me. Can I go?"

Zachary leans back in his chair to think about what to do. Suspending the kid is giving him what he wants; letting him continue to terrorize the school helps no one.

Lucy is not only yapping but is now also spinning in circles. She tugs at her leash, eager to get to Barry. If she were a Dobermann Pinscher Zachary would enjoy watching her tear out Barry's throat. Problem solved.

Barry points to the dog. "What's wrong with her?" "Do not attempt to change the subject, young man." The kid bends to examine Lucy. He holds his hand out, and the dog takes a deep sniff. Zachary doesn't like this. "Barry, listen to me, I don't care for the direction this conversation is going."

The kid kneels on the floor and Lucy puts her front paws on his knees.

Zachary stands, his back clenches, and he sits back down. But knowing he's more intimidating when he stands tall, stretching his five feet nine inches to their limit, he forces himself to endure the pain and rises to his feet. "Listen to me right now. Get back to your chair, please!"

But Barry keeps on petting the dog. "That's a good girl. Yes, you are. You're a sweet girl." Lucy, out of breath, stops barking and sits. "That's a good girl. Yes, good girl. You're such a sweet one." Her tongue lolls out of her head; she blinks happily and then rolls onto her back so the kid can scratch her stomach.

"Good girl." Still kneeling, but looking up at the vice-principal, Bad Barry says, "She's really sensitive." Barry looks up at Zachary. "She's a good dog."

Zachary sighs. "You know I have to suspend you for this."

"Can I hang out in the detention room?" Quietly, he adds, "I don't want to go home." He looks almost vulnerable.

Just outside the office, someone knocks over a stack of boxes and Lucy leaps up and begins barking. Barry strokes the dog's head; she immediately settles and starts to lick his hands.

Zachary falls back into his chair and, gazing down at the kid, has a revelation; it's the perfect solution to two problems.

Tentatively, he says, "I can't make any guarantees, but what if I could convince the principal to let you do community service?"

Barry looks up with a pained expression. "Like those guys who pick up trash on the side of the road?"

"Well, I have something else in mind." Zachary sits up straight, attempting to look authoritative. "I'd pitch it that way, but the *community service* would largely involve looking after pets while their owners work." He glances down at Lucy. "Well, a very specific pet."

Barry looks puzzled. "Is that legit?"

Zachary knows it's a stretch. "It's a bit unorthodox, but I *am* part of this community so—"

"Why would you trust me? You hate me."

"I don't hate you. But to be honest, I don't trust you." He pictures the Epstein Barry Virus rifling through his collection of Robert Johnson records, spilling beer all over his living room area rug, burning the entire house to the ground. "But Lucy seems to. And if you manage to get the job done without destroying my house, I'll even pay you."

Barry scratches Lucy behind her ears. "What about school?

Aren't you supposed to make sure I'm getting educated or something?"

The vice-principal can't help but see Barry's point. Then again, mandatory suspension has always seemed counterproductive; what does any kid learn from *not* coming to school? Zachary allows himself a small smile. "Let's just call this a lesson in economics."

Barry starts to perk up, but then remembers who he is and regains his tough-guy attitude. "Yeah, okay," the kid says. "Whatever."

Zachary wakes at five on Monday, makes himself an egg-white omelet, and focuses on his coffee. He pours in a splash of cream and watches it swirl, forming a Kandinsky painting in his cup. He crunches two pieces of plain wheat toast.

The Epicenter arrives at 6:20 a.m., ten minutes early, and Zachary shows him around the house.

"Here's the fridge. You can eat anything you want, but no cooking." Zachary opens the door and is embarrassed to realize all he has is half-eaten takeout and a jar of pickles. The refrigerator has been mostly empty since his mother died. He looks at Barry, expecting a sneer, but the boy seems unfazed. Zachary shuts the door. "I think there are cookies in the cabinets."

Lucy races in and circles Barry's feet. He picks her up and cradles her; she settles into his arms, her eyes half-closed. She's found her soulmate.

"The TV is here. I have cable so feel free to watch whatever you want." Zachary imagines him watching reality shows like MTV's *The Real World*. Wait, is that even what kids watch now? "The dog treats are here, but don't overdo it. And she needs a lot of exercise so you should—"

"I know how to take care of a dog, okay?"

"Of course you do." Zachary folds his fingers together to demonstrate his composure. "But Lucy is very special."

"She seems like a regular dog to me." Barry pets Lucy for a moment. Finally, he says, "I grew up with a dog, but she died two years ago."

Zachary tenses. "How did your dog die?"

"She was old." Barry exhales sharply. "What, did you think I killed her or something?"

Zachary stutters, "No, no, I just—"

"I love dogs."

Zachary restrains himself from patting Barry's shoulder. "I'm sorry. I can see that. What was your dog's name?"

"Sticky."

"That's an interesting choice."

"Yeah, well, she drooled a lot."

"What breed was she?"

Barry snorts. "Breed. Yeah, right. She was a rusty-colored mutt. About this big." Barry holds his hand down to knee level. "She was great. One of those dogs who always seemed to be thinking, you know?"

"I understand completely. I'm sorry about Sticky."

"Yeah," Barry says. "Thanks."

This is the first time Barry has ever spoken to Zachary without snarling.

The kid picks *The Big Book of Origami* off the bookshelf and thumbs through it. "You really make toys out of paper?"

"It was sort of a hobby of mine a long time ago." Zachary fights off a memory of his lonely college years. He begins to leave but pauses at the door. "Listen son. You mustn't let anyone else know your dog-sitting for me. If it gets back to the principal that you are somehow benefiting from your suspension, it's likely he'll elect to permanently suspend you. Is this clear?"

Barry smirks. "I'm not the only one who'd be fucked if the principal found out about our little economics class."

Zachary crosses his arms over his chest. Why did the troublemakers have to be so smart? "I see we do understand each other."

"Looks that way, chief."

"Wonderful. Then I'll see you after school."


It's Zachary's intention to refrain from checking in on Barry, but not even halfway through the day, feeling anxious, he calls his home number. It goes to voicemail after four rings. He hangs up without leaving a message. He should have gotten the kid's cell. How could he have been so reckless?

At the end of the day, he makes a beeline for the door but nearly crashes into Principal Miner.

"Listen, Zach. I really appreciate you taking care of that dog situation."

Zachary grinds his teeth. "It was no problem, Toby."

"What did you end up doing with her?"

Zachary tries not to scowl. Why was Toby pretending he even cared? The lie materializes even before he realizes he's going to make up a story. "I gave her away."

"Really? I didn't mean to suggest that drastic a step was necessary."

"I didn't have much choice, did I? I looked into hiring a dog-walker, but it was too expensive." He pauses to let that sink in. "So, it was either give her away or put her in a shelter. And you know what they do to dogs in those places."

Toby fidgets uncomfortably. "Well, it's good you found someone to take her."

"I didn't even have time to check them out. I'm really just hoping for the best."

"If you'd told me it was this desperate, we would have worked something out." He *did* tell him how desperate the situation was. "I know how much that animal meant to you."

Zachary says nothing.

The principal deflates. "I'm really sorry."

"You were just doing your job. And actions have consequences."

After rushing up the short path to his house, Zachary turns the key in the knob and then pauses to compose himself. Inside, Barry is lying on the floor, his head propped up on his elbow, thumbing through the origami book. Lucy is lying next to him. Her ears perk up and she begins to growl softly as Zachary enters, but when she sees that the invader isn't a threat, she closes her eyes.

Zachary digs in his wallet and hands the money over to the kid, who shoves the cash in his pocket and stretches.

"So, there were no problems? Lucy was okay?"

"No problems."

Barry seems almost trustworthy. Maybe the two of them will become friends. Barry certainly needs a father figure. And Zachary wouldn't mind. He never wanted kids of his own—that's the reason one of his engagements ended—but when he had first gotten into teaching, he'd loved seeing the delighted eyes of his students when they understood a new concept. He'd forgotten how good that felt. He says, "I'll see you tomorrow then." He waits until Barry is at the door. "You did a good job today."

"Whatever."

And so the days pass like this, with Zachary meeting Barry in the mornings, rushing off to work, and then returning to find his dog and her babysitter curled up somewhere. Zachary feels a twinge of jealousy—why can't Lucy relax when he's the one caring for her?—but after a while begins to concede, without resentment, that the kid simply has a special bond with the animal. In fact, Zachary watches the boy for clues: how he holds himself, how he talks to her, how quickly he moves. But there are none that he can discern. Lucy and Barry just understand each other, plain and simple.

One afternoon Zachary finds the two of them together on the couch, asleep. The boy's face is almost sweet and for an instant he wonders if Barry isn't really a monster after all. He had thought he was beyond feeling anything for a kid like this, especially after more than twenty excruciating years working in the school system. Their parents were trash, the kids were trash, and they would grow up to be trash. It was a consistent, unbreakable pattern—one he'd seen even when he started as a naïve ninth-grade math teacher. But maybe Bad Barry was a unicorn, that one-in-a-million who could defy the odds. And Zachary never would have known had he not invited the kid into his house.

He nudges Barry awake. "Hey!"

The kid's eyes spin. "What happened?"

"It's time to go, Barry. You gotta go."

He yawns. "I guess I fell asleep."

"I guess you did."

Zachary pulls out his wallet. "You know what? I'm gonna up your salary. Another dollar an hour."

Barry rolls his eyes. "Thanks."

Zachary can see through the boy's irony-plated armor; the raise means something to the boy. It feels good to make a difference.

That evening Lucy seems woozy and unstable. When Zachary tries to pick her up, she nips at his hands. Finally, she throws up a chewed sock all over *Whipped Cream*, the Herb Albert album cover he'd left out on the floor. He calls the vet and manages to get her into the Lincoln.

He paces in the waiting room. Thirty-eight-year-old Christy Kim, the vet, is inside checking Lucy. Her wall is covered with photos of her skinny son, Justin: the kid playing soccer, eating ice cream, winking for the camera. He wonders why there are no pictures of her husband, but then dimly recalls she got divorced two or three years ago.

She emerges from the back office in scrubs; she's kind of cute, he thinks. "The x-ray confirms there's nothing else in her stomach," she says. "But watch her carefully just to be safe." Suddenly, Barry's angelic nap seems like neglect. "You're lucky she threw it up."

"Yes, very lucky." He picks up Lucy, hiding his anger. "Thank you for all your help."

On the way home he seethes and thinks that Barry really was a bad kid, but by the time he pulls into the driveway he's decided that some of the blame lies with him. It had been his idea to trust Barry in the first place. And Barry was, after all, still a teenager.

At home, Lucy seems like her usual energetic self, but Zachary can't sleep. He paces in his bedroom, pulling at his flannel pajamas. He trots into the bathroom and stares at his crimson face in the mirror. He cups a handful of water from the sink, splashes it on his eyes and does it again. And again. The water splatters down his pajama front. Finally, he strips off his clothes, gets in the shower, and turns the water on without adjusting the heat.

He calls in sick the next morning and then sits, fully dressed, legs crossed, on the sofa facing the front door. But

Barry doesn't show up. He waits five more minutes and when it's clear the kid isn't coming, he pulls on his North Face parka. With Lucy yapping, the two of them get into the car and pull out of the driveway. Traffic is backed up for a good mile heading toward school, but Zachary is going in the opposite direction.

He tightens and releases his grip on the steering wheel, though he's still careful not to exceed the speed limit by more than five miles an hour. He's angry, but was this really Barry's fault? Lucy wasn't the first dog to swallow a sock; the vet had seemed more bored than surprised by the whole thing. He thinks about what could have been—not just about how Barry could have been a better kid, but about how he, himself, might have been a better man. In his mind's eye he can see himself teaching Barry life's hard lessons. He pictures Barry graduating high school, Zachary convincing Christy Kim to give the kid a job. He and Christy taking the kid to shows in Boston and out for pizza. Later, when Barry is older, the two men reminisce about the old days when Zachary was a cynical wretch of a vice-principal and Barry was a confused teen. Zachary and Christy get married and Barry is best man.

Zachary knows these thoughts are fantasies, but he indulges in them because they soothe some wounded part of himself. He wants to believe he's building a bridge between two men, separated by thirty years, who both see through life's obligations, phony smiles, the jobs that twist your soul, the make-pretend loving families.

Maybe it's not too late. He can go there, forgive him. Lives are built on second chances. He can teach Barry that.

He pulls over and thumbs through the stack of paper on his passenger seat until he finds Barry's file. The boy lives on Fifth Street, only fifteen minutes away.

Barry's neighborhood is in an older section of town; the

homes are smaller, but it's still suburban and the lawns and houses are well-kept—except for one. There is no lawn in front of Barry's house, just dirt. An ancient, beat-up van sits against a picket fence that has seen better days. There are car parts everywhere. Tree branches encroach on the house's sagging roof and most of the paint has worn off the shingles.

Outside the car it's a warm winter day. A light breeze tousles Zachary's hair and puffy clouds roll lazily overhead. He takes a gulp of air and trots up the walkway. The metallic storm door is rusted around the edges and a shard of glass is missing from the lower left corner of the window. The door rattles and threatens to come off its hinges when Zachary knocks. After a minute, a bald man about six feet tall wearing shorts, boots, and a moth-eaten winter jacket appears from around the side of the house carrying a metal cage used for trapping animals. Lines cut deep grooves across his forehead, and his eyes are swollen and red.

He clears his throat. "Can I help you?"

"Are you Mr. Epstein?"

"Who are you?"

"I'm the vice-principal over at Benfield High. I'm wondering if I could speak to your son."

"Barry isn't here."

It's not a surprise. He'll have to remain patient. Persistent. "Would you mind telling me where he is? He was supposed to report to me this morning before school."

"Like I said, he isn't here." The old man begins to turn around.

"This is very important for Barry's future, Mr. Epstein. If you could tell me where he is."

Mr. Epstein turns back and takes a step toward Zachary. "It's important for Barry's future? That's what you said?"

"I'm fairly certain I can help him, but it's imperative that we talk."

His eyes darken. "The fucker is gone."

Zachary pulls his head back as if dodging a punch. "Gone? What do you mean?"

"He was selling drugs. I found out. I kicked him out on his ass."

"Do you know where he is?"

"Like I said. He's gone. You won't have to worry about his future anymore." The old man spits into the dirt.

Zachary nods grimly. "Okay." Brittle branches on nearby trees whisper to each other in the wind. "Okay."

On the drive home, he thinks that none of this is worth it. First Billy, then Barry—he can't help these kids. It's hopeless. There's an opening for a principal at Rogers Elementary. Maybe if he can reach the kids before they get to high school...

He nods to himself.

By the time he gets home, he's paranoid; has Barry left any of his drugs behind? He puts Lucy on her leash and ties her to the bedroom door. She whimpers, but he needs her out of his way. He opens every cabinet and drawer in the kitchen and pulls out all of the food—cans of soup, boxes of pasta, peanut butter, granola bars, and more—but doesn't find anything. He looks under his bed and the sofa, in the medicine cabinet, in the tall cabinet with all his records. There's nothing. Still, you can't be too careful. He pulls open the small drawer under the center bookcase expecting to find his tweezers, some envelopes, stamps, and a few rubber bands and paper clips. Those are present and accounted for, but they're buried beneath at least a dozen flattened origami sculptures. He pulls them out one at a time. The first several are simple—a cube, a swan, a ragged airplane—but the work improves: a violin, a blossoming rose, a Tyrannosaurus

Rex. The last sculpture, of a horse, is the most intricate. A mane runs down its neck. Folds at the base of the feet look like hooves. The eyes are big and inquisitive. The legs are bent to make the horse look like it's galloping. The tail whips in the breeze.

The kid has a knack for this, Zachary thinks. He turns the sculpture over in his hand and sees that there is a small piece still flattened out against the horse's side. Zachary carefully bends the twisting horn that juts out from the center of the creature's head into place.

## DECEMBER 31, 1973

Tara mixed the ingredients in a large bowl and then stirred until the batter was dark brown and thick. She spread it evenly into a baking pan, smoothed the top, and transferred the pan into the oven. Upstairs, Pete was already getting ready for the party; he was tying his bowtie when she entered their bedroom.

"You look nice," she said and kissed him on the cheek.

He finished the tie, lifted his jacket off the thick duvet of their king-sized bed, and pulled it on. "I ought to for what renting this tux cost." He pulled her close. "Are you wearing that?"

She was wearing an apron over casual clothes. She laughed. "I am not."

"Then you better get moving."

"Are we in a rush?"

"Nah. I just wanted to make sure this thing fit." He released her.

"You want to help me pick out a dress?"

"Surprise me," he said. He kissed her on the forehead, checked himself out in the mirror, straightened his tie, and started for the door. "I'll be waiting for you downstairs."

Tara opened her walk-in closet and began to go through dresses: No. No. No. No. No. Finally, she found a long black one with a deep, off-center front slit that would show off her legs. Pete would like that. She loved the contrast of the high neckline with her bare shoulders. After a shower, she sat at her vanity and carefully applied her make-up: shimmering pastel-green eyeshadow, black mascara, and black eyeliner. She swept bronzer with a large brush on her cheekbones, the tip of her nose, her chin, jawline, and hairline; then she coated her lips with a shiny, clear gloss.

She moved slowly down the stairs, imitating the Miss America strut she'd seen on television.

"Whoa," Pete yelped from the kitchen. He was leaning over the pan of brownies and holding one piece in his hand. "Look at you!"

"I'm glad you appreciate fine art," Tara said and kicked out her leg to show off.

"Come over here." He put the brownie down and sat in their leather recliner; she sat on his lap and they kissed.

She licked her lips. "You taste like chocolate."

"Sorry about that." He kissed her again. "I couldn't resist them."

The doorbell rang, and Tara hopped up to let the babysitter in.

"Hi there, Mrs. Blythe," sixteen-year-old Robyn Davis said. "You look so pretty!"

"Thank you, Robyn." Tara twirled.

Pete put his arm around his wife. "There's food and soda in the fridge. Help yourself."

*The girl's eyes widened and she blushed; she'd never seen Pete in a suit before. "Thank-you, Mr. Blythe."*

*The couple walked side by side up the stairs. Shelby was sitting on the floor of her bedroom when they entered, playing war with her tiny, plastic toy soldiers. Her finely attired dolls sat in a circle around them.*

*"Give your dad a hug," Pete said and picked up his daughter.*

*Shelby wrapped her arms around her father. "Can I stay up late tonight?"*

*"You can stay up to watch the ball drop," Pete said. "Then it's bed for you."*

*Shelby beamed.*

*Tara brushed a strand of hair out of her daughter's eye. "Happy New Year, beautiful girl," she said and kissed Shelby's cheek.*

*"Happy New Year, mom." She reached out and Tara squeezed her hand.*

*Larry Foster, head of sales and Pete's boss, greeted the Blythes at the entrance to his huge home in neighboring Stanton. "You two! Come in!" He took Tara's fur and Pete's tailored overcoat. Looking the couple up and down, he said, "I'm amazed what Pete can buy on his salary." Then he vanished.*

*"That was strange," Tara said.*

*"He's a busybody," Pete said. "Don't think about it."*

*The party was already in full throttle; funky music emanated from the furnished basement.*

*Pete held out his arm for Tara. "Shall we?"*

*The room was dimly lit; several goofy souvenir caricatures of Larry and his wife were nailed to the wood paneled walls; red and orange shag carpeting covered the floor. Most of the party guests were gathered around the long bar at the back of the room.*

Pete and Tara stepped into the crowded room and were quickly separated. After a moment of saying hello to colleagues, Pete looked around. Tara was now talking to Larry's wife, Nancy, at the far corner of the bar. He looked past her: a slender, red-headed woman wearing a leopard print dress stood alone, looking lost. When her eyes met Pete's, she smiled. He wondered what she smelled like. What her body against his would feel like. Suddenly, everything else in his life seemed like a lie, and yet he felt he had to resist this thought. Resist the impulse to talk to her. Uneasy, Pete looked away.

As midnight approached, Tara found her husband sitting by himself.

"Hello there," she said.

"Hello," he said.

Tara waited for him to say more. "Are you okay?" she asked. "You seem a little glum."

"I'm fine," he said. "Just tired."

"You, tired?" She pushed his arm playfully.

"I know, right?"

Tara studied him. "This is really fun."

"Yeah," Pete said.

"It's nice to leave the kid with the babysitter."

"It is."

"Maybe we can do that more," Tara said. "Go on a few trips together. Nancy and Larry went to Montreal for Christmas."

"Yeah," Pete said. "We should do something like that." He was distracted, though, thinking about how much he hated sales and loudmouth Larry; he was thinking about trips he'd like to take alone.

They leaned against the wall together, neither speaking.

"Be quiet," Larry yelled suddenly. "The ball is dropping."

*The crowd counted down together. "10. 9. 8..." When the count reached zero, Pete and Tara watched the couples in the room celebrate the beginning of 1974, kissing and clutching each other.*

*Tara leaned in for a kiss, but Pete offered only his cheek. He looked away as everyone else raised their glasses in celebration.*

# MARCH 2014

## PAREIDOLIA

Louis presses his hands over his ears, but it only muffles the sound of his parents' arguing. The air of his cramped bedroom is stale. He closes his eyes and pulls on his headphones. He'd stumbled on *Music for the Royal Fireworks* by George Handel a year before when he'd decided he would only listen to classical music; he'd read online that it made you smarter. He's not sure if he believes that, but this particular piece always helps him sleep.

It doesn't work this time. He can't climb on top of the thunderous chords and float away like he usually does; he finds himself still stuck to his damp bed, stewing. He stares at the yellow-brown stain on his ceiling—it formed a few years back when the toilet in the apartment above his family's had begun leaking—to see if the patterns will transform into pictures. It's called pareidolia: the tendency of the mind to create meaning out of nebulous visual stimuli. He'd learned about it in a report he wrote on optical illusions for Ms. Romano's fifth grade class.

At first, he sees the usual patterns: a hazy angel; a furry animal with three whiskers jutting out at odd angles—maybe the dog he's always wanted; an old woman with a long, twisted nose and flat chin. Slowly, as he allows his eyes to blur, he sees a fat hand reaching out for a trophy, a pair of pursed lips, and then, finally, an airplane ascending into the clouds. It goes higher and higher, breaking through the atmosphere. It keeps going, past Mars, past Neptune, out of the solar system, out of the Milky Way galaxy, deeper and deeper into space.

He falls asleep and loses all sense of time. Then a door in some far-off universe slams and wakes him up. His mother, Melissa, stands over his bed. Her tangled dark hair hangs down, clinging to her sticky forehead and cheeks.

"Are you awake?" she asks.

"Yes."

His mother sits on the edge of the bed, then tucks a stray strand of hair behind her ear and looks away.

Neither of them speaks. His father hadn't had a drink for a blissful year, but he'd started again a few weeks before the trial and the family had fallen back into a familiar routine: Mom, lethargic and depressed, wearing her dingy bathrobe everyday like a uniform. Dad, sober and sad, happy after two drinks and angry after four.

But now there was a new kind of darkness in the house. His father's drunken rage had always frightened Louis, but last week his dad had actually slapped his mother. The next day, his father was ashamed. Louis had heard him crying—saying something about how everyone would be better off if he were dead. That "apology" was almost as upsetting as the rage...and anyhow, his dad was drunk again a few hours later.

Louis sits up. He wants to ask if his father is going to be okay. If his mother will be happy again. But all he says is, "Things will get better soon."

She continues gazing into the corner of his room. "Do you think so?"

"Definitely. Once the trial is over, he'll be okay." Louis's father, Tim, had testified for the prosecution in the Billy Lawson trial the week before—something to do with why Billy had gone to the Blythe's house in the first place.

His mother exhales and a flicker of relief tugs at her cheeks. Louis likes the way she looks when she smiles; something comes alive behind her eyes.

His mother stands. "Get some sleep."

He rolls over, pulling his blanket around him.


Louis gets off the bus to find Adam Liu, his new best friend waiting for him. "Hey," he says.

"Hey," Adam replies. Adam is really his only friend. They'd met in the gym during recess at the beginning of the year, two kids standing alone trying to be inconspicuous. Outsiders. Adam's family, it turned out, had just moved to Benfield.

There's time before the first bell, so they walk behind Rogers Elementary to the pathway through the woods. The cold air cuts into Louis's face; it feels like tiny mice are gnawing at him. The tree branches on both sides of the path are barren and jut out in a thousand directions. "Well? Should we get started?" This is Louis's signal to his friend that he's ready to play their favorite game.

"Once upon a time," Adam says.

"Roger walked to the supermarket."

"To buy a roll of toilet paper."

"The sun was shining."

"The birds were chirping."

"Then suddenly, one of the birds pooped on his jacket."

"Then another bird did it too."

"Hundreds of birds went after him."

"So he ran."

"And ran and ran."

"But the birds followed him."

"He ran into a grocery store."

"But they broke in."

"He ran into a car."

"But it was a convertible, and they ripped the roof off."

"He hid under a picnic table."

"But a bunch of eagles carried it away."

"He ran and ran some more until he ran into a dark alley."

"It looked like he was trapped."

"He didn't know what to do."

Adam thinks for a while and then smiles slyly. "He reached into his coat pocket and pulls out something scary." Adam, using his thumb and index finger as a gun, points it at Louis.

Louis pauses. Suddenly, instead of the story, he can only think about his father, who owns a handgun that he keeps in the bottom drawer of his nightstand.

"What's up?" Adam nudges Louis's shoulder.

Louis shrugs. "Nothing."

"Really?"

"I mean, you know. My dad."

"Are you okay?"

Louis bends to pick up a branch from the footpath. He hadn't told Adam about his father hitting his mother. "I'm fine. It's just...everyone in this town hates him."

Adam looks down and kicks a rock. "Everyone makes mistakes."

"But he was the chief of police a long time ago and people trusted him and... and... They were just starting to get over that when he got caught up in this trial."

"But he's not the one who killed those people."

"I know. But he was kind of part of it. All the papers—everyone

—says he told those kids where they should go that night. That they'd find lots of money there." Louis clicks his tongue with regret.

The boys stand together without speaking for a stretched-out minute. Adam wipes his nose. After another pause, he says, "It's really cold out here."

"Yeah." Louis lets out a puff of air.

Adam picks up a branch and leaps in front of Louis. "En garde," he says.

Louis smiles. "I don't think I can fight you today."

"Okay." Adam nods and throws the stick to the ground. "No problem."

Louis drops his stick as well and they walk silently back to school.


That evening, on autopilot, Louis makes macaroni and cheese and sticks a plate of frozen vegetables in the microwave. As usual, his mother is sprawled out on the couch in the tiny living room; still in her shabby robe, she's reading what Louis is pretty sure is a romance novel. The cover displays a chiseled man with flowing hair leaning over a blonde damsel in a long green dress. Both of their chests appear to be busting out of their clothes.

Louis carries a full plate into the living room and places it on the coffee table. The local newscaster on their old TV is going on about a riot in Boston. The radiator clicks as it heats up, but the room still feels cold. Even the metal fork Louis uses to eat is like a slender piece of ice in his fingers.

"Where's dad?"

"Still at work."

His father loaded and unloaded trucks for some construction company a few towns away. His mother didn't work; she described herself as being "between jobs." She looks at the food and then turns her attention back to the novel. "Thanks, honey."

Louis watches her read for a moment. "You need to eat something, mom."

"I will," she says without looking up.

Louis goes back to the kitchen, sits, and eats his dinner. The cheese is extra hot, the way he likes it. Afterwards, he puts his dish in the sink and reaches for the dish soap. They're out. Typical. Louis never knew whether there'd be a light bulb when he needed one, bags for the trash, or even food in the fridge. Part of Louis is angry with his parents, but mostly he just feels irritated. He gets a bar of Ivory soap from the bathroom and scrubs his plate. He looks to see if his mother has eaten her meal, but she still hasn't touched it. Louis rinses, dries, and puts his plate in the cabinet and his fork in the top drawer.

Looking at a pile of dirty dish towels, he thinks about doing laundry in the basement, but there are no quarters left in the soup can next to the door that separates their apartment from the hallway.

He glances at the clock. It's after eight, which means that his father has stopped off at the bar for a drink. Louis tenses, afraid. He's not sure if he prefers his father sober and sad, or drunk and angry. Both scare him. Both bring his mind back to that stupid gun in his father's nightstand.

Louis glances at the couch; his mother has dozed off, the book resting on her cheek. He sneaks into his parents' room and quietly closes the door behind him. Without turning on the light, he kneels next to his father's nightstand and pulls open the bottom drawer where he finds the shoebox. He pulls it out and tucks it under his arm. It is heavier than he expects. He'd felt calm and collected—like a secret agent—just seconds before, but now his arms and legs shake. He realizes he's holding his breath.

He pokes his head out; the book has fallen to the floor and his mother is snoring softly. He slips through the door and moves as fast as he can into his own room. His limbs are still trembling as he shoves the shoebox behind a stack of comic books in his closet. As he feels his heartbeat slowing, he realizes that he isn't absolutely sure that the gun is in the box; he hasn't looked inside. He forces himself to retrieve it from the closet. He sits on the floor for a minute, and then musters the courage to remove the cover. The gun is there, all right: a black snub-nosed revolver with a rubber grip and silver chamber. He hates the sight of it. He always has, even when his father had dragged him to the shooting range to fire off a few rounds.

He covers the box and shoves it back behind the comics in his closet. When he lies down, he begins to feel satisfied. His father can't wake now in the middle of the night in a fit of fear and self-pity and reach for the gun. Everyone is safe.

Louis lies in bed that night waiting. A few times he hears a creaking on the stairs outside their apartment, but the doorknob never turns, and he finally gives up hoping that his father will return.

In the morning, he goes to the bathroom to get ready for school and finds his father passed out on the floor. The smell of alcohol mixes with the acrid odor of piss and burns his nostrils. "Dad?" Louis begins to panic. "Dad!?"

His father snores but doesn't move. Louis races into his parents' bedroom and wakes his mother.

"Dad's passed out in the bathroom again."

She wipes sleep out of her eyes. "What?"

"In the bathroom. Come quick."

She lets out a pained moan and then plops her head back

down onto her pillow. "Let him sleep it off," she says. "He'll be fine."

Louis glumly retreats to his room and texts Adam.

"OMG. Dad super drunk."

Adam replies immediately. "That sucks."

"Totally."

"What r u gonna do?"

"Idk."

"U going to school?"

"idk."

A moment passes before Adam texts again. "U should come to school."

Without hesitating, Louis types, "Yeah. OK."

School is long and boring. Louis spends most of it at his desk in Ms. Romano's class, head on his chin, trying to stay awake. He thinks about his father on the floor of the bathroom. Will he wake up and notice the gun is missing? He tightens his lips to keep from crying; he pictures the revolver like it's a cartoon character with angry eyes and downturned lips.

After school, Adam and Louis meet up as usual on the pathway through the woods that leads to Cranberry Street. Louis takes the late bus, so they have twenty minutes to kill.

Adam says, "Here's a big question. Who is Tom and who is Huck between you and me?"

Both had been assigned *The Adventures of Tom Sawyer* in school even though they had different teachers. Louis thought it was the most interesting book he'd ever read, totally unlike all the kid's novels he usually took out from the school library, which were full of clear villains and heroes. It was hard to know who was good and who was bad in *Tom Sawyer* and that made him like it even more.

"I'm definitely Huck," Louis says.

"But I thought I was Huck."

"Come on. Huck's father is the town drunk. My father is the town drunk. It's pretty obvious."

Adam nods and they walk in silence until Adam says, "It would be weird to go to your own funeral, you know? Like they do in the book. I wonder what people would say about us."

Louis thinks. "I bet my parents would be really sad. Especially my dad. He'd bawl until his eyes fell out of his skull."

"My parents would probably bring my math homework and shove it into my casket."

Louis laughs. Then he braces himself. "I stole my dad's gun."

"What?" Adam grabs his shoulder and they stop walking.

"I took it from his night table."

"Are you crazy?"

"Probably. But next time he looks for it, it won't be there—it can't hurt anyone."

Adam nods seriously. "That makes sense. Wow. What are you gonna do with it?"

"I hid it in my closet." Louis looks up at the sky. A puffy cloud overhead looks like a skinny, grinning man. "All I want is to forget it's there."

Adam rubs his hands together for warmth. He looks away from Louis and when he speaks again, his voice is cheerful. "I forget things all the time," he jokes. "Like last week I forgot I was human."

Louis laughs. "That must have been hard."

"It was. I looked in the mirror and I was like, 'whoa! Wasn't I a cheetah when I went to sleep?'"

Sitting at the kitchen table Saturday morning, Louis watches the last two Cheerios in his bowl circle each other like gladiators. He wipes his chin and then snatches both pieces of cereal in his spoon and swallows. His mother yawns and stretches. She has dark circles under her eyes and she's moving slowly, but she'd made the effort to be up in time to sit with him as he ate his breakfast. She was always better in the mornings.

"You okay over there?" she asks.

"What do you mean?"

"I'm not sure. You seem off."

He forces himself to sound upbeat. "I'm fine."

"Are you worried about your dad?"

His father had spent the entire night out somewhere and still hadn't returned. "He'll be okay," he says yet again. "Once this all passes."

His mother chews at her thumbnail. "Sure," she says. "He's a good man. Deep down."

"Yeah," Louis says.

He goes to his room, paces for a few minutes, then manages to settle onto his bed. He watches an old episode of *Justice League* but can't focus on the plot. It's dumb anyway. They always are. If he got to write his own superhero show, his stories would be better—more action, less talking. He pictures a kid about his own age with twelve gangly squid arms who can clean and cook and fight bad guys at the same time. He runs away from home to the big city. That's where he can do the most good. When the boy goes to school during the day the other kids make fun of him for having so many gross arms. But he doesn't care because he knows he's been put on earth for a reason.

Louis curls his knees into his chest. His mother knocks and then enters.

"I'm going to the supermarket," she says. "Why don't you

come?"

He was planning to meet up with Adam at ten, but he's happy his mother wants to get out of the house; he doesn't want to disappoint her. "Okay, mom," he says.

"Put on your coat. Come on, hurry up."

Louis texts Adam. "Slight delay. Will text when free."

"Kk."

At Stop & Shop, squeaky shopping carts seem to be muttering to each other. Customers, mostly women, stand with hands on hips, posing like statues as they stare at shelves of food, trying to decide what to buy. Louis follows his mother at a distance, looking around, wondering if anyone can tell he's not the same since he did what he did; he feels guilty, but also brave. How many boys would risk getting caught with a gun to protect their family?

His mother suddenly leaps back from the cart. "Oh my god," she says and points. Louis catches up to her and looks: a long-legged spider dances over a box of generic chocolate chip cookies. Louis laughs. "It's okay, mom." He bends over the cart and holds out his hand; the arachnid climbs onto his knuckles. Louis brings it close to his face. Its entire body trembles.

"Keep it away from me," his mother calls.

Louis gently puts the spider onto a shelf of canned fruit. "Spiders are good luck," he says.

In the check-out line, Louis rests his hand on the mountain of food in their cart.

His mother pulls a scarf out of her coat pocket and wraps it around her neck. "Louis," his mother says. "I wanted to talk to you."

"About what?"

Her face looks strained. "I just wanted you to know that I love you." He must look puzzled because she says, "It's not so out of the blue, hon."

His mother's face has been vacant lately, like someone had emptied all of her feelings out onto the kitchen table the way you'd empty a purse. But now a crooked crease runs down the center of her forehead, her skin turns red, and her eyes get wet.

Louis hates when his mother cries. It means he's supposed to make her feel better, but he can never figure out how. "Everything will be okay. Please, mom." He's tempted to tell her how far he's already gone to protect them all, but he knows that would be stupid.

His mother wipes her eyes and then composes herself. "Okay," she says. "I'm okay."

Louis looks up at his mother. "I love you too, mom."

When they pull into the parking lot of their apartment complex, Louis is surprised to see Adam hop out of a parked car right near the side entrance to their building.

His mother parks the car and Louis leaps out to greet his friend. "Hey," he says.

"I figured I'd come over and save you a trip," Adam says. "We never hang at your house." It's true, but it was on purpose—any time Adam's mother dropped Louis off after school, he made an excuse for why they shouldn't go inside. Louis didn't want Adam to see his family's sparse, tiny space; Adam's family lived in a big house with a landscaped front yard.

He tries to hide the fact that he's embarrassed. "You're brilliant," Louis says.

"So totally."

Adam waves to his mother who returns the wave and then backs out of her space.

His own mother stands next to the now open trunk of their Chevy Malibu applying lip balm. "Is this your new friend?"

"Good to meet you," Adam says politely.

"You two boys can handle the bags, then?"

Adam kisses his tiny bicep as if he's the Hulk. "No problem, Mrs. Pearson."

"Okay, then," she says, seeming energized by Adam's good spirits. "Excellent!" She puts her lip balm in her purse, turns and walks toward the apartment.

Adam picks up the two heaviest bags like they're nothing and follows. "Your mom is funny," he says.

Louis smiles awkwardly.

Inside, as they put away the groceries, Louis watches Adam for any signs that he's repulsed by his family's apartment.

Adam says, "You have a really cool view of the woods."

Louis used to stare out into the woods all the time. Now all he ever notices when he looks back there are the dumpsters behind the building piled high with garbage. "Yeah. It's nice."

Adam stacks a can of soup. "Do you ever see eagles or hawks or anything?"

"Not yet, but I'm on the lookout."

When they're finished with the groceries, Louis's mother makes them peanut butter sandwiches. Louis cringes. This is the only snack they can offer Adam, even after shopping.

Adam takes a huge bite of his and then grins, his teeth and lips covered with peanut butter. "Grrrrrrrr," he growls, holding his hands up like claws.

Louis laughs and then takes a messy bite of his own sandwich and growls back.

When they're done eating, they go to Louis's room and decide to play chess, a game Louis's father taught him. After a handful of moves, it's obvious Louis will win. But he can tell that Adam has improved since their last match; it won't be long before he's the better player.

As Adam studies the board, Louis notices a knot tightening around something in his chest. He can feel the gun there in the closet, a big, heavy weight.

He stares at his friend. "Have you ever seen a revolver?" The words just come out; he didn't plan them.

Adam looks up. "What?"

Louis realizes he doesn't want to be the only one who has seen the ugly weapon. "Just take a look at it, okay?"

Adam tenses. "Yeah. Okay," he says.

Without saying a word, Louis goes to his closet. He shoves aside his comic books and pulls out the shoebox.

Adam looks at it and then back at Louis. "This is weird," he says.

"It's okay." Louis peels off the lid; just the sight of the weapon causes a spasm of fear to run through his body.

"Whoa!" Adam instinctively reaches for the gun.

Louis pulls away. "No," he says. "No one touches it. It's too dangerous." He puts the lid back on the box.

Adam exhales. "Thanks for showing it to me."

"Sure," Louis says.

After chess, they decide to come up with an idea for a comic book.

"Let's do this outside," Louis says. "I think better in the woods."

They gather materials and dash outside. They wander through the woods until they come to a small clearing. A shallow ice puddle reflects a ray of light from the sun, which is already descending. "This looks like a good spot," Louis says.

Without a word, Adam drops to his knees, pulls out a pen and paper and begins sketching.

"He should be tall, but thin," Louis says.

"Yeah. Ordinary."

"Exactly."

"A superhero that everyone will understand."

Louis releases a breath in a long, thin stream. "You'll draw them and I'll write the stories."

That night, Louis has a dream. He's in Benfield, but the entire town looks different. Industrial, brick, windowless buildings line every street, wide fields of manicured grass seem to stretch for miles, and airplanes constantly roar overhead. The people are all young and grim and seem to be rushing to get somewhere. He's rushing too, to school—there's a math quiz that day —but he's lost. There are no buses, the streets are wide and long, and every building looks the same. He hurries into one entrance, then another, and then another. He realizes that all of the entrances are exact copies of the lobby of his family's building, except instead of a dirty blue rug that leads to the elevator, there's a sparkling red and gold one. He finally gives in and goes into one of the buildings, bypasses the elevator, and heads up the stairs. For some reason, his math test is being held in his family's apartment. He runs down the hall, but then suddenly a man steps in front of him. He has square shoulders, dark hair, and a bushy beard. He's holding the snub-nosed revolver in his hand.

Louis wakes, sweating.

A couple of days pass. His father goes to work, comes home, eats dinner with the family. His mother sleeps and reads her book. They even laugh a few times. Maybe everything will be okay, Louis thinks. Maybe there was no reason to worry after all.

One evening, he goes with his father to gas up the car. The old Malibu looks bad from the outside, but the engine hums and gives a pleasant ride. Louis always feels secure sitting in the passenger seat.

His father clenches his teeth. He turns on the radio, tries out a few stations, and then turns it off.

"I know I've been working long hours and that's been hard

on you." He stares through the windshield, squinting at the headlights from oncoming traffic. "I want to thank you for taking care of your mom." He pulls his eyes off the road for a second and looks at Louis. "I'm proud of you."

Louis stares at his father. He's never felt happier. Not when he'd won a writing award in fourth grade and his story was published in the *Benfield Weekly*. Not when he'd gotten his first (and only) hit in a little league game last summer.

When they reach the Sunoco station, his father parks the car at the pumps. He holds out his hand. "Men shake," he says.

His father's hand is smaller than Louis expects, and more delicate.

"Good," his father says and opens his car door. "I'll be right back." But then a loud beeping sound emanates from his coat pocket; he pauses halfway in and out of the car so he can check his phone. As he looks, his eyes narrow and he purses his lips. Louis feels that knot around something in his chest tighten again as his father looks up from his phone; he looks out the windshield for a couple of beats, his jaw getting harder, his face redder. Then he slams the phone onto the seat. "I'm gonna run in the store a minute," he says.

Louis watches his father go into the convenience store connected with the gas station. When he's sure his father can't see him, he grabs his father's phone. Several people have posted nasty comments on Facebook. "You should hang yourself," someone wrote. "Go to hell," wrote another. Another wrote, "I'm watching you. Believe me, I am watching you."

Louis closes his eyes, but that just makes it worse; he can hear his heart thumping. He tries to think about the superhero that he's developing with Adam, but they haven't gotten very far. They'll do more soon.

When his father comes out of the store, he's carrying two six-packs of beer. He gets in the car, closes the door, and slams on the accelerator, making the tires squeal; he never even got gas.

As they drive, Louis, feeling his father's rage grow, is afraid to talk.

His father hits the brakes, and then peels down a side road. "We're getting something to eat," he says. "Your mother isn't gonna cook."

"Okay."

Louis waits in the car in the parking lot outside Town's Pizza. He stares out the window. The sky is clear. Black. If there were clouds, he thinks, he could imagine them transforming into something that would save him in this moment. Save them all.

When his father returns, he cracks open a beer and climbs behind the wheel. He drinks the entire can in a continuous series of gulps. "Here we go," he says.

His eyes are crazy, Louis thinks.

At home, his father pours another beer into a glass, plops the pizza on the kitchen table, and starts gobbling it down. "Eat," he says to Louis.

Louis hesitates.

"Come on. Eat!"

Louis takes a few small nibbles of the pizza. His mother watches like a frightened dog from the living room.

His father looks over at his mother. "What are you staring at?"

"Nothing," she says.

"You want a slice? Or are you fat enough?"

"Tim, please."

"If you cooked something besides macaroni and cheese, maybe you wouldn't look like a jumbo jet."

"I..." His mother sounds scared.

"You're so fucking out of shape." He grunts like a pig.

"Tim—"

"Am I wrong?"

"That isn't fair."

He slams his fist on the table. "You heard of jogging? It's a new craze sweeping the nation."

"Leave her alone," Louis says. He's surprised how small his voice sounds.

"You too? Is the world against me?"

His mother stands. "Tim, in a few months, everything will seem..."

"Fuck both of you." He slams his drink onto the floor. Beer shoots up into the air like a fountain and shards of glass fly all over the kitchen.

His father stands and grabs the doorknob, but the door won't open. "What the hell!" He kicks at it. Then, in a moment of clarity, he unlocks the deadbolt that had been keeping it shut and leaves, slamming the door behind him. The metal door hums.

His mother looks at Louis and tries on a comforting smile, but she can't manage it. Louis begins to pick up the broken glass on the floor.

"I'll get that." She kneels next to Louis and together they clean up the mess. His mother's hands shake.


Louis texts Adam later that night. "Dad losing it."

"R u ok?"

"Not sure."

"Did he find the gun?"

"No."

"U r a master thief."

Louis stares at his phone, unsure what to write next. He looks around his room: a pair of crumpled jeans lie on the floor;

a tall stack of used comic books teeter like the Leaning Tower of Pisa next to his closet; a pile of his friend's drawings, mostly of ideas for a new superhero, are scattered over his desk. He types, "Our superhero won't use guns."

"Ha. Yeah. He won't need to."

"How do we make that work?"

Adam thinks, then answers, "How about something to do with water?"

"Bullets go right through him!"

"Exactly."

"He's a normal looking kid, but he can take any shape he wants."

"He's Salt Man! He can dissolve in water!"

Adam gives a thumbs up.

Louis types, "Start talking about story tomorrow at school. K?"

Adam texts a GIF of a kid screaming with joy.

Louis tosses and turns that night. He thinks about the trial in *Tom Sawyer*. Muff Potter is accused of murder, but he's really just a sad drunk and didn't commit the crime. Tom Sawyer feels bad for him and even thinks about helping Muff escape, but the man is pale and hopeless and would just get himself caught. When Tom bravely takes the witness stand and accuses Injun Joe of the crime, the real murderer jumps out of the courthouse window and escapes.

Both men are bad, Louis decides, but Muff is worse. He's weak. It's good to be a man of action, like Injun Joe. But it's better to do the right thing, like Tom Sawyer.

The next morning, before the sun comes up, Louis rummages in his closet, pushing all of his comic books out of the way, and takes out the shoebox that holds the gun. Carefully, he slides it under his bed where he can reach it if he needs to.

## MAY 26, 1978

P ete got home from work at 4 p.m. feeling like his body had been wrung out like a damp washcloth. Tara and the kids weren't around, but she'd left a note saying she'd be back soon. He took a shower and then raced off to the diner for a quick meal. The place was nearly empty, which he took to mean most folks were home having dinner with their families at this hour. The new waitress was stunning—curly brown hair and clear, blue eyes—but he didn't have enough time to rev up the charm. He already had a date.

The drive to the Landon Hotel in New Haven took longer than he expected because of an accident on Route 95, but he didn't mind much. It was ironic that all the excitement of his adult life happened in his hometown—the place he had once been so relieved to escape. With the windows rolled down, he sang along to the Beach Boys' "Good Vibrations" and pictured Marianne's narrow shoulders, tiny breasts, and round ass. She was a bit of a talker, too, which he liked. She usually got going on something to do with feminism, which he thought was funny considering what they were doing together. He would lean in closer and closer as she talked, until his lips were lightly pressed against her neck. Then she'd stop talking.

The Square Lounge was crowded and smelled like hairspray. Pete pushed into the bar and ordered a gin and tonic. Marianne was due at nine-thirty so when ten passed and she still hadn't arrived, he called her number. No one answered. For ten seconds he contemplated the possibility that something had happened to her, then laughed to himself. Women had broken up with him before, but usually they had the courtesy to tell him he'd been dumped. He thought about the waitress at the diner and wished he'd taken his time there.

He ordered another gin and tonic. When his drink arrived, he caught a glimpse of himself in the mirror behind the bar: a well-dressed man with meticulously groomed hair and a practiced smile that could close any sale. There was no reason he should be sitting there alone. He scanned the room. Most of the women were with men or with friends. He needed a plan. He could separate one of these women from the herd like a lion falling on the weakest prey; he'd done that before, but it would require more work than he felt like putting into it tonight.

Marianne had stumbled as she stepped away from the bar one evening and he'd caught her; a smile and a drink led to their first time together. It didn't get easier than that. So he waited. After eleven, a new sort of woman began to appear in the bar. Tired looking. A little sad. He picked the best looking of them, a blonde, and sat next to her; he listened to her labored breathing, smelled her damp sweat, watched the mole on her cheek bob up and down as she talked. The lounge bustled with noise. The dim lights made everything seem like a hazy black and white movie.

* * *

Tara, wearing tight blue jeans and a blouse, sat down with Shelby, her oldest, and served her string beans and meatloaf while the baby slept in her crib.

"What do you say?"

"Thank you."

"Good. Now eat."

Shelby gobbled up her mashed potatoes. She was in a rush to finish so she could watch an episode of Wonder Woman that was starting in ten minutes.

"How was school today?" Tara lit a cigarette and took a puff.

"It was okay."

"Did you learn anything interesting?"

"Not really."

"Nothing?"

Shelby rested her fork against her lips and thought about it. "We got to order new books from the reading catalog. That was fun."

"What did you order?"

"A mystery book. With ghosts."

"Oh. Scary."

"I'm not scared."

Tara took a long drag on her cigarette. "You're not afraid of ghosts?"

"There's no such thing, Mom."

"You'd be surprised."

"Really?"

"Ghosts are everywhere." Tara sipped her wine. "They're over there. And there. And here!" She tickled Shelby, who giggled and pulled away.

"Quit it." After a moment, she took another bite of her meatloaf. "You don't really believe in ghosts, do you?"

Tara didn't answer for a stretched-out minute; Shelby waited without moving. "Who knows what's real and what *isn't?" Tara looked over her shoulder as if she expected to see a ghost looking back. She crushed her cigarette into an ashtray.*

*"I don't believe in them," Shelby said to reassure herself.*

*"Well," Tara said. "You're young."*

*"So?"*

*"You believe in bad things more when you get older."*

*"Why?"*

*"Because life happens." She noticed Shelby looking toward the living room television. "Real life."*

*Shelby was playing with her potatoes. "I don't understand."*

*Tara laughed bitterly. "You will." Instinctively, she lit another cigarette. If only Pete would come back from his trip, she thought, she could get a break from answering these insane questions for ten seconds.*

*"Okay." Shelby reached for a napkin, but her elbow struck the glass of soda that sat on the edge of the table and sent it to the floor; it shattered, sending a streaming shower all over the floor and onto the flowered wallpaper.*

*"Fuck," Tara said. "What's wrong with you?"*

*"Mom, I—"*

*"You have to pay attention to what you're doing, Shelby."*

*"I was paying attention." The girl bit her lower lip.*

*Tara flicked the fresh cigarette into the sink. "Don't give me that. You wouldn't have spilled your soda if you'd been paying attention."*

*"But I was."*

*"Goddamnit, Shel!" Tara grabbed her daughter by the hair and forced her to look at the mess on the table. Shelby reached out, her hand shaking, and tried to clean up the spill. She let out a muffled shriek as a splash of red blossomed on her palm.*

*Tara said, "Stop being so dramatic." But when she noticed how pale her daughter was, her breath caught in her throat. Tara let her lungs fill with air. "Did you cut yourself?" Tara reached* for Shelby's hand, but Shelby pulled away." Tara deliberately made her voice softer. "Come on, hon, let Mommy see."

Shelby tried to choke down her sobs. Sniffling, she held out her hand. Tara tried her best not to cringe. It wasn't deep, but it looked nasty. She led Shelby upstairs to the bathroom and carefully washed out the cut with soap and water, dabbed it with a washcloth, and covered it with a bandage. "Does that feel better?"

The girl looked at the wound. "Yes."

The tub was filled with plastic dolls left there from Shelby's last bath. Tara grabbed her daughter into a hug. "I'm sorry I lost my temper."

"It's okay."

"You know Mommy loves you. I just want everything to be nice."

Shelby nodded.

"Forget dinner. We'll just have ice cream. How does that sound?"

Shelby nodded again.

"Do you forgive me?"

"Yes."

Tara lifted Shelby's chin. "Promise?"

The girl couldn't hold back her tears anymore. "I forgive you."

Tara hugged Shelby again. Just then, the baby started wailing. The sound came in waves. The girl could feel her mother's body slacken. Suddenly, Tara was crying too.

# APRIL 2014

## BATTLE HYMN

Wendy flips on the light switch in the dingy gym of Benfield High. One of the lamps that hangs from the ceiling pops and sizzles. She leaps away, but it's only another damn bulb needing to be replaced. She collects herself, pushes back through the swinging doors, and stares at it for a ponderous moment. During the day, sunlight would pour in through the large windows that skirted the top of both long walls; running a dance class at night had not been a consideration of the architects who designed the building.

Inside the storage closet she finds the usual: several janitor uniforms suspended on hangers, a stack of plastic buckets sitting next to an old mop, a balding broom, a locked toolkit, and a wet/dry vacuum. But the ladder isn't in its usual spot on a hook in the back. She pushes aside the uniforms to see if she's just not finding it in the dim light, but it's definitely missing.

"Great," she whispers.

She cycles through the contact information on her phone—Vice-Principal Zachary Rivers, that administrative lady, Viki

Sobchok—until she finds the janitor's phone number. She presses the button.

"Hello?" He sounds groggy.

"This is Wendy Watson, the ballet teacher." She's aware of her uptalk; she is working on sounding more definitive.

His own voice perks up. "Wendy Watson. Wow. How can I help you?"

"Another bulb went out." That made it four since February. "And the ladder is MIA. Do you know where it is?"

"Oh shoot. Sorry about that. I chucked that old thing in the garbage last week. It was getting dangerous."

She rolls her eyes and then looks around the gym. The ragged basketball nets on either side of the room hang off their respective rims like cobwebs. Cracked padding runs along one wall. Retractable bleachers from half a century ago, chipped and worn, run along the other.

"Listen, Nick, I really, really hate to ask—I know this is your off time—but is there any chance you can swing by here with a ladder and change the bulb?" She hopes she isn't asking too much of him.

"Sure thing," he says. "I'll be right there."

"Really? That's great. I appreciate it."

"It's no problem at all. That's why I get paid the big bucks."

"Right!" She likes that he's so helpful; kind men are difficult to find these days. "We're all getting fat and rich, right?"

"You're funny," he replies and hangs up.

When she pictures Nick—an acquaintance from her high school days—she can only imagine him sitting home by himself eating old-fashioned foil-wrapped TV dinners and watching cop shows. So maybe she's giving him something to do with his time and she shouldn't feel guilty?

Wendy pulls a portable speaker from her backpack, sets it up on the first row of the bleachers, and attaches her phone.

She starts and stops a few numbers: "Don Quixote, Act III, No. 24," and "Pas de quatre ballet: Coda." She wants to find something with the right tempo for class. They're not fast learners, she thinks. When she settles on "Pavane, Opus 50," she pulls out her compact and admires her auburn hair and smooth skin; if she didn't look so tired, she could pass for twenty-five. Is thirty-three too early for bags under your eyes? Taking a breath, she pushes a stray silver hair into the bun on the back of her head. Now, divorced and back in Massachusetts, what she wants more than anything is to be left alone—to live a quiet life in the town where she grew up.

"Wendy?"

Nick's brown hair is messy and tangled, like a child's, and he's wearing beat-up brown coveralls under a grease-stained quilted vest. His face hasn't changed much since high school.

"That was fast," she says.

"I live a few blocks away."

"Oh, I didn't realize." Now she *really* doesn't have to feel bad. She thinks for a moment. Why does she always feel like everything is her fault anyway?

He gives a friendly nod. "I'll be a second."

"Take your time."

He drags a folding metal ladder to the center of the gym. "You always get here before class like this?"

"I like to set up without having to run around while the students are arriving."

He steps onto the ladder. "That makes a lot of sense."

"It pays to be prepared."

As Wendy says this, she realizes she no longer believes it. She used to be the type of woman who looked forward to the future, sure she could get the life she wanted if only she checked all the boxes along the way—and she had: she'd diligently put herself out there—dating, making small talk on commuter trains and in coffee shops—always ready to meet the right man. It had all fallen into place when Dan came into her life. He was perfect—masculine, but sensitive. She'd been sure he would never hurt her. After their wedding he landed a job in San Francisco developing software for a start-up, and she followed him there, excited to start a family.

Nick pulls a new bulb from its soft cardboard case. "How many teachers does it take to change a light bulb?"

"Nick..." and she is about to say, *I'm sorry, but I need to finish setting up*, but stops herself. He did come by to help during his off hours and he's being awfully nice, so she re-engineers her reply. "I don't know. How many teachers does it take to change a light bulb?"

He says, pointing a finger at her like a scolding teacher, "You need to figure that out for yourself, young lady." He waits for a reaction. After a beat he says, "Don't you get it?"

She's heard the joke before but pretends she's just understanding it now. "Oh, right. That's funny, Nick."

He begins descending the ladder. "You're not laughing."

"Well..."

"I know. Light bulb jokes aren't really funny. They tend to go over your head."

Wendy lets the pun drop without comment. She doesn't want to be rude, but she really needs to get ready for class. "I *so* appreciate you helping me tonight. I don't know what I would have done without you." She does know. She would have taught the class in the near dark and apologized to her students for the inconvenience.

He shuffles his feet. "Can I tell you something?"

She can see no polite way of stopping him. "Sure. What is it?"

"I almost asked you to the senior prom," he says. "Did you know that?"

She'd had a doting boyfriend, Harris, whom she had dated for three years, so she didn't think much about other boys back then. It had rarely occurred to her that anyone else could have a crush on her anyway, especially with her braces and plump frame. She didn't have the braces anymore, but in spite of eleven years of dancing she felt that her body was still a little too round. No matter how much she flexed her arms or calves, a layer of puffy flesh covered the muscles she knew lay below the surface.

"What stopped you?" she asks.

He looks down at the floor. "Things got complicated and I ended up skipping the prom."

"You didn't miss much," she says.

"I still wish I'd gone. You only get one chance at those things in your life."

"That's true."

She hopes agreeing will end the conversation, but he says, "We should get dinner some time."

Some men cannot take a hint. Scratch that. None of them can. She wants to give a flat no, but doesn't want to be mean. She decides to drop an obvious hint. "How about coffee instead of dinner? Like Dunkin' Donuts?"

He thinks. "How about the diner?"

A diner is the best compromise she's going to get. "Benfield Diner near the library?" It had been a popular place for the kids to hang out after an evening of parties, but she hadn't been there since high school.

"That's the place."

"Well, then, sure. That'll be fun."

"Terrific!" he says.

Wendy feels her face reddening. "Great!" Why did she still worry so much about being nice to everyone?

She plans to arrive before seven that Friday night to find a table near the door for a quick getaway but falls asleep in the afternoon and is now running late. She curses herself as she pushes through into the damp warmth of the diner at quarter past to find Nick waiting for her in a booth by the window on the other side of the room. She hurries past the old counter. The vinyl upholstery on the row of stools is cracked and patched in places; yellow, formless stains cover the linoleum floor; the lights above flicker, though they've done that for as long as Wendy can remember.

She sits down, rubbing her hands together. "It got really cold out."

"Yeah, it's crazy how fast it changes this time of year. I like it, though. It feels like something important is happening. Like potential. I wish I could feel that all the time."

He's smiling at her. "I know what you mean," she says. "But spring always leads to green trees and grass everywhere you look. You can't stay in potential forever."

"I know." He opens his menu. "Summer's a pretty good time of year, too," he says. "Nothing will help you beat the heat in August like driving down to Nelson's Pond for a swim."

"I used to go there as a kid." It's where Wendy had passed her lifeguard certification test—another place she hasn't visited since high school. She opens her own menu. "We really should figure out what we're going to eat. There are way too many choices." She remembers vividly the pancakes and vanilla milkshakes she would eat at 3 a.m. here. Tempting as those are, however, she wants to find something that won't make her look like a pig in front of Nick.

"The specials are good. Chicken pot pie especially."

"Thanks for the advice." She decides on a salad. "You eat here a lot?"

"Every night."

This strikes her as strange, but she says nothing. Small talk is her best bet. Stick to the weather. The local headlines. "I came back to Benfield because I thought it would be peaceful," she says, "but I didn't know about those murders. Benfield has really changed."

"Nothing really changes," he says matter-of-factly. "People always hurt people."

"This guy killed an elderly couple in their sleep, though."

"He was only eighteen years old," Nick says.

"But he didn't have to *kill* them. He's horrible."

Nick raises an eyebrow. "We don't know the full story." He looks down at his menu. "Anyway, I'm starving."

"Me too," Wendy says quickly. She realizes she'd been getting worked up for no reason. She's happy to change the subject.

After they order he leans forward. "You still look really good, you know."

She can't remember the last time she'd received a compliment dropped casually into a conversation like this. And she hadn't felt at her best; it was just what she needed to hear. "Thank you, that's really nice of you to say."

"It's my pleasure."

Nick doesn't look half bad himself. He's wearing a worn-out blue flannel shirt that fits snugly around his shoulders. His hair is combed flat to one side, and he shaved, revealing a strong jawline. But the last thing she wants is a fling with an old schoolmate.

She works up the courage and then says, "A quick heads-up. I'm off the market, dating wise. I hate to be blunt about it, but I didn't want there to be any misunderstanding."

Nick rearranges the salt and pepper shakers so they're in a single line with the ketchup. "That's okay. I don't really date anyway."

"Oh yeah?" She's relieved. "Why's that?"

"Don't you know about me?"

She tries to remember but can't. "What are you talking about?"

"I thought everyone knew." After scratching his chin, he looks straight up at her. His eyes are the darkest she's ever seen, yet they're bright and sad. "I hung with some bad kids in high school. You probably remember that."

A bad crowd is putting it mildly, she thinks. One of Nick's pals had been a notorious shoplifter, and another sold an assortment of drugs near the dumpsters behind the high school.

"We used to skip class and go to the deserted tracks across from the junior high school and smoke," Nick says. "We mostly goofed around, talked about girls...you know."

"We all did silly things back then. It shouldn't stop you from dating now."

"Well, that's not really what I meant." He moves the salt and pepper shaker with the ketchup into a triangle. "I hung out with those guys because I wanted to do something to make me feel tough. I really needed that then." He shoots his eyes up at her. "You really don't know about this?"

She feels the muscles in her neck tighten. "Know what?"

"When I was little, my dad used to... He...you know...I didn't want to talk about it, but they made me see the school counselor and after that it seemed like everybody knew. The counselor didn't help, anyway. I've never been able to be intimate with anyone. I can't."

She remembers what Nick had said earlier. *We don't know the full story.* No one can escape their past, she thinks. "Oh my god, Nick. That's awful."

"Thanks." A thoughtful beat. "You really didn't know?"

She's touched that he's opened up like this. "I guess I heard rumors and stuff, but I never knew the details. I'm really sorry."

And the truth was, she'd forgotten about those rumors until he'd brought them up. Which was worse, to remember him as the abused kid or to have forgotten all about it? She cast her eyes down at the table.

"It's okay," he says. "We all have a cross to bear."

"I guess that's true." She looks at her hands and then, for something to say, asks, "Are you religious?"

"Because of the cross to bear thing? No, I'm not. That's just a figure of speech."

"I'm not religious either. I think it's all a bunch of lies so people can hide their heads in the sand."

He tilts his head like a curious puppy. After a moment of thinking he says, "I have nothing against people who believe in God. If it helps you get through the day, then you should do it."

"I agree with that. Hey, maybe you should give it a try."

Nick grins good-naturedly. "Give God a try? Is there a one-week trial or something?"

They both laugh, but Wendy feels like an asshole. Who's she to tell Nick how to fix his life?

Nick's expression turns thoughtful. "It is a really nice thing to think about, but no. I don't think I could fool myself like that."

"I hear you." She releases all the air in her lungs. "I suppose we all have to face up to things eventually."

"I guess so." His smile is crooked. "But I wish I had some kind of story to believe in."

This is not at all how she imagined the evening going. She'd worn a baggy sweatshirt to encourage small talk and avoid intimate revelations. She feels the weight of the years that have passed since the last time she saw Nick. But that was a long time ago—before she'd left for San Francisco. Back then she'd been certain her life would go exactly as she'd planned.

There's a welcome break in the conversation as the waiter delivers Nick's vegetable soup.

"That looks good," she says.

He holds a spoonful in front of his mouth and, after gently blowing across the surface, takes a sip. "It's a bit salty." He looks up at her. "Wanna try?"

She leans forward and he feeds her. Normally this would seem weird, but somehow it's okay with him. She follows the warmth all the way down to her stomach. "Not bad," she says. "But you're right, a bit salty."

Nick says, "You want some more?"

"It's your soup. You eat it."

He takes a few delicate slurps. He's a sweet man, she thinks. It's terrible what happened. Nick probably never had the chance to feel that his life would go exactly as he planned it.

Wendy suddenly wishes she'd dressed up for their date, or at least worn some makeup. She pulls her hair back and ties it into a ponytail. "You look different from how you looked in high school," she says. "But in a good way."

He doesn't stop eating. "You really think so?"

"More grown up."

"That's a good thing?"

"Definitely. The more distance I get from all that youthful beauty, the happier I get."

"Aw shucks." His sarcasm is charming.

"I'm sorry, I only mean, instead of perfection in the shiny faces of kids, I see innocence and stupidity. Wisdom is the real beauty."

"I like that." He smiles, perhaps flirtatiously. "You're very wise."

"Why, thank you." She flips her ponytail like a teenager. "You really wanted to ask me to go to the prom with you?"

"You always seemed so happy in those days." She doesn't remember being happy. "But I couldn't ask you," he says. "I was a bit of a mess."

"Of course, I'm sorry." She watches the way he eats, not spilling a drop. "It's nice to know all these years later that you were interested, though. It still feels good."

"Does it?"

"Yes. I've had a pretty shitty time of it lately."

"What happened?"

"Divorce."

"Oh, I'm sorry."

"He left me."

"Oof. That really sucks."

"That's okay."

"What happened, exactly?"

"What happened? I don't know. I guess he got bored. That's what people say, right?" Wendy sits quietly for a moment. "He called a few weeks after he left and said he was sorry. He wanted to stay friends." Wendy chuckles ruefully. "Friends? You can't go back to trusting a person after something like that." She shakes her head. "When other women used to complain about their guys losing interest, I gave them my shoulder to cry on, but secretly I was sooo happy it wasn't happening to me. I was dumb."

An awkward pause follows, and Wendy wonders what Nick is thinking. The waiter arrives with the rest of their food and the sound of plates clicking down onto the table snaps Wendy out of her anxious reverie. When the waiter leaves, Wendy says, "I was going on and on, wasn't I?"

"It's okay." Nick pokes at his steamed vegetables, which look desiccated. "I like that kind of story."

"What kind of story exactly?" She pushes her wilted salad aside.

"Stories about real life. You know, people doing the things I can't do." He must sense that she pities him because he rushes to add, "I didn't say that to make you feel sorry for me."

"I don't. Really." Strange that Nick thinks he has intimacy issues. She and Dan dated for two years before marriage and never had this open a conversation.

"Thanks. People always want to feel bad for me. Don't get me wrong, I understand that. I'd feel bad for me too if I was looking in from the outside, but if I'm being honest, I'm kinda used to my situation."

"You shouldn't give up." She hears herself sounding like a Hallmark card and cringes.

"I haven't. I've accepted things. There's no undoing what happened. I'm stuck with who I am now."

"I'm stuck too," she says impulsively.

"Well...we're not the same." His voice isn't unfriendly, but it has an edge. "You know what I mean?"

"Of course. I shouldn't have said that."

"That's okay," he says. "Maybe we should eat."

She worries that she has offended him as she pokes at her salad. It actually tastes better than it looks. Nick seems to be enjoying his pasta. She starts to speak, but then stops.

"What?" Nick asks.

"Do you *ever* date?" she asks. "Or is it completely out of the question?"

"I never date." Without looking up he adds, "But I pay for it once in a while."

Wendy instinctively leans away from him. She has said during more than one cocktail conversation that prostitution should be legal, believing it would be better for women if the practice were regulated. But now that she is confronted by a man who has actually slept with a prostitute, she isn't sure how she feels. Finally, she says, "What's that like?"

"It's exciting the first few times, but after a while it gets kind of terrible. You start to think, even before she arrives, that this is all it is. Just this hour. No dinners, no movies, no kisses on the doorstep before saying goodnight. It makes you feel like an animal." He's a romantic, even about prostitution, she thinks. "But I guess we're all animals. And animals have drives that insist on being fed."

He looks at her when he says this, perhaps hoping she'll explore her own animal impulses with him later that night. She's warming up to the idea, but not for animal reasons. She'd like to be the one who breaks through his outer shell. She imagines them embracing, crying together. She could help him find a therapist, a new job...She'd be the one who turns his life around.

There's a break in the conversation and she listens to him chewing. His jaw clicks like a metronome. Click. One chew. Click. Another chew. After a moment she detects a soft humming sound.

"Are you singing?"

"Oh yeah. Probably."

"I recognize the tune, but I can't quite place it."

"It's the 'Battle Hymn of the Republic.'"

"That's it. Yes! Why the heck are you humming that?"

"It's something I do. It keeps me calm. I'm sorry if it's bothering you."

"Not at all," she says. "You might have heard the rumor: I like music!"

"Yeah, that's right." He points his fork at her. "How did you get into dancing?"

"I got swept up in it at college and kinda fell in love. So many things make us numb to the world. TV. Movies. Drugs. But dancing makes you more alive. It's pure happiness." She hears how Pollyanna sounds, but he simply nods in agreement.

"I guess we would have danced at the prom," he says. "If we'd gone together."

"Yes, I guess we would have." She wants to reach out and take his hand. But no, that would be wrong. Instead, she looks down at her food. "This salad ain't half bad."

"I'm glad you like it."

Later, outside in the crisp air, cautiously hugging, they say goodnight.

Her students annoy her the next evening, in particular Shelby Blythe, the town librarian, who stays past eight asking for advice on ways to improve her balance. Wendy has no desire to stay late, but Shelby has been struggling since her parents' violent death. How can Wendy turn her away, especially after her talk with Nick? She grits her teeth. There's that guilt again. She forces a smile and says she can stay a few minutes longer.

At home in her small apartment, Wendy sits on the couch sipping apple juice from a bottle. She'd deliberately rented a tiny place when she moved back to Benfield, thinking the closeness of the walls and ceiling would help her feel safer and more in control. And it had been working until tonight; now she mostly feels numb.

Cardboard boxes full of her things are strewn about. A layer of dust, like the first snow of winter, lightly covers the tables and chairs and the cheap lamps she bought at the discount market. In an effort to shake the immense feeling of fear and loneliness that has awakened in her, she rips open the nearest box and pulls out the photo album from her wedding. It feels nice to hold solid proof of her past life. The pictures are standard: Dan and her feeding each other cake, the two of them leaning awkwardly against the railing outside the wedding hall, the bride surrounded by her bridesmaids. She runs her hands over the single shot of Dan standing alone under a cherry blossom tree in full bloom, his chin jutting forward, his eyes bright and expressive, and tries to find evidence of the man he would soon become.

She slams the book shut, shooting dust into the air. She pulls open other boxes, tossing books onto the floor until she finds her high school yearbook. Pictures of her with the debate team. At the prom with thick-haired Harris. Her goofy headshot revealing, in vivid color, her pimply skin poking through layers of make-up. She reads the words she chose to appear next to her picture: *Summers with the fam on the Cape. No debate, debate was great. Ready to take on the world!* She stares at that last phrase, then thumbs through the gallery page by page until she finds Nick's picture. He was definitely intense-looking, but cute. He'd written, *Jazz Band fun, Marching Band not fun. The goofaphone. It's all so....*

She removes her smartphone from her pocket and holds it, hovering her finger over Nick's number. She decides to text him instead.

"Hey, it's Wendy, what's up?" She feels like a coward, but is excited when the response comes seconds later.

"Home watching *The Sopranos* for the hundredth time. What's up with you?"

"I'm feeling itchy tonight." She deletes "itchy" and replaces it with "restless." "Do you want to hang out for a bit?"

"What do you have in mind?"

She didn't have a plan when she picked up the phone, but one appears like a light bulb over her head. She smiles at the vision, remembering Nick's joke. "Let's meet at the high school parking lot. You know, where the cool kids used to hang out."

"I wouldn't know," he responds.

Wendy parks along the edge of the lot next to the steep hill that runs up to West Street. The darkness swallows her car, the only one in the lot, and she hums the last song she heard on the radio —"Video Killed the Radio Star"—to keep herself company. She doesn't particularly like the song, but it's one of those tunes she can't get out of her head. She rolls down the window. The air is cold and wet; she begins to feel drowsy and starts to regret her decision to go out in the middle of the night to meet a man with intimacy issues.

He pulls up in a noisy old Honda Civic and backs into the spot next to hers so the driver's side of each car faces the other.

He shuts off the engine and rolls down the window. "How's it going?"

"Pretty good. How about you?"

"I'm fine." He rubs his forehead with the palm of his hand. She's seen him do this a few time, but isn't sure if it's a tic or that his head hurts. "Just fine."

"Good. I'm glad to hear it." The comfortable rapport they shared at the diner is gone. Now they have a history, and she feels pressure for this conversation to go well. "Can I sit over there?" She points.

He looks at his passenger seat and then back at her. "I'd better come over there. This thing isn't set up for humans." She giggles, and he adds, "My dog Filly chews up the seats pretty bad."

She watches in the rearview mirror as he passes by the back of her car; he has a smooth, athletic gait. He folds himself in and closes the door behind him. He smells like sweat and aftershave lotion. She checks out his crisp jeans and what appears to be a brand-new black windbreaker that he's zipped all the way up to the neck like a priest. Moving closer she asks, "Why'd you name your dog Philly? You can't be an Eagles fan."

"Definitely not an Eagles fan. I call her that because she's brown with long legs, kind of like a horse."

"*Filly.* Now I get it."

"You have any pets?"

"I can barely care for myself right now."

"I'm sure that's not true."

"I'd like to get a cat someday."

"Cats are good company."

"They are."

A moment passes in silence.

"So..." He pulls the zipper on his windbreaker halfway down and then back up. "What did you want to talk to me about?"

She isn't sure what to say. "The other night was fun."

"It was." He continues zipping and unzipping.

"It's nice to talk to someone from the old days."

"Yeah. It is."

"I wish we'd gotten to know each other when we were younger." He's cute, and she wants to trace her fingers over his face. "I feel like I missed a chance there."

"I don't know. I wasn't that fun back then."

"I bet you *were* fun."

"I really wasn't."

She feels her heartbeat against her ribs. "I bet you're fun now."

He lets go of the zipper, leaving it halfway down. Underneath he's wearing a ragged T-shirt; it might be the same one he had worn to the gym to change the light bulb.

She takes his hand and squeezes his rough fingers.

"Wendy, I..."

"Come closer."

He doesn't budge, but the heat builds between them and she can't stand it a moment longer. She leans toward him, her body loose and happy for the first time in too long. "Nick," she says.

He pulls back. "I can't. I'm sorry."

"Just come closer," she whispers.

"I thought maybe when you called we could...but no. I can't." He tugs his hand free.

The moment is broken, but she persists. "I really want this."

"I know you do." His smile is warm and sweet. "But I told you. I can't."

"Listen, Nick. It doesn't have to mean anything." A car passes up on West Street, dimly illuminating his face for a second. He looks more thoughtful than hurt. "Shoot, that didn't come out right," she says.

"If we do this, you'll wake up tomorrow morning and think, 'What the hell am I doing with *this* guy?'"

"You can't predict the future."

Nick shrugs. "What I do know is that my past isn't going anywhere. I'll never be that happy guy you want to marry someday."

"How do you know what I want?"

His eyes are sad. "You really haven't changed. You might not remember that much about me—" Wendy begins to protest, but he puts a coarse finger to her lips. "You don't have to say anything."

A salty lump fills her throat, forcing tears down her cheek. He gently pulls his hand away and they sit looking at each other. She wipes her face. "You know something, Nick. I'm really sorry about all this. I don't know what I'm doing."

"It's okay." He takes the last couple of tissues from a box on the passenger side floor and offers them to her.

She blows her nose. "Whooo," she exclaims. "I feel stupid." She crumples the tissue. "Thank you."

"No problem."

She gathers herself. "You know what?" she says. "Someday in the way-off future, you and I will meet again. I can feel it. We'll meet right back here and talk about our lives and laugh about how foolish we used to be."

Nick doesn't reply. After a quiet moment he begins softly humming "The Battle Hymn of the Republic." There's a childish simplicity to the tune; it's eerie, a song from a different time. Wendy observes the tiny muscles in Nick's jaw twitching. A drop of perspiration slides down his cheek. She feels a raw dread rising from her stomach into her throat as every second passes like a ticking bomb. She cautiously touches his shoulders, and he immediately stops humming, but remains silent for another beat.

"Are you okay?" she asks.

He tilts forward and glances through the windshield at the starless sky. "Here's what I think will happen someday, way off in the future," he says. "You'll move away somewhere and have a real life, then return to Benfield on vacation to show your family the place where you grew up. One afternoon on your way to get lunch, you'll pass by the high school and remember what happened tonight." He blinks slowly; he looks peaceful. "Later you'll go and visit my grave, and for just a second I'll be alive again."

# JULY 23, 1983

P ete and Tara strolled, arm in arm, through the Stardust Room of the Nevele Grand Hotel resort in the Catskills. Pete wore a light-brown suede leather jacket with jeans; Tara wore a black and white polka dot dress with a wide, red belt.

When they sat down, Pete glanced at the stage. "I think it's a Barry Manilow cover band."

"That sounds great," Tara said. "I love him."

They ordered cocktails and sat silently for a minute taking in the atmosphere. The other guests filling the hall chattered quietly. Warm lights cast delicate shadows on the floor. Pete took Tara's hand. "You look lovely tonight," he said. "Really. Just beautiful."

Tara was used to Pete's compliments, but she sensed he meant this one. "Thank you, hon. You do too."

Pete leaned closer to his wife until his face was only a few inches from hers. "It's so much easier to be us here, isn't it? I feel so much more relaxed."

"I know what you mean." Tara squeezed his hand. "I feel so happy."

Pete's gaze drifted toward the stage. "I wish we could stay here forever."

"Me too," Tara said. Neither said anything for another minute. Tara, overwhelmed by the moment, finally spoke. "I have to say something terrible."

"What?"

"Don't get angry."

"I won't. I promise. I wouldn't let anything spoil a night like this."

Tara squeezed his hand tighter. "I think our lives have become all about the kids. It's 'Shelby and Sam' this and 'the kids' that. We don't have time for ourselves."

Pete caressed Tara's hand. "I'm not angry at all. You're absolutely right." Jovially, he added, "We've become too unselfish. Those kids owe us!"

Tara laughed, but then, after reflecting, became serious again. "It's a different world here. The kids can go to the bowling alley or the swimming pool anytime they want and—"

"—they have their own room—"

"—and they're out of our hair."

"Yes."

"That leaves us free to do things... Adult things." Tara placed Pete's hand on her thigh.

"Yes." He dug his hand into her leg and dragged the chair closer. "It's like old times."

* * *

As the ice cream party was coming to an end and everyone was wandering out, Shelby stopped to talk to three kids she'd met that day playing pinball. Two of them were high school boys, a few years older than Shelby. One was tall and lean with dirty-blond straight hair that fell to his shoulders. The other was also tall, but his shoulders were already broad like a man's, and he had dark, curly hair. The girl was thin with freckles and a few years younger than the boys. The four of them spoke excitedly, planning to go to the arcade, but Sam, Shelby's six-year-old sister, began to complain; she was tired and wanted to go to sleep. Irritated, Shelby told her new friends that she'd leave her sister in the room and come right back. But the boys gathered the girls into a circle; for a moment they spoke conspiratorially. When Shelby turned around, she looked inspired. She took Sam's hand and led her out.

The air conditioner was blasting in their room because Shelby preferred it cold at night, and Sam didn't mind piling blankets on top of herself. But Dirty-Blond immediately shut the air off when he entered. "It's freezing," he said.

The teenagers decided to play charades. They wouldn't let Sam play but said she could watch; she propped herself on her own double bed. The rules, as she understood them, were simple: Your opponents suggest a movie. Your teammate then acts it out using only gestures. No talking aloud. It was boys against girls and you had just sixty seconds before time was up. Curly-Hair went first. He stood on Shelby's bed while the three other teens sat on the floor. He pretended to crack a whip once and then again and Dirty-Blond answered, Raiders of the Lost Ark.

"That was too easy," Curly-Hair said.

The boys high-fived.

Freckles, Shelby's partner, tried to act out her movie, but nothing she did made much sense and when time expired the boys were gloating. "The Godfather is a classic," Curly-Hair said.

The game went back and forth for about half an hour. The room started to warm up and the teens giggled and joked. Occasionally, Sam saw Dirty-Blond and Freckles exchange glances. She wasn't sleepy anymore; she felt like she was watching a nature documentary on TV and if she paid enough attention, she would learn something important about life.

"We're way ahead," Curly-Hair said.

Dirty-Blond added, "You're no match for the Death Star." That was the name they'd given their team.

The boys high-fived again and, as Shelby studied her next suggestion, they began pushing each other and wrestling around the floor. Shelby looked determined and stood on the bed. At first, she tried to act out her movie, gesticulating and making wild faces, but it was hopeless. Freckles just shrugged and giggled; it was like she was trying to lose. After about half a minute of this, Shelby's expression changed; her face softened, she pouted her lips and closed her eyes. Then she began gyrating her hips in a wide circle. Freckles looked more confused, but Shelby wasn't doing this show for her. Slowly, she tugged at her Madonna T-shirt—it showed the pop queen sucking on a lollipop. She pretended to pull it up over her head. The boys stopped wrestling and yelled and hooted. Dirty-Blond screamed, "Yes, please," and Freckles giggled nervously. Sam, not quite understanding what was happening, screamed with the others. When Shelby ripped her T-shirt off, exposing her bra, everyone got quiet. Curly-Hair stared, his jaw slack. Freckles pulled her knees into her chest and looked scared. Dirty-Blond grinned.

"You shouldn't do that," Freckles said.

But Shelby didn't stop. She continued swinging her hips as she pulled her bra off.

Sam began to panic; she felt there was something she should be doing. But what? Her sister tugged down her red shorts next and only her underwear remained; they were white and lacy with little blue flowers. Sam thought they made her sister seem small and vulnerable.

Freckles stood up and tried to tug Dirty-Blond toward the door. "Let's get out of here," she said. "This is stupid."

*"You go," he said. "I'll catch up with you later."*

*"We both will," Curly-Hair said.*

*Freckles slammed the door behind her. And then Shelby slowly and gently pulled her panties down until they were around her ankles.*

*"Stop," Sam said. "Stop it!"*

*Shelby's face didn't change; she still looked sad and strange as she swung her panties around one ankle and then flung them across the room with a kick.*

## MAY 2014

## NOTHING TO DO WITH REAL LIFE

Shelby lurches out of the prosecutor's office onto the sidewalk and nearly collides with another pedestrian. Catching her breath, she turns, wiping rain from her eyes, and shuffles around the building to the parking lot in the back. She can't believe the ruling; yes, the judge handed out a thirty-year sentence, but that's lenient for a double murder. All because some cop had roughed the kid up a bit when he was taken into custody? Her hands shake; the lawyer can't appeal the judge's decision, so she will have to find her own way to deal with this. She's not sure how, but she pauses there, letting the water soak her shirt, her loafers, and vows that somehow or other she'll get revenge.

She drives with the windows down. Stretched-out raindrops, like streaks of light, bite at her cheeks. Every once in a while, thunder rumbles. She grips the wheel with both hands, ignoring the pundits chattering away on NPR. After a short trip she pulls into the Taco Bell drive-through a mile from her condo and orders three soft beef tacos. Still inside her car, she eats quickly; she hasn't eaten meat in more than five years, but it feels good to break the rules. When she's done, she tilts the rearview mirror, dabs at the corner of her lips with a napkin, and then drives the rest of the way to her condominium complex. The building hasn't changed much since the '70s when it was constructed, but the exterior was recently repainted beige with dark brown trim. Shelby feels proud every time she looks at it; she was vice-president of the condo board when they made the decision to refurbish the exterior.

Inside, she collapses onto the floor with the lights out. Then something in her chest unclenches. It's over, at least. Billy Lawson is going to jail for a long time. That's good enough, isn't it? Is it worth spending her life finding a way to hurt a guy who is already in prison? Her anger would burn up like jet fuel in a year and she'd be left tired and sad. But would she be letting her parents down if she gave up too easily?

An image from her childhood pops into her head. Shelby is eight and has brought home a report card with a B-minus. Her mother is at the stove stirring a pot of stew and holding the evidence of Shelby's inadequacy in her other hand. She turns to her daughter. "Jesus Christ, Shel, you can't do anything right, can you?"

Shelby flicks on the lights and hoists herself to her feet. Her apartment is decorated with yellow-brown paintings, a gray area rug, and fully stocked bookshelves on all four walls. She begins practicing ballet, a new hobby she picked up to take her mind off losing her parents, but gives up after ten minutes, thinking her balance is simply hopeless.

Instead, she pulls a book down—it's a collection of the best short stories from 1987, her sophomore year in college—and starts reading one of her favorites. The details blur and after re-reading the third paragraph several times, she puts the book back on the shelf and goes to sleep. She wakes in the middle of the night, anxious, pulls her laptop onto her crossed legs, and goes online.

OkCupid is more of the usual. Two messages say, "How's it going?" another says, "Are you really forty-six?" and another two just say, "Hey." There's one from a guy in Boston that includes a link. Against her better judgment, she clicks on it and is unsurprised, but still shocked to see an entire Instagram account full of dick pics. She'd been hoping to hear from an archivist for a museum in Boston, but the woman hasn't written in a week. Dating is hopeless. She goes to *The Boston Globe* website, but the news is typically depressing. And she won't read the *Benfield Weekly*; it's full of stories about her parents' murder, including yet another interview with Billy Lawson's mother. She tries the local news from Stanton, a neighboring town; it's always less sensational, more concerned with simple facts. She reads the coverage of the trial.

*There was noticeable outrage in the courtroom when the sentence of thirty years was announced. Judge Klepper's controversial decision to forgo a life sentence for the eighteen-year-old did not sit easily with those who had come to see justice handed down. Shelby Blythe, the elder of the Blythes' two daughters, stormed out of the courtroom, slamming the door behind her. Samantha, her sister, began weeping from her seat in the back row.*

The story is written by a female reporter—somehow that figures—named Emilia Stone. There's a black-and-white picture of her next to her byline; her eyes are tiny, but intense. Shelby touches the picture with her fingertips.

Mr. Wictor checks out a couple of Hercule Poirot mysteries the next morning and Mrs. Freeman returns seven recipe books—"I really have to learn to cook something or my husband is gonna run for the hills"—but otherwise the library is quiet. Shelby catches up on a bit of inventory work but finds herself staring at the *Stanton Journal* byline again at lunch time.

On a whim, she checks out the reporter's Facebook profile and finds a few photos from several years before of her holding hands with a pretty young woman. Shelby's face flushes. Making sure no one is lurking nearby, she finds the number for the paper and calls. She's surprised when she's transferred directly to the reporter's line.

"Emilia Stone speaking."

"This is Shelby Blythe. I'm calling about..." Her mind goes blank.

"Hello?"

She clenches her eyes shut. Doing so has always helped her focus. "I appreciate the way you wrote about the trial. It was almost elegant."

"Thank you." Her voice reminds Shelby of the teenagers who chatter too loudly in the library. "That's nice of you to say."

She pictures the reporter's round cheeks and straight, chin-length hair. "Anyway, I thought you'd want to know that. You're a really good reporter."

After a beat, Emilia says, "Is that the only reason you called? To compliment my writing?"

Shelby is too embarrassed to admit that she's really on the line because she thought Emilia's byline picture was cute. "I don't know why I picked up the phone, to be honest." She hears the buzz of the newsroom on the other end.

"Maybe you finally want to talk to a reporter, Ms. Blythe. Let people know what you're thinking about this tragedy."

"Maybe."

There's another long pause, although Shelby thinks she hears the reporter whispering to one of her colleagues. "Listen.

Why don't we meet for a cup of coffee and chat for a bit. You don't have to decide right now if you want to do an interview. What do you think of that idea?"

"Meet in person?" Her mouth is dry.

"Why not?" When Shelby doesn't reply, Emilia continues. "What about Dunkin' Donuts—the one in Benfield? Can you meet there at five-thirty tonight?"

Shelby grips her leg to stop it from shaking. "Okay, I'll meet you there. Look forward to it."

"Great! Me too!"

Shelby spends the afternoon resisting the impulse to chomp her fingernails down to the bone. She leaves promptly at five-twenty-five and races to her blue Nissan. She pulls out of the library parking lot, drives two miles, and then pulls into the lot for the donut shop.

Emilia parks just as Shelby exits her car, and they share an awkward handshake. The reporter is even younger than Shelby had expected—no more than thirty—and wears a neat military coat, gloves, and a wool hat even though it's warm for May, close to seventy-five degrees. The intensity Shelby saw in Emilia's eyes in her byline photo is not as obvious now, but she looks kinder and less intimidating in person.

"I know you drove all the way down here, but do we have to go inside?" Shelby crumples half her face to show she's ashamed to ask this question. "I just don't have a lot to say."

"I was hoping you'd decided to give me an interview." She smiles warmly; Shelby looks away. "People want to hear the victim's side of things. It makes them feel like there's a little more justice in the world, maybe more than there really is. If we sit inside where it's warm, you might relax. I promise, I don't bite."

Shelby tries to smile. "I know. I should have been...I shouldn't have let you think...I'm not doing any interviews." It crosses her mind to recommend Emilia call her sister, but Shelby doesn't want the reporter asking questions about her relationship with Sam. It's none of Emilia's business that they're not close; her conversations with her only remaining relative over the years had become contests over who had it worse with their parents. Now they almost never talked.

Emilia pulls at a loose thread on her coat; she seems to be thinking. "So you wanted to meet your favorite reporter in person? That's it?"

Shelby shuffles from foot to foot. "I think so. I'm sorry."

"Well, there are worse reasons. At least you're not a serial killer."

"Oh, no, I was, but I only killed the bad reporters." Shelby can't believe she's joking about her parents' murder. "I'm done with all that now."

Emilia raises both eyebrows. "Reporters are a shitty bunch. I'll give you that."

Shelby nods. "But your writing is very honest. Most reporters can't resist inserting themselves into the story or trying to make it more dramatic than it already is. You let the story tell itself. I mean..." Shelby catches herself sounding too much like a smitten schoolgirl. "Sorry, I was rambling."

"That's quite all right. Unless I call my mom, it's pretty rare that I get someone telling me how wonderful I am."

It's the reporter's writing she was complimenting, but Shelby doesn't correct her.

Emilia, after a moment, says, "Are you sure you don't want to sit down and talk for a bit? Even off the record?"

Shelby's stomach flips over. Is this the invitation she's been hoping for? Why else suggest talking off the record? She imagines how nice it would be to tell someone what she's really feeling: *I hate that this happened, I hate Billy Lawson, I hate my stupid life. I hate my perfect little sister. I hate my stupid dead parents.* She wants to scream until her face and neck are purple and have someone there to console her. To kiss her. But Shelby knows reporters can't be trusted. She manages only a shy shrug.

Emilia considers her. "Why don't you think about it?" She hands Shelby her business card. "You can call me anytime you want."

Shelby stares at the flimsy card. She isn't sure she'll have the courage to call Emilia again after today. Impulsively, she says, "Can we talk out here in the parking lot? I don't want people staring at me."

The reporter tilts her head; she seems genuinely sympathetic. "Do they do that?"

"Yes. A lot."

The reporter places her hand on Shelby's forearm. "It's chilly out here. Let me take you to my place."

Emilia lives in a clean, sparsely furnished apartment on Bluejay Circle. A widescreen television fills one wall; Shelby can't understand other people's obsession with TV. Sometimes when she finishes a novel, she feels a longing to return to nineteenth-century London or 1960s Oklahoma or wherever the story has been set; occasionally, she returns to page one and starts the book over again. Television shows make her feel dull and drugged, less alive. She senses the way each episode is built to stimulate her desire to watch the next one, which would be okay with her if the universe of the shows felt at all real. The only reality she believes in is the one she can see in her mind's eye.

Emilia fixes them both a cup of coffee. Shelby can't stand the stuff but sips hers politely as they sit side by side on the loveseat. Shelby points to the stereo system below the television —not many people have a component with real speakers anymore. "What kind of music do you listen to?"

"Techno mostly."

"Really?"

"Yeah. Do you want to listen to something?"

"No, that's okay."

After a second. "I know, people hate techno. Even I think it's stupid most of the time, but there's something about it that gets me. It's great to dance to."

Shelby shrugs. She doesn't want to seem judgmental. "Everyone likes what they like."

"What do you listen to?"

"Mostly classical." She hears how pretentious that sounds. "I like Bach."

"Bach is cool."

"Yeah. He's very cool."

Emilia holds the coffee cup with both hands against her chin, letting the steam warm her face. "So tell me what you'd like to talk about. Off the record."

"Well...I hate Billy Lawson." Shelby puts her hand over her mouth to stop more words from spilling out.

Emilia doesn't even blink. "I know. He's an evil son of a bitch."

"When I left the court the other day, I wanted to kill him."

"That's only natural. If it were me, I'd want the same thing."

"I want to take a gun and put it against his head and pull the trigger." Shelby covers her mouth again.

"I know. He deserves it."

After a breath, Shelby says, "I feel bad for his mother, though. She doesn't deserve this."

"Maybe she does," Emila says. "I met her once at the courthouse and she was really, *really* drunk. She didn't exactly seem like mother of the year."

This strikes Shelby as unfair, but she doesn't want to find herself defending Billy's mother. After a moment of silence she says, "I should probably get going."

"Are you sure? You just got here."

"I know. I feel weird."

"I won't publish anything unless you want me to."

"I appreciate that." She really doesn't want to leave. She needs a pretext. "Would you want to help me write a letter to Billy Lawson?"

Emilia taps her finger on the edge of her coffee cup. "Why do you want to write to that fuckwad?"

"I want to find out why he did what he did."

"I don't think you'll get the answers you're looking for."

Shelby wants to kiss Emilia. She pictures them together, snuggling under the covers, reading in bed, walking along the beach at Nelson's Pond. "I'm not looking for any particular answer. I want to write to him, that's all."

"Listen, it's generally my experience that it's best to stay away from people like that. You'll only get yourself hurt." Emilia seems to realize what she's just said. "I mean, I guess you're already... I'm sorry."

"It's okay. It's not your fault. Please, will you help?" She senses Emilia's hesitation. "I like to read, but I've never really been able to write very well." She tries to sound cheerful. "You're a great writer. Remember we established that?"

"Am I going to get an interview out of this?"

"Probably not." She shrugs. "Sorry."

Emilia laughs, a sound like wind chimes. "I probably shouldn't. My editor would kill me if he found out. Ethics and all that." She pauses and for a moment Shelby thinks something important is passing between them. "But you know what?

Sometimes you gotta say *fuck it* in this business. I'll help you write a letter."

She doesn't let herself sound too enthusiastic. "You will?"

"Yes. But not tonight."

Shelby feels dizzy. She's not ready for what she thinks is about to happen. But Emilia only says, "You need to think about what you want to say. You throw together a first draft and I'll read it over. I can't do all the heavy lifting."

After work the next day, Shelby follows Emilia's suggestion; she jots down ideas for the letter so the reporter will have some raw material to edit when they meet up again. She's looking forward to that. After scribbling gibberish for several minutes she finally forces herself to write a few complete sentences. Once she gets going, she can't stop.

> *Billy,*
> *I want to let you know that you've hurt me and nothing*
> *will change that. But when I think about it, I forgive*
> *you. You must be suffering yourself. I'm sure you*
> *couldn't have been in your right mind when you did*
> *what you did. We all do crazy things in life and we have*
> *to suffer the consequences. When I was eighteen years*
> *old, there was a boy I really liked in college. We were in*
> *his room together and he started kissing me and instead*
> *of staying there and letting things happen, I ran away. I*
> *always hated the version of myself that would do that*
> *and I wonder what would have happened if I'd stayed.*
> *I've missed so many opportunities because of fear.*
> *Another time I could have taken a job at the Boston*
> *Public Library. It was entry level, but it's an amazing*
> *place to work and there's nothing wrong with starting*

*from the bottom. But again, I ran away. Or rather, I was
afraid that commuting all the way into Boston would be
too difficult. Why didn't I move there? I know most of
what I'm writing here probably sounds stupid, but I
wanted to say that many of us live in prisons. Anyway,
that's how I feel. I hope you'll write me back.*

Shelby re-reads her letter and is taken aback; what was
supposed to be an angry screed had turned into a personal
confession. She realizes most of her anger is directed at herself.
After a cup of chamomile tea, she lies in bed and wonders what
kind of life she's led. Is it really her parents' fault that she hasn't
gotten married, that she turned down her dream job, that she
hasn't told anyone about her bisexuality? Parental encourage-
ment would have been helpful, but Shelby is an adult. Adults
determine their own destinies.

When Emilia comes over the following night, Shelby tries
to sit near her on the couch, but the reporter is all business.

"What do you got for me?"

Shelby nervously hands Emilia the letter.

Emilia reads it, then slaps the paper down on the table.
"You want to make him feel bad about himself. This sounds
like you're writing in your diary."

"You're probably right." Shelby wants to caress the dark
circles around the reporter's eyes; poor thing probably doesn't
sleep much. "But isn't he getting punished now? Isn't that what
prison is for?"

"What the hell are you talking about? The other day you
were saying that you wanted to kill this guy, right? If this was
Texas he'd be on death row. He's a murderer!"

Shelby looks down. "Want to know something funny? It
was all for nothing. The kid thought they were rich. Everything
he stole was costume jewelry. None of it was real."

"This is my point," Emilia says. "When we write the letter, we'll be sure to let him know he's a fucking moron."

"Yes, you're right. You're so much better at this than I am."

Emilia helps her craft another letter. In it, they call Billy a cretin. They liken him to the devil. They tell him that school-children will talk about him the same way they talk about the boogeyman and he should never forget that. For the rest of his life he'll be the incarnation of evil. It's fun writing these things, mostly because Emilia seems to enjoy coming up with darker and more perverse rants.

*I hope you get shivved on your first day in the yard! I hope a psychotic 300-pound neo-Nazi makes you his bitch!*

Taken with Emila's giggling, Shelby shifts closer to the reporter. "Are you sure it's okay to write like this?"

"Listen to me. The world is full of people dying to be victims. They're lining up to feel aggrieved. It's a fucking national pastime."

Shelby flinches when Emilia swears.

Emilia pulls a Twizzler out of the front pocket of her jeans, removes the plastic covering, and takes a bite. "But *you* really *are* a victim. You can say whatever the fuck you want to say. You can do whatever you want to do. The last thing you should worry about is what this scumbag thinks about you. Do you understand?"

Emilia's crass language and casual demeanor make Shelby feel uneasy, but she tries not to let it show. "Thank you, Emilia. You're really helping me."

"I'm happy to do it if I'm being completely honest. Most of my life is spent talking to shitty people about the shitty things they've done. It's a nice change of pace."

A warm moment passes between them, and Shelby is tempted to put her hand on Emilia's knee. But she doesn't.

The following morning, she looks at the two versions of the letter and decides to send the first. Writing the second was like playing some childhood game: Who can say the meanest thing? The first letter, though not as well-written, is honest. She feels satisfied when she puts it in the mail.

Over the next two weeks, Shelby and Emilia go to the movies, the mall, and the diner. Emilia teaches Shelby how to play tennis. They become friends. But that's all. And Shelby wants more. She lets her arm lightly caress Emilia's arm when she wants her attention; she compliments her outfits; she pays for meals. Still, these are only friendly gestures. Telling someone you want them is a chasm the librarian cannot seem to bridge.

One day, Emilia surprises Shelby by showing up at the library and offering to take her to lunch. She's wearing bright red lipstick and a side ponytail.

"I'm glad you came by."

"I'm glad, too. Because the alternative is work."

Shelby giggles. "Let me grab my purse."

They sit across from one another in the diner. Other customers come in and out looking haggard. Shelby feels she's better than them; her crush is like a beautiful secret.

She pushes her salad around her plate. "You look nice today."

"We should go shopping again soon." Emilia takes a bite of a huge roast beef sandwich. Cheese drips from the bread to her hand. "You have a knack for picking out clothes that look perfect on me."

"We should definitely go shopping again." Shelby hates herself for how stilted her voice sounds. If robot lovers ever come into being, they'll sound exactly like her.

"Do you like road trips?" Emilia wipes the cheese off her hand, but another glob oozes over her forefinger and thumb.

Shelby has noticed that there's an ongoing war between Emilia and the splatters, spills, and crumbs that accompany eating.

Shelby hasn't been on a road trip since B.U. when she and a few pals rented a car and drove to little Warwick, New York, to go wine tasting and attend the drive-in theater. She remembers Cheryl and Theresa getting hammered at a tasting and going back to their room with a couple of frat dudes, sending her and mousy Alexandra off on their own to see *No Way Out* on the big screen. She had heard it was a great film and was surprised by how predictable it was. The trip was memorable for all the wrong reasons, so Shelby says, "No, but I've always wanted to go on one."

"I used to go on them all the time. I kinda hate the idea now. Just give me my couch and some food that arrives in a box."

Shelby fights her disappointment. "Oh yeah. Staying home is fun too." She wonders why Emilia asked her about the road trip, but the reporter reads her mind.

"My friend Ken is having a road trip movie marathon at his house in Putnam this Friday. *Thelma and Louise, Little Miss Sunshine, Vacation*, and that Spanish one about the girl with cancer."

Shelby hasn't seen any of the films except the last one, *Y Tu Mamá También*, and she's pretty sure it's a Mexican film, not Spanish. "That sounds fun."

"Ken is kind of a dick—he's a sportswriter—but it might be fun to go."

Shelby is flattered that Emilia wants her to meet her friends. And the idea of being trapped together in the car for the twenty-five minutes or so it will take to drive to Putnam, the small town west of Benfield, is thrilling. In the quiet, enclosed hum of the car she can finally tell Emilia her feelings. "Yeah, I would definitely be into that."

"Terrific. I'll pick you up at your place at six."

"Awesome!"

Shelby takes the day off from work Friday and spends the afternoon practicing what she's going to say to Emilia. *I've been thinking about something. I've been enjoying spending time with you and wanted you to know that I like you a lot. Can we go on an official date?* She feels better after each time she recites her speech, but then, after an hour, a kind of tension grows inside her stomach, and she has to practice again to lessen the stress. This cycle repeats itself all day, so when Emilia is forty-five minutes late, the tension she'd relieved by practicing at six has already built back up. She's sweating when she opens the car door and blurts, "You look great!" Emilia is wearing a leather jacket and white jeans with pre-made tears along the front of each leg. Shelby had helped her pick these out on their last shopping trip.

"Thanks," she says. "Sorry I'm late. My editor cornered me about a feature story about the old Benfield police chief."

A flickering anger ignites in Shelby's belly. The old police chief was the one who'd told Billy Lawson that her parents' place had jewelry there and she hated him for it. She doesn't understand how Emilia could bring it up just before their date. It's callous. It's inconsiderate. But she says, "It's okay. You have to earn a living."

"Don't I know it." Emilia flashes Shelby a smile. "Are you psyched for this marathon? It looks like we're gonna miss *Thelma and Louise*."

"Whatever happens happens." She clenches her jaw but refuses to let the anger consume her. Emilia hadn't brought up the police chief intentionally. She has her own busy life, and she can't be expected to monitor every word that comes out of her mouth. It's even a little flattering that she slipped like that; it means she's comfortable with Shelby. She takes a breath and flushes away her anger.

A throbbing techno beat plays, but when Shelby climbs in, Emilia switches to a classical station. Shelby smiles.

She watches Emilia's face as she drives. Blonde, downy hair lightly covers a section of her cheek. The words are right there. *I've been thinking about something...*But she can't force them out at this moment. She fights her frustration, but then decides she'll be more relaxed at the party; maybe she can have a few drinks, practice her speech once in the bathroom and then get Emilia alone and say it for real.

Ken is tall, reed thin, and friendly. His house is a large log home with an all-glass atrium and several wings. There are five bedrooms, a game room, and more than one marble sculpture. It's not at all what Shelby had pictured. She wonders how he can afford this kind of place on a reporter's salary, but it turns out his wife, Amber, is a surgeon.

There are no seats left in the expansive, finished basement, so she and Emilia sit on the floor close to the TV. The room smells like beer and salty snacks; it reminds her of her college dorm.

"This is cozy," she whispers to Emilia.

"Ooh. My back is killing already. You might have to give me a massage later."

Shelby takes a short breath. "Emilia, I've been thinking about something."

Amber enters carrying a baby and most of the guests jump up to greet her. Shelby lingers on the floor watching the movie. She'd missed most of it, but at the moment two women are sitting in a car deciding if they should drive off a cliff. Not a great omen for her romantic prospects, she thinks.

The party is still going strong at one a.m., but Shelby is

dozing off. Emilia offers to drive her home, but Shelby says, "You're enjoying yourself. Stay. I'll call a car." A wretched stew of self-hatred bubbles up in her stomach.


Billy Lawson's letter arrives on Wednesday evening. Shelby props it up against the gooseneck lamp on the coffee table in her living room. Then she tears it open. It's full of typos and misspellings, but his handwriting is almost elegant. She copies the letter into her computer, correcting the spelling mistakes.

> *Dear Shelby,*
> *I was really surprised that you sent me a letter. I almost*
> *didn't open it. But I'm really lonely. I cried when I read*
> *it. It was really nice of you to say the things you did. You*
> *didn't have to say that you understood me. You probably*
> *don't understand me. I don't understand me. But it*
> *doesn't really matter because I'm here now. I wish I*
> *hadn't shot your parents. They were good people. You*
> *probably heard that I was with Barry, my friend, that*
> *night and we were planning to break into your parents'*
> *house because we heard they had a lot of valuable shit.*
> *But Barry decided he didn't want to do it. Did you know*
> *he actually came all the way to the house with me? But*
> *he said it was stupid and he left. Sorry, I'm sure you*
> *remember that from the trial. Anyway, he was right. I*
> *wish I'd listened to him because then your parents*
> *would still be alive and I wouldn't be in prison. But I'd*
> *probably be screwing up my life in some other way.*
> *Because I'm a screw-up. I'm sorry you didn't have sex*
> *until you were twenty-four because you were too afraid.*
> *And that you didn't take that job. Maybe you and I are*
> *like opposite sides of a coin. I jump into things when I*

*should hold back. And you hold back when you should*
*jump into things. Yin and Yang. I'm really sorry for what*
*I did. If you want to write me again, I would like that,*
*but I will understand if you don't. Enjoy your life. Billy.*

Shelby stares at the typed words on her computer. She feels like she should text Emilia to say she got a response, but hesitates to share the candid note. She saves the document, closes it, and burns the original letter before texting Emilia. The reporter writes back immediately. "I'll be right over!"

Emilia arrives and, before Shelby can say anything, begins pacing around the apartment like a panther, smelling strongly of tobacco. "I can't wait to read what this asshole has to say."

Shelby holds out the bowl full of burnt ashes.

"That's the...? Why'd you do that?" Her face is red.

"He wrote awful stuff. I can't say what, but...I don't want to..."

"I understand."

"I figured burning it would be a sort of revenge." She hopes Shelby will like this answer.

"Thata girl! Fuck that guy."

"Yeah. I feel much better."

"We should go out and celebrate."

Shelby's legs quiver, but she forces herself to say, "Or we can stay in and order something."

After a long pause, Emilia says, "Yeah, okay. I could go for some pizza." Shelby prefers Thai food, but says, "That's perfect."

When Domino's arrives, they sit together on the carpeted floor. Emilia munches a large pepperoni slice, then tosses it down and grabs a napkin to wipe a grease stain off her chin. "Ooh. That's hot."

"Yeah."

Emilia nervously tears at her napkin. Shelby has never noticed her doing this before. It's a little annoying.

Emilia gives up on the napkin, crumples it, and tosses it onto the floor. "This pizza kind of sucks, doesn't it?"

Shelby looks at the slice in her hand. "It's the worst pizza I've ever tasted."

"Are you sure you don't want to go out?"

Going out is the last thing Shelby wants to do. She gathers herself. "I like your glasses."

"These? Really?"

"They make you look like a movie star."

"I'm too fat to be a movie star."

"You're not fat."

"No, I'm not. But movie stars are starving bitches with giant cartoon heads. Did you ever notice how big their heads are?"

"I guess I never noticed that." Shelby isn't getting her message across. "But I still think you could be one of those superhero types. Like Catwoman."

"You watch a lot of those movies?"

"Well, no, I—"

"I hate those films. They have nothing to do with real life."

"What kind of movies do you like?"

"I like gritty. Real. You ever seen *Ace in the Hole?* I'm a sucker for movies about reporters."

"That makes sense."

"Lately, I've been spending more time surfing the web than watching movies. The internet is kind of addicting."

"Yeah," Shelby says.

"Do you ever get sucked into the vortex?"

"Not really. I read a lot, actually."

"What do you read?"

"Novels mostly."

"Novels. I've heard of those."

Shelby's fingers trace a path across the carpet toward Emilia. "Can I kiss you?"

Emilia hesitates; a surprisingly shy smile brightens her face before she says, "If you want to. That'd be nice."

Emilia is anything but shy once they move to the couch. She begins to unbutton Shelby's shirt.

Shelby retreats. Whispers. "Slow down."

"Are you okay?"

"I need to move slowly."

"That's fine. It's okay."

Eventually, Shelby relaxes into Emilia's embrace. She makes love for the first time in four years. Afterward, as she lies next to the reporter, who snores when she sleeps, Shelby wonders what's going on in the young woman's mind. Maybe a dream about her next interview, her next car ride, or her next meal.

There's something chaotic about Emilia, unfocused; she plummets forward without reason. She's like an unfinished novel someone tossed into a bottom drawer and forgot about.

Shelby tiptoes into the living room, fixes herself a cup of tea, and sits at her computer. She feels almost giddy.

*Dear Billy,*

*I made love tonight to one of the reporters who covered your trial. I feel like a few prison bars have been bent back and I'm making an escape. The affair has helped me realize that I want love in my life, and I know now that I can never love the reporter. She's too dispassionate, too immature. She's the type of person who passes through your life and in ten years you barely remember her. I need someone who I can trust. Someone who understands what these prisons of the mind feel like.*

Someone who knows what it means to feel powerless. I'd like to visit you some time. How would you feel about that? I think it could be good for both of us.

All my best,
Shelby Blythe.

On a clear night, stars twinkled over the amusement park on the edge of Benfield. Tara was eating cotton candy off a stick. It was blue. She took a bite and wondered who decided that "blue" was a flavor; what was "blue" supposed to taste like? Pete sat on a bench with a map of the park pointing out the various rides to Sam.

"I don't want to go on the roller coaster," Sam said.

"What do you want, kiddo?"

Sam shrugged. "To go home."

Pete and Tara looked uneasy. "But honey, you've always loved it here."

Eight-year-old Sam said nothing. Shelby had been the one who insisted on coming every year; she liked the rollercoasters and loud noises and games. Sam had just pretended she liked it too. "I don't like rollercoasters," she said. "I've never liked rollercoasters."

"Maybe we should start with something a little less daunting," Tara said. "Like the Ferris wheel."

Pete snorted. "The Ferris wheel is bullshit!"

*Tara, with pretend exasperation, said, "Language, Pete!"*

*He leapt from the bench and pretended to bite her neck. "Bullshit," he growled. "Bull. Shit!"*

*Sam grimaced as Tara pretended to fight him off. "Stop!"*

*Finally, husband and wife kissed, leaning into each other.*

*"Quit it, you guys." Sam said plaintively.*

*"Did I hear a comment from the peanut gallery?" Pete asked. "You might not think kissing is so icky someday."*

*"Okay, dad."*

*Pete swept Sam up in one of his famous bear hugs. Over his shoulder, she saw the admiration her mother had for her husband. Then, still holding Sam against his chest, Pete spun around and snatched her mother's cotton candy from her hand, swallowed it with one bite, and tossed the sticky cardboard cone in the garbage.*

*"I was still eating that!"*

*"Men need sustenance." He grunted like an ape.*

*"Ladies do too." Tara laughed.*

*Pete put his youngest daughter back down. "What do you say, Sam? Are you game to conquer the great Ferris wheel of Benfield?"*

*"Do I have to?"*

*He tried to tickle her with his free hand. "Lighten up, kiddo," he said. "It'll be fun!" But he'd tried this tactic so many times that she was no longer ticklish. Arching one eyebrow to a ridiculous height on his forehead, Pete asked, "You're not a scaredy-cat, are you?"*

*Pete patted his daughter's shoulder, smiling.*

*Sam rolled her eyes. "Right. I'm scared." She would never admit it, but she was afraid of heights.*

*Pete winked at Sam, put his arm around Tara, and led them toward the ride.*

*The sound of giggling children bubbled up around them,*

along with terrified and delighted screams, as they strolled through the park. Thousands of colored bulbs, affixed to the rides, flickered on and off. Behind the water pistol shooting gallery, a young couple pressed their faces together. Past them, at a distance, Sam spotted her parents' friend, Evelyn, alone and looking glum, waiting in line for the carousel. Sam raised her hand to get her attention, but before she could call out, Pete yanked her arm down. "We don't need a wet blanket smothering our big adventure," he said quietly. When Sam looked back, Evelyn was gone.

Sam stole a glance up; it was definitely scary. She squeezed her father's hand. "I really don't want to go."

"You shouldn't give into your fear," Tara said.

"If she's really that worried, maybe we can skip it this time," Pete said.

Tara turned. "I really think she should go. It'll be good for her."

"It's just a ride, hon."

"She has to learn to try things."

"Does she?" He made a sound like a chimp and pretended to pull bugs from Sam's hair.

"Pete. I'm serious."

Sam felt something change in the air between her parents, like a sudden drop in air temperature just before a storm.

Pete stood straight. "I can see that. Jesus."

"Well?"

"I guess you're in charge."

The line stretched past the entrance to the Tilt-A-Whirl and just short of a small hut with dilapidated siding and posters of freaks: a bearded lady, a strong man, the world's smallest horse.

"What's that?" Sam tugged at her mother.

"Nothing," she said. Her earlier joy was gone. Pete's too. They were both avoiding eye contact.

Sam looked at the posters. "Can a lady grow a beard?"

"It's just a bunch of ugly freaks in there," Pete said.

The seat on the Ferris wheel was enclosed in a metallic cage and painted fire engine red. Sam sat on the inside, Tara squeezed in next to her, and Pete sat on the outside. The wheel rotated them up bit by bit as the staff unloaded and reloaded passengers. The car rocked in place every time it stopped. Sam stared out over the town; she pointed in the direction of their house.

"Pretty good, Sam. You have a great sense of direction. You take after your father."

Tara giggled. It was well known in the family that Pete had a terrible sense of direction. "Sure," she said.

Pete didn't mind. "You know me better than anyone." He took her hand.

Sam was surprised by how quickly they seemed to be happy again; her head was already spinning and the real ride hadn't even started.

They soared all the way up to the top. The dark sky looked unending, the stars like sparkling torches.

Sam's chest heaved. "Heaven is so far away."

"It's not that far away," Tara said.

Pete leaned toward Tara. "Yeah." They kissed.

"I wish..." Sam reached, childishly, toward a star.

The wheel turned quickly; it seemed like they would crash, but then the entire apparatus lurched to a halt to let on new passengers, with the three of them left hovering over a storage pen behind the freak show. A yellow light illuminated broken, rusted bits of an old Ferris wheel strewn about the long grass. Barbed wire ran across the top of a decaying metal fence. A brown Rottweiler lay on its side, scratching at fleas. A rat carcass festered a few feet away.

Sam leaned forward to get a closer look.

Tara looked away. Pete put his arm around his wife. "I've got you."

Sam looked back at her parents. "That's bullshit," she said.

"Hey!" Tara said.

"Language!" Pete said. "Christ!"

Finally, the Ferris wheel began to move again. It carried them to the top and dropped them to the bottom, over and over, in an unending loop.

# JUNE 2014

## BLACK AND WHITE

A s he empties the trash into the dump truck, Carlton spots Tim Pearson's rusty Chevy Malibu cruise past, music vibrating the sealed windows. In that moment, the garbage man, infuriated, knows he will confront Pearson that night even though he'd promised Samantha he would leave the disgraced former chief of police alone. But seeing the man looking happy and carefree is more than he can take. Something has to be done.

Carlton is still standing there, alone, gripping the Brown's old-fashioned metallic garbage can as the Chevy disappears around a sharp curve.

Knowing he will be face-to-face with the drug-dealing ex-cop brings a new kind of clarity to the rest of Carlton's day, and nothing can bother him—not the pothole on Winslow Drive that tosses him ten inches into the air or the Walker's uncovered garbage can reeking of disposable diapers.

After the last pick-up on the edge of town, he climbs into the cab. Dave, a white-haired, lifelong garbage collector, is blaring 100.7, WZLX, the classic rock station. It's Led

Zeppelin's "Fool in the Rain." He scratches his gray, stubbled cheek. "Why are they playing *this*? It's not even raining."

Carlton takes note of the crisp air, the blue-yellow haze of a clear spring day. "How the hell should I know?"

Dave puts the truck into gear. "You know what the other dumbass is up to today?" Mikey, the usual third man on the truck, had called in sick that morning. "No way he's sick, right?"

"Who cares?" Carlton stretches his arms and smiles. "It's a beautiful day."

At home, Carlton takes a quick shower to wash away the stench of garbage. He puts on a pair of comfortable jeans and his white polo shirt that shows off his biceps, then jumps into his Ford pickup to see Sam; it'll feel good to talk to her knowing he'll be doing something to make things right, even if she's too stubborn to see that he's helping her.

After his mother and father-in-law were killed, Carlton and Sam had stopped communicating. They went to the trial day in and day out, and it was always the same: Sam was sad, and Carlton was angry. He thought he'd used up all his anger on Billy Lawson, but had nearly lost his mind when it came out that the only reason the kid broke in was because Pearson had let on that the Blythes had money. Sure, Lawson was in prison, but why should Pearson—who had gotten away with a slap on the wrist for a drug charge years ago—get another chance? Carlton's mother and father-in-law are dead, and he and his wife are separated. How could he and Sam ever hope to start again until they get past this gray area, and all guilty parties are punished? *These Arms of Mine* comes on the radio as he pulls into the parking lot, and he quickly switches to an '80s channel. He wants to keep his good spirits; it's a beautiful day, he's about to see his wife, and by the end of the night he'll have taken care of the last thing standing between Sam and her future. *Their* future.

Samantha's Beauties, his wife's hair salon, sits between Town's Pizza and Soaks & Folks, a laundromat with a full bar, in Benfield Commons, a strip mall off Woodside Boulevard. As he enters, the bell above the glass door jingles. There's only one customer, and Colleen, one of Sam's beauticians, looks up with couldn't-give-a-fuck eyes when she sees Carlton. "What do you want?"

"What do you think?"

She flashes her eyes toward the back room. "She's in the office."

That's typical. With all the media coverage since the murder of her parents, Sam prefers hiding out in the back to cutting hair. It's a shame because she used to love chatting up customers; being social was the point of starting the business in the first place. "Thanks."

Sam is sitting in front of the computer, her bifocals tilted so she can read the screen. "Look what the cat dragged in." She places her glasses on the desk. "You need a trim?"

"Nah," he answers. "Just stopping by."

"Well, that's a ten-dollar haircut." One of her expressions, which roughly translates to "bullshit."

"I was in a good mood; thought I'd say hello."

"*You're* in a good mood?" She spins so she can see him better. She's chewing gum, a habit she picked up after the murders to deal with nerves. Carlton hates it; it makes her seem cheap. "Must be the Fourth of July."

"It is. Let me sing the "Star-Spangled Banner" for you." He used to enjoy their playful banter, but now it feels off somehow, like milk past its expiration date.

"So you came by to share your jolly mood with me?"

"Pretty much." Carlton looks at Sam more closely; she is even more pale than usual, and she looks thin. "Really Sam... I just wanted to see you. Maybe even convince you to come outside, get some sun." Carlton speaks up, concerned. "Have you been eating?

"My freezer is still busted. You know that. Remember I asked you to send someone over to look at it?"

"Shit. I forgot."

"I'm eating out every night." She slaps her thigh. She's put on a few pounds, but Carlton still admires her shape, all hips and ass.

He looks around the cluttered office, feeling helpless. "Sorry about that, hon."

"That's okay. You got your busy life of driving around spreading sunshine."

"True enough. It's exhausting being an inspiration all the time." He puts his hands on his sides, unsure what he's really doing here. "You want to go on a little ride with me? Spread sunshine together?"

She picks up a sheet of paper, studies it for a moment, and then puts it back. She looks up at him. "You got the heat fixed in your truck?"

"I'm working on it." He didn't see the need since it was nearly summer.

"So your truck's an ice box. That's perfect." She pauses for a moment, then almost cracks a smile. "Maybe you can throw my groceries in the pickup and save me from having to fix the freezer."

It's good to see that she can still make a joke once in a while. "I'm game if you are! Let's go grab those veggies."

She takes a long breath. "So," she says. "How are *you* doing?

"Well..." He hates this question because he knows she

won't like his answer. "The usual," he says. "Thinking a lot about us."

"Please don't."

"What?"

"Carl." There's a note of exasperation in her voice. "Let's not talk about that."

"Of course." But the truth is, he never stops thinking fondly of life before they separated back in February, remembering days they would go on trips to the Cape, swim in the ocean, walk on the beach as the sun set. He doesn't mind his life; he has a good job, he plays shortstop on the invincible Sanitation softball team, he goes to happy hour with Mikey and the guys on Fridays. But sometimes at night, as he sits up in bed, he feels like a buoy that has become unmoored and is drifting out to sea. He misses what they used to be. One Monday morning, just before their separation, he realized that they hadn't spoken to each other over the course of an entire weekend; they'd just passed each other like strangers in the hallway, in the bedroom, in the kitchen. But it still seemed sudden when she'd asked him to move out.

He tries to believe that their time apart is not the beginning of the end. The one thing he knows is he still loves her.

He strikes a dramatic pose like a hammy community theater actor. "It's spring, a time for new beginnings!"

She snorts. It's close enough to a laugh for him to take it as a tiny victory. She cracks, "I'd like a whiff of whatever you're smoking."

"I'm sober as a priest," he says. "A dead one."

"I guess you are," she says, her voice dropping into its familiar melancholy. That's how fast it happens now, on a dime.

He decides to change the subject. "How's business, hon? Seems kinda slow out there." He regrets asking before the words are out of his mouth. He'd had high hopes for an easy chat, and the next thing he knows, he's drilling her about business. There's a tense silence before she asks, "What are you *really* doing here, Carlton? Do you need something?"

"I'm good." To avoid looking her in the eyes, he surveys his fingernails. They're jagged and cracked, but there isn't a speck of dirt under them.

"I might just go for a drive tonight."

"What for?" She squints suspiciously.

Shit. His resolve is so firm it feels like his plans are printed on his forehead. Was she reading his mind? If she guessed what he was up to they'd get in another big fight. But he realizes that's crazy. She's not the one who can't stop thinking about Pearson. In fact, Carlton has no idea what Sam thinks about these days. But he does know that no answer he gives her will be right.

He doesn't want to fight and so he says, "I don't know." He stares at her self-consciously; even blinking feels deliberate. "It's a beautiful day. I feel like going for a drive."

"Uh huh." She bites the corner of her lower lip.

"It's only a drive," he insists. "You should come." If she goes with him, he won't have to confront Pearson. As he suggests this, he realizes just how much he means it. Carlton wouldn't have to play vigilante if Sam would just let him help her. If she would let life go on. But he knows she won't.

"So, you just dropped in out of the blue?" she asks.

He looks around the room for something more to say. "Not everything's gotta be a special occasion. Can't I swing by and say hello?" He wants to put his hand on her cheek, comfort her, and say everything's gonna be alright. He'd told her that after the murders, but he was lying then, and he'd still be lying if he said it now.

Life is a broken jaw, always aching.

Carlton prefers the winding side roads to Route 42. The streets are still crowded with rush hour traffic, but Carlton feels at ease and the delays don't bother him the way they usually do. He holds onto the wheel with two hands and taps along to the music from the radio. The ZLX DJ is playing the old Wings song, "Silly Love Songs."

He stops off at a gas station across from yet another mini-mall and picks up a roll of antacids. There are taller buildings, more glass, and brighter lights near the border of Stanton, a large neighboring town, and yet Carlton feels it's somehow darker. As he pops one of the antacids into his mouth on the way back to his car, a familiar voice calls out.

"Hey Carl!" It's Mikey. He waves a loose-limbed arm and jogs toward him, his curly hair bouncing with every step. He's wearing tight jeans and a button-down shirt and munching a half-moon, his favorite cookie; it's more like a small, circular cake, really, with black icing on one side and white on the other. "I saw you and came over."

"Yeah, I figured that out," Carlton says. "I'm quick on the uptake that way."

Mikey stretches his mouth into a goofy grin, wipes a sheen of icing from his lips, and shrugs. He isn't the sharpest nail in the toolbox, but somehow he's figured out the meaning of life; the kid is always grinning.

"How was the run today?" he asks.

"Nothing special," Carlton says. "I managed to survive without you."

"Yeah, sorry about that. I wasn't sick, I guess you can tell that too."

The kid has gotten his hair cut, and the jeans and shirt look hours old. He smells like cheap cologne. "You got a date or something, Mikey?"

The grin again. "We met online. Her name is Adia." He

catches his breath. "This is our third time going out. I really like her."

"That's great." Somehow Carlton's become a sort of father figure to the kid, so he adds, "I'm proud of you." As far as he knows, Mikey has not gone on a date in the four years since they started working together. "What's she do?"

"She works register at the supermarket in Stanton, near the mall." Mike grins again. "She's a painter. Isn't that cool?"

"Paint? You mean, like houses?"

"Watercolors and things like that. They're really bright and weird and great."

Carlton pictures a bunch of boring landscapes. He prefers paintings of people doing things. You can see their souls. "I bet they are."

"She's gonna paint me, too." He beams. "She says my face is unique."

Carlton stifles a laugh. Mikey looks like someone who caught a few too many pucks to the face playing street hockey as a kid; he just got rammed in the gene pool lottery. "What's your game plan for tonight? Where are you taking her?"

"We're going to a movie at Starwheel." He points as if they can see through the thirty-story brick apartment building in their way and then three miles past that to the cinema across from the mall. "Then, well..." His pale skin turns to beets.

Carlton puts his hand on Mikey's shoulder; that's what fathers do, he figures. "That sounds really good."

"Thanks." Mikey looks as though he wants to say thank-you but doesn't have the words.

Carlton gives him a playful shove. "You should probably get going. You don't want to be late."

Mikey takes another big bite of his half-moon; he's working his way around in a circle so the cookie stays symmetrical down to the last bite. "Yeah, yeah, I don't want to keep Adia waiting."

He gives one last twisted grin and begins jogging back to his car, which is still parked at the pumps.

As he turns his key in the ignition, Carlton begins to feel a bit uneasy about what he plans to do later. If he gets caught, what will Mikey think of him? But shouldn't a man seek out justice? Won't Samantha see that doing the right thing matters? With a new sense of confidence, he puts the car in reverse and backs away from the gas pump.

Tim Pearson lives in a dilapidated apartment complex that stands behind a McDonald's at the border of Benfield and Stanton. Near the restaurant, three roads intersect. Carlton drives into the wrong parking lot on his first try. A mistake like that would normally frustrate him, but he feels purposeful and calm as he U-turns into the correct parking lot.

There's a space across from the apartment building under a red maple tree. Carlton backs in and shuts off the pickup. He isn't sure what Pearson does to make a buck, but he knows he usually gets home at seven-thirty. Carlton has staked the place out four times already.

By ten-thirty, his leg starts to tingle and he has to piss. He hops out of the truck and runs behind the apartment complex to be out of sight. There is an overflowing dumpster adjacent to a row of pine trees in the rear parking lot and he resists the urge to pick up the stray paper bags, beer cans, and condom wrappers littering the ground. People have a way of pretending the shit in their lives is invisible. Sanitation workers don't have that luxury. As he stands behind the dumpster, a dim light flickers on above the rear exit to the apartment door. He freezes. The door opens and then slams shut. Heavy footsteps grow louder. A plastic bag lands on top of the pile of trash and, defying the laws of physics, stays there. The sound of a cigarette lighter—

three tries. Then a long silence. Carlton closes his eyes and sips long, quiet breaths. He remembers that his fly is open and stifles a laugh. After a few minutes the heavy footsteps recede, followed by the slamming door and he finally manages to relieve himself. When he gets back to the pickup, he feels a chill and pulls on his windbreaker.

Pearson pulls up in his Malibu at eleven-thirty and finds a parking space near the side entrance to the building. He's patting down his jacket when Carlton stealthily gets out of the truck and approaches, his fist clenched, thinking about justice.

"Lose something?" Carlton asks. Carlton vaguely remembers Pearson's hair used to be thick and blond—now it's graying, thin, and tangled.

"Oh," Pearson says. His eyelids droop closed and then reopen, first the left and then the right, as if there's a crane operator operating each independently. "My keys." He's clutching a bag of McDonald's.

"You need any help?"

Pearson shakes his head. "I'm good, man, thanks." Up close, he looks craggy and thin, like beef jerky; his sweater and pants sag off his body.

A silent beat. Carlton studies the man. "Are you sure I can't help you find anything?"

"I took my damn keys out of the ignition and I don't know what I did with them."

"I do that all the time." Carlton pats his own jacket pocket.

"If my head wasn't attached to my body..."

"I know what you mean. My head would be rolling down the middle of Main Street."

"Yeah, anyway." Pearson's eyes dart nervously. "I'll find them, I'm sure."

"Maybe you dropped them on the car mat," Carlton says. "Every time I think about dropping my keys in the car, I think about this episode of *Starsky and Hutch*. You ever seen that show?"

"I don't know, maybe. The two cops?" as if that narrows it down. Carlton watches reruns of every cop show he can find on the streaming channels, even the old ones: *Columbo, The Rockford Files, Streets of San Francisco*. He likes the utter clarity of them; there are good guys and bad guys and it's never confusing which is which.

"Starsky—I think it was Starsky—is about to put the key in the ignition of their Gran Torino, but suddenly, as if God smacks his hand, drops them. I remember the close-up on his fingers as they slip out. When he reaches down to the mat, he sees a wire coming out of the floor that shouldn't be there, you know? He tells Hutch to get out of the car slowly 'cause it's rigged to blow. You recall that one?"

"I don't know. I guess not." He stops searching for his keys and thrusts his chin forward, inspecting Carlton.

"That's not how it works, is it, Pearson? In real life things just blow up in your face."

Pearson's eyes widen with alarm. "Do I know you?"

Carlton takes a step forward. He towers over Pearson, who drops his bag and a large cup; French fries, packets of ketchup, and napkins spill out of the bag. A milkshake oozes out of the cup. His eyelids begin to flicker.

"Oh man," Carlton says. "You dropped your shit."

"What do you want?" Pearson wipes his nose. He's breathing heavily. "I don't want anything."

Pearson stands as tall as he can and puffs out his chest.

The garbage man steadies himself. And then he's ready. "Why'd you do it?" he asks.

"What are you talking about?" Pearson jumps back. "Get out of here, man," he says. "I don't want any trouble."

"Come with me." Carlton grabs Pearson's arm and tugs him toward the back of the apartment building.

Pearson tries to shake him off, but Carlton is too strong. "Fuck you," Pearson says. "Get the fuck out of here."

"Just come with me!" Carlton's voice cracks. He gives Pearson a shove, and the haggard man gives in. They walk together—Pearson in front, limping, and Carlton behind him.

"Come on, man," Pearson pleads. "What is this about?"

Carlton stops on the far side of the dumpster. His puddle of urine is still there, glistening. He pushes Pearson up against the hard metal. The trash looks even more precarious now; a feather could land on top and send the bags tumbling everywhere.

"Are you telling me you don't know what this is about? You don't recognize me?"

"I really don't."

Carlton takes a minute; he wants to make this last. Savor it. "You told those kids to go to my in-law's house. It was your idea."

Pearson seems surprised. "You're here about that? I had nothing to do with what happened to them."

"Bullshit. I was in the courtroom when you testified."

"I never said they should break into the place."

"Then how'd they get it into their heads? They didn't get that from you?"

"I guess they did, but—"

Carlton holds up his fist.

"Wait, listen." Pearson's pupils are the darkest pools Carlton has ever seen. "I was at Center Bar. I was pretty drunk, I guess, and I stepped into the parking lot for a smoke and those kids, Billy and Barry, were there, leaning against a Camaro. I got a light from Billy and just then a squad car whizzes by, and because I can't keep my big fat mouth shut, I tell them I used to be the chief of police. Billy and the other kid look nervous, angry even, like they think they're in trouble or something. So I start babbling, telling them how I got busted for selling cocaine—to show 'em that I'm no one they have to worry about. But they're high off their asses and coming at me, so I go into how I could help them. How I know things. I tell them lots of stuff, most of it garbage. Like the best places to get drugs, the easiest people to rip off." Carlton clenches his jaw and Pearson throws up his hands defensively. "Really, I was just rambling; I didn't mean to talk about Tara. But for some stupid reason, I started remembering out loud about the one time she invited me into her house." He suddenly slumps. "It was probably the best moment of my life."

"What are you talking about? You didn't say any of this in court."

Pearson seems at a loss. "I guess in some way I wanted to protect her. You know, her reputation."

"What the fuck are you talking about?" Carlton growls.

Pearson, his voice just above a whisper, says, "Tara and me..." He hesitates, then says, "We made love. Just once."

Carlton isn't a confessor and is far from giving absolution. "This all just sounds like a story you're telling to keep from getting your ass kicked." It's a cool night, but Carlton is burning up. He wipes a trickle of sweat off the side of his face with his forearm.

"Listen," Pearson says, changing tacks, "I probably said that she was glamorous. Yeah, I said that." He hurries to add, "But it was them who took that to mean the Blythe's had expensive jewelry socked away somewhere. I never gave them the idea. I just said that night was the last really good thing that ever happened to me."

Carlton squeezes his fist; he can feel his fingernails tearing into the skin of his palms. A trumpeting war cry rings in his ears.

"You want to kill me? Is that it?" Pearson asks. "You'd get caught," he says. "You're a good man. You don't want to screw up your life. Lots of good men inside, I'm telling you. The good ones always regret it. You want to hear about prison? Look at this knee." He points to his left leg. "Guy smashed it on the pavement 'cause I sat too close to him in the cafeteria. After rehab—I'm talking about six months of painful bullshit—this guy found me and fucked it up again."

Carlton laughs.

Pearson clasps his palms in front of his chest, as if praying. "What's so funny?"

"Shut up," Carlton barks.

The ex-cop frantically shakes his head back and forth. Carlton steps forward and grabs Pearson by what's left of his stringy hair.

"I should toss you right up there." Carlton points to the impossibly unstable mountain of garbage. "Right on top."

Pearson tries to pull free. "Come on, man. I didn't tell them to do anything." He clamps his eyes closed. He's shaking. "Come on," he says. "I got a kid. Louis. He's in fifth grade. Listen. Listen. Come on, don't do this. My wife's right in there, man. My wife."

"Don't talk to me about your fucking wife." Carlton is angry. But then memories of Sam—how things used to be with her—cut through his rage. He remembers one of his favorite days with her. She had lived her entire life in eastern Mass-achusetts without visiting Fenway Park before she met Carlton. After they'd been dating a few weeks, he announced, "I'm taking you to a game. This travesty has to end!" It was an over-cast, cold spring day. They sat in right field, and he pointed out all the famous landmarks: the Green Monster, the red seat where Ted Williams hit his 502-foot home run, the dugout where the Red Sox players milled about. Carlton remembered huddling together for warmth and sharing a box of popcorn and a hot dog. It had always been a perfect memory. But now he remembers the rest of it. Sam shivering and wanting to go in the seventh inning. "Leaving early's for tourists," he'd said. By the end, her teeth were chattering, and they began to have an argument; it had been their first.

Carlton looks at the pathetic man in front of him. Pearson, his eyes still closed, sniffles, but he isn't crying. "Please," he says. "Please."

Carlton wants to hold onto his anger; it's a salve on his scorched flesh. But he can't. Everything that had seemed black and white before dissolves into shades of gray. His anger floats away from him like a ghost. "What's your wife do?" Carlton asks. He feels like smoking a cigarette, though he gave them up more than five years ago.

Pearson's eyes flicker open. "A little of this and that. She used to be a teacher."

"You'd think she'd be smart enough to stay away from you."

Pearson offers no argument. He looks Carlton in the eye. "I'm really sorry about what happened. I really am."

"Sure you are." Carlton releases the ex-cop. "I bet you feel real bad."


Carlton staggers back to his pickup. Once there, he tries to steady his hands against the steering wheel. He starts the truck.

As he drives out of the lot, Pearson is stumbling around the corner. His spilled milkshake is streaming down the driveway.

With rush hour past, the streets are clear on the drive back. The sky suddenly spits a few fat raindrops onto the windshield, promising a storm, but it's only a passing cloud and the air dries up. At a stoplight, a car pulls up behind him, and Carlton catches a glimpse of himself in the rearview mirror. His eyes are cold and dead. Why is everything so complicated? Why can't there be a simple button he can push that will make everything all right?

As he calms down, he's glad he didn't rough up Pearson. Beating him up wouldn't have been worth screwing up his own life. But he still feels deeply unsatisfied; it's all so fucking unfair. Then he has a thought. Maybe he can call the cops and report Pearson for something. Make up a story—they'd want to believe it and put that prick behind bars again. And maybe Sam will see that there is a little bit of justice in the world.

At the next intersection, he grips the steering wheel and turns left instead of right. He isn't sure why, but he wants to see the house he and Sam lived in during their first year of marriage. He clears his mind as he drives down the dimly lit roads.

It's a small house with a cross-gable roof. A basketball hoop now stands alone on an extension of the driveway. A modest chandelier illuminates the living room from within. He remembers the young couple who bought the house. Both are tall, thin, and good looking. He wonders what's going on inside. Carlton gets out of the pickup and leans against the truck door. A slight breeze tousles his hair. He pictures them cuddling together on the couch, watching a movie. Afterward, they caress each other the way only intimate lovers know how.

Carlton pulls out his cell phone and holds it for a moment, unsure. Then he presses the numbers.

As the phone on the other end rings, he sees a few years into the future. The young couple now have a girl old enough to shoot baskets. She plays one-on-one with her father. Her mother watches from the stairs that lead to the front door, proud. The girl has nothing to fear; her life is a long, smooth road that stretches into an unencumbered future.

It's all a fantasy. Reality is harder; it calls for difficult decisions.

A woman's voice answers the phone. "Jesus, Carl, I just fell asleep." Sam says. Then, more gently, "What's up?"

"Nothing much," he answers. "I just wanted to hear your voice."

## NOVEMBER 17, 1994

Something in the engine popped, and the car stalled.

"Shit." Pete fiddled with the key in the ignition, but the engine wouldn't turn over.

Tara pointed to the parking lot of a 7-Eleven. Luckily, their Lincoln Continental was perched at the top of a steep hill; when Pete put the sedan into neutral, he was able to glide into the lot and ease into a space. Sam, sitting in the back seat, nervously crumpled her UVM catalog. "What do we do now?"

Pete adjusted the rearview mirror to see his daughter's face. She looked tired. "Don't worry, we'll get there."

"How?" She batted the catalog into her palm and crossed her arms over her chest.

Tara crossed her arms too. "Yes. What now?"

"Give me a damn minute to figure it out, okay?"

Tara looked back at Sam. "Why don't you go and grab us all a snack in the store?"

Sam opened the back door and slammed it shut. "Fine," she said, loud enough to be heard through the window.

With a grimace, Pete said, "Once we get to the campus and she sees what a great school it is, she'll be okay."

"If we actually get there."

"We'll get there."

"I hope so."

Pete pinched his lips together to keep his composure. "Whose side are you fucking on?" Pete lightly hit his fist against the steering wheel. Tara opened the glove compartment and took out a cigarette.

\* \* \*

Sam leaned against the door frame of the 7-Eleven, watching her parents' bicker; she was relieved to be at a distance. From where she stood inside the store, she could see her mom puffing away on a cigarette and chattering. Tara had warned Pete to get the car checked, but he'd insisted it would be fine, and now she was pissed. For his part, he was probably denying responsibility. "Cars break." Sam watched as Pete rested his hands on his lap and then stepped out of the car, pulled open the hood, and began checking the engine. He poked and prodded, but Sam knew he wouldn't solve the problem; it was all a show. He knew as much about cars as she did about nuclear physics. Still, he stood there looking, rubbing his hands to stay warm. After a moment, he sat down on the bumper and her mother joined him. Of course, the car broke down on the way. Of course they were going to argue, even after she'd overheard them promising each other they wouldn't.

Sam exhaled and caught sight of herself in the glass of the store. She wore no makeup, and with her blunt bangs, gray coat, and plain hiking boots, she was not the picture of an angst-ridden seventeen-year-old rebel. And yet all she could think about was running away. It would be more like leaving behind *abrasive siblings than leaving the security of a parental home. She could hitchhike all the way up to Vermont, check out the school herself, and then find someplace to live until she could start college in the fall. That would set her apart from her sister; Shelby had always talked about running away but had never done it. She'd ended up back in Benfield, a librarian of all things.*

*She watched her parents as they talked. Even in the cold air of mid-winter, red-faced, they were stunning, and Sam wondered why neither she nor Shelby had inherited their parents' bone structure. Her father wiped his eyes, then reached over and took the cigarette from her mother. Or was it offered? It was difficult to say at this distance.*

*He handed the cigarette back. Sam pulled her headphones on.*

* * *

*Tara held her half-smoked cigarette tightly between her first and second fingers, occasionally flicking ash onto the pavement.*

*Pete looked over his shoulder to make sure Sam was out of earshot. "I know we said we weren't going to talk about it on this trip, but I just want to say that I'm sorry."*

*Tara wiped her tears. "I hate you."*

*He ran his hands through her hair. "You don't hate me."*

*"Why do you keep doing this?" She forced herself to stop crying. "What do you get from these women that you don't get from me?"*

*Pete angled his face toward the sky as if there were answers there. Instead, his eyes landed on a solitary seagull circling above. There was something mesmerizing about the way it rose and fell on the wind currents. "I guess because it feels good," he said.*

*"That's not an answer, Pete."*

He compressed his thick eyebrows; he wanted to answer honestly. "I suppose I just can't help it. When I go on sales calls, the women ...The way they look at me...They want me and, even though I know it's wrong, I want them too. It's this intense feeling and...If I was ugly and fat and no one ever—"

"But that's just normal temptation. Everyone has that. You make it sound like you don't have a choice."

Pete squeezed his fist; he hadn't thought about choice before. "Yeah," he said. "It feels..." He tried to think of a word that would exactly capture it. He deserved a little sympathy at least. "It feels inevitable."

"Inevitable?" She tossed the cigarette into the parking lot.

"Try to see things my way. You're an attractive woman. Men notice you."

"I'm not an animal, Pete. I have willpower. I love you. Do you even think about me when you're...?" She couldn't finish the sentence.

Pete closed his eyes for a moment, but the morning sun penetrated his eyelids. "I do think about you." He opened his eyes, looking again for the seagull.

Tara followed Pete's gaze upward. When she saw the bird, she felt a sudden rage. She wished she had a rifle so she could shoot it right out of the sky. "I'd feel awful if I did what you do. I would never sleep with someone else." Tara looked back down at the pavement; she began crying again. "I'd feel like something was eating away my guts from the inside."

Pete wished he could cry that easily. Just spill out all his pain, like his wife did. Maybe that would change his plight.

Tara continued. She couldn't help it. "You've broken my heart."

If he held his head steady, Pete could see the breeze rippling the individual feathers of the seagull. It stretched its wings and *began to fly higher. A tense moment passed.* "I should probably leave. Strike out on my own."

Sure, Tara thought. On the open road, free and happy. But she forced herself to stay calm. "If you think that's best," she said.

She could hear Pete's breathing; it always got slow and deep when they talked this way. She took it as a sign of his passion for her. A sign that he didn't want to leave her. She focused her eyes on a few loose pebbles near her feet. "Where would you stay?"

"A hotel, I guess."

"Which one?"

"I don't know. The idea occurred to me only this second."

"You can't stay in a cheap hotel."

"Why not?"

"Those places are terrible."

He found her concern for him touching. He pictured the double bed in the Landon Hotel, could smell the cleaning solution that didn't quite cover the odor of vomit. The place was haunted by those who'd spent the night there and never spoken to each other again.

Tara let the thought of Pete leaving her sink in. How large the house would feel, how long the nights would be without him. She followed his gaze upward again. She could see a tiny dot far above. Was that the bird or a trick of her eyes? Tara shivered. "Should we call a tow truck?"

"Yeah," Pete said. "I guess so."

"I don't want you to leave."

"I know," he said, still looking at the sky.

Resigned, Tara trotted over to the payphone, called AAA, and got them to send a truck.

After she returned, she lit another cigarette. "Where the hell is Sam?"

He looked back at the 7-Eleven. "Moping in the store, I'm guessing."

"I hope she's buying something decadent," Tara said, trying to relieve the tension. "But she'll probably come out with a bunch of lettuce and a few bananas."

"Yep." He patted his wife's arm. "Inedible garbage."

The tow truck arrived. The driver looked over the engine, checked a few connections, and said he'd have to take it to the garage to figure out what was wrong. He gave them a business card and attached the Lincoln to the back of the truck. "Call us tomorrow morning," he said and drove off.

Tara called a taxi to take them to the nearest car rental place. Pete hopped up and down next to the payphone to keep warm.

"Okay, the cab will be here in ten minutes," Tara said as she hung up.

"We'd better get Sam."

It was colder in the store than it was outside, but brightly lit. There were only a few aisles, none higher than five feet.

"Where is she?" Tara asked, annoyed.

"Like we don't have enough to worry about," Pete said.

Tara checked the bathrooms, opening the stalls one by one, but they were empty. Pete, beginning to panic, approached the cashier. "Have you seen our daughter? She's about this tall with long, brown hair. She was wearing..." But Pete couldn't remember what Sam had been wearing, and neither could Tara.

The pimply-faced cashier shrugged. "She might've been here for a second."

"What the fuck?" Pete said.

"Oh my god," Tara said. She covered her mouth with her hand. "Where is she?"

They rushed outside and looked around, now frantic. Sam was sitting on the grass next to the store, sipping a ginger ale. "I got you some water and a couple of apples." She waved them over. "Someone has to make sure we don't starve to death."

# JULY 2014

## OPPOSITE FIELD

R on claps three times. Sweat beads prickle his forehead, slide over his thick brow, and plunk onto the third base coach's box. "Let's go!" he shouts.

Tony nods from the batter's box and then, with a swing that would make Ted Williams proud, shoots the ball down the right field line on a rope and past the outfielder, a tubby fireman whose name Ron can't remember. Alex easily scores from second and suddenly Tony is the winning run. As soon as the right fielder turns to chase the ball, Ron knows it's over.

But Tony goes into a cocky jog as he cruises past second and heads for third; he can't see that the ball got hung up in the grass, and the outfielder is already throwing it to the relay man. Ron leaps up and down and waves his arms—he'll strangle that fucking prick if this costs them the game. But Tony only grins as he cruises past third and heads for home. Ron gapes as the ball arcs toward the plate and reaches the catcher an instant before their star third baseman. Somehow he has the presence of mind to slide, kicking a cloud of dirt into the air, and taking out the legs of the catcher, old man Steve Kenison, team captain for The Tinders. From his place in the dirt, Stevie holds the ball up to show the world that he has it. The crowd—about fifteen or twenty wives and kids—goes quiet. The umpire raises his hand as if he's about to call Tony out, but then a light beam from another galaxy penetrates his head and alters his brain cells. He reaches his arms apart and bellows "safe." Fuck yeah. Ron scrambles toward home plate along with the rest of his teammates, but stops short of the mob of elated cops piling on top of Tony. They were *supposed* to beat the fire department in the semis, Ron thinks. The finals will be another story.

The firefighters are friendly as they line up and shake hands with the police. Ron, as team captain, brings up the rear of the line and pats Stevie on the back as they pass each other. There's real respect there, Ron thinks, and he congratulates his opposite number for a great season. "Good luck in the finals," Steve Kenison says.

As Ron packs up his equipment, Miguel Anders, the pitcher for the Sanitation Trash Talkers, taps him on the shoulder.

"Nice game." Miguel is tall and lanky, but his arms are weirdly thick; it's like Dr. Frankenstein dug up a body and transplanted giant arms onto the Sanitation star.

Ever hear of leg day? Ron thinks. Then says, "Thanks, man."

"I thought he was out, though." His brown eyes are hard. "You paid off the umpire or what?"

Ron seethes. "Of course not." He wants to point his finger into the chest of the freakish science experiment and tell him to take it back, but he's a cop, and Miguel is a garbage man and he doesn't want to come off like a bully. He hates bullies. He attempts to level his voice. "I'd never do that."

Miguel chuckles. "Jesus H. Christ, Ronnie. Look at you. All worked up. I'm only kidding."

Miguel has been captain of the Trash Talkers for fifteen years; he's *definitely* not kidding. "Yeah, me too," Ron says.

"Sure, you were." Miguel pats him on the chest. "You're always kidding."

Fucking dick, Ron thinks. "We'll see you in the finals."

"That we will."


Center Bar and Grille is packed and humming with chatter. He finds Tony on a stool, clutching a pint. Firemen and police mill about swapping stories.

Ron leans over Tony's shoulder. "You gave me a scare at the end of the game, kiddo." He raises his hand to get the bartender's attention, but the man doesn't notice. Or pretends not to. Another prick. It's a new guy, so Ron cuts him some slack.

"I had it all the way, coach."

Ron tolerates Tony's sarcasm because he's the best player on the team, but he wishes the Slammers were a real team and he was a real manager. He'd suspend Tony's ass. Instead, he pats his third baseman on the shoulder. "It was pretty close, though. Maybe next time run hard all the way."

Tony looks irritated. "We won, didn't we?" Tony's funny. Confident. Like his shit doesn't stink. So why does it matter if he gets thrown out at home in the semis? He'll still enjoy his pint, and everyone will say it was too bad—a good try. It must be nice to walk on water, Ron thinks. But Tony isn't as popular as he believes. His wife runs the local paper and people tend to be nervous about what they say around him.

Ron knows he should leave it there, but can't help himself. "We can't afford to make those kinds of mistakes against Sanitation."

"What mistakes? We fucking won."

Ron wants to say, *You have to hustle on every play or Sanitation will kill us in the finals*, but instead, biting his tongue, says, "You're right."

"Fuck," Tony says. "Lighten up." Tony holds up his beer. "I'm gonna enjoy this right now, if you don't mind." He begins chugging.

"Yeah, you do that." He pats Tony on the shoulder. "Good game, today."


He sits at his desk outside the courtroom the next day, making sure only authorized personnel enter. He'd gotten stuck with this assignment after the arrest of Billy Lawson. That collar should have made his career, but he'd brought the kid to his knees with a gut punch—for all he'd known, the kid was still carrying a loaded gun. Next thing you know some public defender is crying *police brutality!* and what should have been a commendation becomes a demotion. It had cost the prosecution a life sentence, too, and had made Ron a joke around the office. Police Chief Earley had been right to take him out of circulation for a while, but checking IDs is tedious as hell and it's already been more than six months. He'd begged for a new assignment, even offering to take a midnight desk shift, but the Chief shook his head and mumbled, "Sorry, Eagle Scout. You're lucky you're still on the force."

He hated that nickname.

To distract himself, Ron scribbles down lineup combinations on a piece of paper; if he jumbles the order for the championship game, it'll light a fire under his players. The guys who move to the top of the lineup will get a boost of confidence, and the guys he moves down will be pissed and want to prove he's wrong. Basic psychology.

But who is he kidding? There's a reason the undefeated

Trash Talkers' closest game was still a seven-run win. Ron loves his pitcher, Alan "Pee Wee" Connor; he takes the game and himself seriously, but he's nowhere near Miguel's level. Miguel can buzz a fastball, whip a riser, and K you with a drop ball. It's as simple as that. A pitching matchup that overwhelmingly favors Sanitation. Ron should be happy he'd gotten his team this far; the finals will be a massacre. The cops haven't won it all in six years, which was a year before Ron joined the team.

He pours himself a scotch and soda that night and paces around his cramped apartment; it's all he can afford after his divorce. It's full of mismatched furniture: a scratched-up desk and a chair held together, in part, with packing tape, an old metal filing cabinet, a beat-up couch. It still smells like cigarette ash from the prior tenant. Ron finds himself standing in front of the empty glass case adjacent to his forty-eight-inch flat screen. There's one trophy there and it's not his; it's his daughter Edith's. She'd pitched her high school team to an undefeated season and a state championship. She throws for Arizona State now. He's proud of her, although they haven't spoken a whole lot over the past five years.

Ron has an idea. There are no rules against ringers, so why not stick it in Miguel's eye? The next day he digs up Edi's number. How great would it feel helping the old man win a championship? Softball was the one thing they'd had in common; he remembers how his daughter looked the last time he saw her—all lanky arms and legs, wild hair, and a round face like her mother's. He feels the five years of estrangement melt away as he envisions father and daughter lifting the trophy together.

After work on Sunday, he cranks up the air conditioner,

pours himself a drink and calls Edi to ask her about playing the game.

"Who is this?" She takes a bite of something, possibly a cracker.

"It's your dad."

"Oh, it's you. Wow." Another crunching sound. "What's up?"

"I'm sorry if I caught you in the middle of something. I can call back."

"It's okay. I was finishing my workout."

Ron gathers his thoughts. How can he put this in a way that will sound appealing? Play up the father-daughter angle. Pour gasoline on her competitive fire. But before he can speak again, she says, "I'm glad you called."

"Yeah?"

"Well...yeah. I mean, I hoped you'd call me at some point."

This throws him off track. "I'm sorry I didn't call sooner."

"Crime fighting is a busy job." She giggles.

"So..." He doesn't know what to say. "Are you home for the summer?" He's been assuming all along that she is; if not, his plan is over before it begins.

"Yep. I fly back to Arizona in a few weeks."

"That's nice."

"Mom is driving me nuts."

"I bet."

"How are you?"

He puts down his scotch. He wasn't expecting this reception from her; he quickly changes course. "Do you want to meet up?" If Roberta finds out, shit will hit the fan, but it'll be easier to convince his daughter to join the Slammers if she sees him in person. There'll be tears. Maybe real affection.

"Tonight?"

"What do you think?"

"Okay, I guess." He can hear her breathing. "I'm starving, though. I get that way after a workout."

"Dinner's on me." His mind races. He needs a place with candles on the table and a separate wine menu. That's how professional GMs entertain potential free agents. "How about Di Napolis? You like Italian, right?"

"I don't know. That place is kinda fancy, isn't it?"

He feels a burst of pride; she's a meat and potatoes gal. "You're right. I don't know what I was thinking." Before he can suggest another restaurant, she says, "The Benfield Diner is nice. And they have huge portions."

He laughs. "You can't go wrong with huge portions."

"Does seven sound okay to you?"

"Sure." There's a beat. "I'm excited."

"I am too."

He stares at his cell. What the fuck just happened? His daughter *wants* to spend time with him? After his divorce, he had seen a therapist for a short time. Alexandra Waverly. She told him he had to learn to go with the flow. Accept things. He'd never really gotten the hang of that, but maybe he'd picked up more from her than he realized. He takes a quick shower, shaves, and puts on a pair of slacks and a snug fitting Polo shirt.

The diner is crowded, but he gets seated in a booth by the window and stares out; waves of heat drift up from the tar parking lot, cars shuttle in and out, a young couple stand near the entrance kissing. He wishes summer would never end.

Edi arrives thirty minutes late wearing a long skirt and a blouse. Her hair is pulled back into a ponytail. "Sorry if I'm running behind." She slides in on the other side of the table. "I'm always late. It's kinda my thing."

"I get everywhere early." He doesn't mean it as a rebuke, and to show her he's on her side, he forces a happy grin.

Her rosy cheeks brighten. "I guess we're opposites."

"I guess so." A fly buzzes near his ear and he swats at it.

"I hope they're stocked up back there. I'm hungry enough to eat the whole kitchen."

"Go nuts." He slides a menu over. "It's on me."

"You said that already."

"Well, I'm just happy to be buying you dinner."

"It's been a while since *that* happened," she says.

That isn't fair, he thinks. "I paid child support, you know."

Her face changes. "That's because the law made you."

He sees his mistake. "That's not true. I wanted to pay it. I never stopped caring about you."

She looks down at her menu.

He says, "Losing touch wasn't my plan. Even when you were in high school, I tried seeing you. Your mother wouldn't let me."

"That figures. She hates you."

He's tempted to launch into a few anecdotes about his ex, how she once stole his wallet and denied it for three days, but he's got bigger fish to fry.

Edi tosses the menu on the table and gracefully moves a strand of blonde hair behind her ear, exposing her pretty face. She looks less like Roberta than he remembers, more angular now, less like a baby.

"Looks like you made a decision there." He picks up the menu. "What's it gonna be?"

"You'll see!"

"It's gonna be a surprise, then?"

"Yep."

When the waiter arrives, he orders veal parmigiana, and she orders the chicken cacciatore special, an order of sweet potato fries, and a chocolate milkshake.

"You really *are* hungry."

"I don't mess around."

She's got his appetite; he's impressed. "I used to eat like that."

"What happened?"

"I got old."

"You're not *that* old."

"Tell that to my gut."

She rests her hands, folded together, on the table; they're thick and strong. She got that from him, too.

He takes in the diner. A few older couples sit at booths opposite each other picking at their food. A fluorescent light flickers on and off. The Formica countertops are stained with coffee rings. There's something sad about the place. He remembers taking Edi here when she was a kid, how much she loved climbing up on one of the stools that run along the counter. Now each one lists, one way or another, not totally anchored to the ground, miniature towers of Pisa.

Ron feels tongue-tied. When Edi was small, he could just pick her up, make a funny face, or playfully kiss her stomach. All he needed to say was, "I'm your daddy," and she would cackle with joy. Now, all he can manage is, "It's really hot out there, isn't it?"

"It's not Arizona."

Dinner is overcooked, but neither mind, and there are mostly laughs; both avoid serious subjects. Finally, Ron says, "This has been a great summer for softball."

"You still play?" She seems surprised.

"Of course. I'm the team captain."

"That must be a lot of work."

"Not really. I like whipping those boys into shape. When you're passionate about something, it's contagious. Right?" He leans forward. "You must really miss it while you're on break."

She looks down at her food.

He pauses as if he's thinking about something that just occurred to him. "We have a pretty big game coming up. Do you think you'd like to play with your old man?"

She stares at him incredulously.

He tries to sound nonchalant. "It's the championship game against Sanitation. Those guys have been killing us every year, and it'd be great to beat their asses for once. You could be our secret weapon."

She doesn't say anything. He asks again. "What do you think? Want to help us out?"

"Playing with a bunch of old cops doesn't sound that fun to me." The ping has gone out of her voice.

"Don't you want to show off what you can do?"

"I don't know." Edi turns her body and looks out the window. A pick-up truck pulls into the parking lot; its headlights blind her for a moment. When it passes, she's hanging her head. "It would mean a lot to me."

She takes a bite of food. After swallowing, she says, "I really have a lot of studying to do."

"During the summer?" He makes sure his disappointment doesn't show.

"I switched my major to biology. I'm thinking of going to veterinary school after college."

"Veterinary school. Wow."

"You look surprised."

"Not surprised, really. Just wondering where that came from."

"Maybe it was begging you and mom for a dog every year." She looks up.

He doesn't remember that. And it's his experience that vets are harried and overworked. But fathers are supposed to be encouraging. "That's a great idea. I can introduce you to

Christy Kim. She works at the Benfield Vet. We sometimes bring her injured strays."

"That's okay. I've already talked to a bunch of vets and everything."

"Terrific. I'm happy for you."

"Thanks." She sips her milkshake.

He waits for an appropriate amount of time to pass. "Well," he says. "There's no pressure. I just thought you'd want to get out on the field with the old man one more time."

She puts the milkshake down and looks out the window. "Actually dad..." Her voice trails off.

"What?"

"Nevermind. Can I think about it?"

He can't ask for more. "Absolutely."

Later, as they stand next to her battered silver Buick Century in the parking lot, he feels a thousand pounds fall off his shoulders—he's happy with himself. This is what it feels like to recruit players professionally, he thinks.

"This was fun," he says.

"It was."

He watches her climb into her car. "Talk to you soon, kiddo."

"Thanks, Dad."

On the way home, he detours down Furman Lane, stops at the ball field, and gets out of his car. It's a perfect night: a steady buzz of insects from the woods beyond the far fence. A light breeze. He takes a jog around the diamond, picturing himself hitting a game-winning grand slam, embracing Edi when he crosses home plate.

On the drive to the courthouse the next day, however, he begins to feel uneasy. If his daughter decides she doesn't want to pitch for the Slammers, what will he do then? Real general managers always have a plan B. Just in case.

After his shift, he drives to Tom Armstrong's place, a ranch house in a wooded area of town behind Rogers Elementary School. Tom, a twenty-two-year veteran of the police force, had been the clean-up hitter for the Slammers for a long time, but when he got into his forties, developed diabetes and stopped playing. Adding him to the lineup wouldn't guarantee a win, but it would certainly improve their chances; he had been their star player last time they hoisted the trophy. Play all the angles, he thinks.

Part of the roof seems to be slowly collapsing, but the yard is pristine. The lawn is green and evenly mown, the woodchips in the garden around the house are fresh, and all the bushes and trees are groomed.

Tom opens his front door wearing a T-shirt and shorts. His face looks wan, but he's still a hulking figure, about six-four with a barrel chest and tree stump arms and legs.

"What's up, Ron?" There's a touch of suspicion in his voice.

Ron figures there's no point pussyfooting here. "I want you to rejoin the team."

"Ron—"

"Before you say no, hear me out."

Tom rips open a bag of peanuts and starts munching on them. "Come on, then." He steps outside and they sit side by side on the stairs.

"Did you know we added a DH to the lineup last season?"

Tom looks up at a squirrel bounding along a branch in a nearby tree. "I hadn't heard."

"You wouldn't even have to play the field. It's one game."

He chews on a peanut. "I don't think so."

"But softball is great exercise."

Tom shrugs. "I don't play anymore, Ron. You know that."

Ron clasps his fingers tightly together. "This is a chance to beat those assholes in Sanitation."

"I haven't lifted a bat in years."

A glimmer of hope. "Don't be modest, Tom. I'm sure you can still crush the ball."

Tom scratches his head. "Like I said. I don't play softball anymore."

Ron nods. He needs a different strategy. "Can I ask you why you never played in the majors?"

"I messed up my knee in high school sliding into third base; it couldn't stand the constant pounding."

"But you were drafted, right?"

"By the Dodgers." He stares at the open bag of peanuts but seems uninterested in eating them. Ron takes this as a good sign.

"So, you never really got to see how good you could be." Ron holds up his finger, stopping Tom from interrupting. "Miguel Anders struck out seventeen in three different games this year."

"Town softball isn't the major leagues. Not by a long shot."

"Of course not." Enthusiastically, Ron adds, "But remember the bombs you used to hit off that fuck? He won't know what hit him."

Tom tosses the bag of peanuts into the shrubs with the flick of his wrist and pops a toothpick into his mouth. "You should get a life, Ron." He stands and opens the door to his house. "Good luck."

At home, he sits on the couch, tapping his foot nervously on the hardwood floor. Fuck that guy, he thinks. What's wrong with needing a win?

An old black-and-white Barbara Stanwyck movie is playing on the television; her costume sparkles and shines as she sings in front of a big band. But Ron can barely follow the plot. He clicks off the television and begins pacing. Finally, he decides to call Edi. She's really his only chance.

"How's it going, daughter of mine?" His mind is racing.

"It's going great. How's it going with you, sorta-father of mine?"

"Not half bad. Not half bad at all." There's something fragile in her quiet breathing. His eyes dampen. He wants an answer, but after their supper, he feels like he should try to be a good dad and not pressure her. "I was thinking, we should get ice cream tonight and talk some more. How about I meet you at Sweet Edge in an hour?"

"That sounds fun. Thanks, kinda-dad!"

The ice cream parlor sits on a farm in Putnam. Cows graze in the fenced-in pasture. Fireflies flicker. Ron and Edi sit on the hood of his Jeep.

His ice cream cone is heaped three scoops high and he tries to figure out how best to attack it. "I don't remember you liking mocha chip."

She bites into hers. "I don't remember you ever taking me out for ice cream." He doesn't know what to say, but she laughs. "Don't worry. It's not that big a deal."

Her gentleness makes him see her as an adult for the first time. He knows he hasn't earned it, but he feels proud of the way his daughter carries herself. "Veterinary school is a great idea," he says. "I don't think I said it before, but I'm really proud of you."

"Thanks." She squints as she watches the sun vanish over the horizon. "Why'd you become a cop?"

He looks toward the pasture and fixes his gaze on a grazing cow. His reasons for becoming a cop seem part of a different life now. "It's complicated," he says to Edi as evenly as he can manage. "It doesn't matter anyway; it's a good job. I get to make the world a better place."

But he knew, being a policeman hadn't changed anything. No one, especially his colleagues, cared about justice. They just wanted a paycheck and a pension. That was the real reason he was on courthouse duty. It was to punish him for caring.

"That makes a lot of sense." She resumes eating and her face brightens. "It's good to be practical."

There's a break in the conversation. He feels like he needs to explain his life to her, but he isn't sure there's anything he can say that will make sense. As casually as he can, he asks, "Any thoughts about pitching for us?"

She's still squinting. "I don't know."

What's so difficult about deciding whether or not to play in one little game? Frustrated, he hops off the Jeep, and his ice cream falls back onto his shirt. "Goddamn it," he says.

Edi laughs. Then, as she seems to consider him, readjusts herself on the hood of the Jeep. "Well," she says. "Maybe it could be fun."

He turns. "You mean it?"

"Sure," she says. "As long as it's okay with the rest of the team. I don't want to step on any toes."

"Oh, don't worry about that. Everyone wants to win. Our toes have been stepped on enough by those Sanitation guys anyway."

"Uh huh," she says.

"Great, then. It's settled."

The air conditioner is broken in the station the next morning. Chief Earley wants the staff to stay professional, but the walls are melting. The men unbutton their top buttons and roll up their sleeves. Several buy fans and put them around the station and fill coolers with ice cubes to sit on instead of chairs. Ron is unaffected, though, striding through the halls. His uniform is buttoned to the top, and he wills himself not to sweat.

"What the hell is wrong with you?" Tony is fanning himself with a magazine at his desk, his forehead a swamp.

"We're gonna win the game on Saturday."

"Bullshit."

"I've got us a pitcher. The real deal."

Tony laughs.

"What's so funny?"

Tony calls across the office so everyone can hear. "Ron recruited a pitcher for the Sanitation game. You believe this shit?"

Chief Earley's expression doesn't change. "Is that true, Ron?"

"We're gonna win."

"That's good news, then." The Chief strides away.

Ron doesn't care that Tony is laughing at him—the Chief isn't laughing. Maybe he'll see that he's wasting Ron at the courthouse; he's a guy who can get things done. Ron imagines himself cruising past the high school. There's a kid in torn jeans, hunched over, ragged. He walks up the short hill to the railroad tracks. Ron gets out of his car, talks to him, buys him lunch, helps him get a job. Policemen should be able to do these things.

Ron texts Edi a quick note on his way to the courthouse, but she doesn't reply. Worried, he tries calling. She doesn't pick up. He gives it a few hours and tries again. Still, no answer.

Why did I brag to the guys? He thinks. How could I be so stupid?

He calls Roberta.

"What?" she asks tersely.

"I was looking for Edith. She hasn't been answering my text messages."

"I'm sorry to hear that."

"Can we cut out the sarcasm? She's my daughter and I'm concerned."

"Sure you are."

He sniffs. "Please, Ro. Help me. I'm really trying."

"She went back to Arizona."

"What? When?"

"Last night."

"She didn't mention anything. Jesus."

"Why would she mention anything to you?"

He wants to slap his ex right through his phone. That impulse is what got him in trouble in the first place, though. He takes a breath. "I'm sorry. I shouldn't have called."

"It's okay," she says. Her tone changes. "Take care of yourself, Ron. Will you do that?"

"I will. You too."

He tries calling Edi again, but now he's not surprised that she doesn't answer. He flips on the nature channel for a few minutes—it's a documentary about elephants—and then turns off the TV. He calls the Arizona State University Athletics Department.

"Hello. I'm trying to reach my daughter. I think her cell phone isn't working. I'm Ronald Miller."

"What's her full name?" It's a young woman's voice, probably a student.

"Edith Miller." In a moment of pride, he says, "She pitches for the softball team."

He hears a keyboard clicking on the other line. "Found her! Edith Miller. She lives in Palo Verde East." The woman gives Ron the number for the dorm's front desk. "Are you sure she pitches for the softball team?" she asks.

"Positive," Ron says. "Why?"

"I just thought all the players lived together."

"Well, she has a mind of her own." He's surprised by how defensive he sounds.

"Sure," the girl says. "Can I help you with anything else?"

"No, that's all."

Feeling a tightness in his belly, he goes online and finds the page for the Arizona State softball team. Edi's name isn't listed on the roster. He realizes he could have checked on her like this at any time; it had just never occurred to him to look her up.

Ron calls in sick the next day and gets on a flight to Arizona. On the short cab ride from the Phoenix airport, he notes the strange, bushy trees scattered around. It's so different from the pines and oaks in Benfield. The air is different from Benfield too—dry and clean, but hotter, like it's on fire. The cab leaves him in front of Palo Verde East. There are students everywhere. He texts Edi: *I'm at your dorm room. Downstairs. Can you come down and talk to me?*

After a few minutes, she comes outside. She's wearing blue jean shorts and a T-shirt and somehow looks much younger in this context than she did back home in Massachusetts.

"What the hell are you doing here?" She looks around nervously.

"I was worried. You just left."

She scoffs. "Worried about your softball game?" As she says this, he realizes that softball was the last thing on his mind. She continues, "You can't show up like this out of nowhere."

"I know. I'm sorry. Can I come inside?"

"I don't think so." She still won't look at him.

"Just for a few minutes?" He breathes the dry air. "Please," he says.

She puts her hands on her hips. "Fine. Come with me."

He follows her through the doors where she signs him in at the desk. There's a café down the hall. They order their drinks and sit. Edit takes a packet of sugar from a plastic holder on the table and begins fidgeting with it. "So? What do you want?"

"I don't know. This, I guess." His mind is suddenly clear. "I want to know you better."

She holds the sugar packet up to the light, like she's discovered a secret message written on the side. "You want to know why I quit softball."

"Sure, I want to know why you quit." He studies her nervous fingers. "I want to know everything about you."

"Yeah?" She narrows her eyes. "Aren't you going to miss your game?"

"Yeah, I will. But I've decided softball sucks," he says.

Ron enjoys the wry smile that passes over her face. She says, "Yeah, me too."

"The guys will hate me for this, but who cares?"

"I doubt they'll hate you."

He laughs. "You know what? They already do. They always have. I'm thinking of retiring from the force anyway." As soon as he says this aloud, he knows it's true.

She leans forward; her voice is measured. "What will you do then?"

"I really don't have any idea." Edi is still fiddling nervously with the sugar packet. He gently takes it away from her and puts it back in the holder. "But I don't want to worry about that right now. I'd rather talk about you."

# AUGUST 9, 1995

Everyone had been complaining about the heavy, humid August afternoons, but Tara liked the weather. She spent hours sunning herself on her front lawn, reclining on a deck chair like a satisfied cat. She was past the age where she would attract swarms of men but still in good enough shape to elicit a few car honks.

One afternoon, Police Chief Tim Pearson pulled into her driveway and stepped out of his patrol car. Built like a tree stump, he took short, powerful strides. Tara stayed in her recliner and waited for him.

"Hi, Chief," she said. "How are you?" He'd been on the force for about nine years, if she remembered right, and had only been Chief for the last two, but he had a confident swagger like Gary Cooper in High Noon.

"Hi Tara." He shaded his eyes. "How're you doing?"

"I'm well." She crossed her legs at the ankle and caught him glancing down at her lean flesh. It was nice to know a younger man—she was almost forty-nine—could look at her that way. "What can I do for you?"

"Well," he said. He removed his hat. "This is a bit awkward."

"It's okay," Tara said. "Tell me what's on your mind."

"A few people have been complaining about you sitting out on your front lawn nearly naked every day."

"Really?" When Evelyn, her closest friend, mentioned something like this to her, she'd felt a warm rush of blood to her face, but then defiance. Let 'em look.

"It's a shame," he said, "but small-town people have small minds."

"They do, indeed," Tara said.

"It's your property and you can do whatever you want. I should make that clear."

"Thank you, Chief."

"But if it's no difference to you, you might want to sun yourself in the backyard."

She shifted her legs to see what effect it would have on him. "Do you think that would be best?"

"Well. Personally, I'd say you have plenty to be proud of and I don't blame you for showing off."

Tara sat up, arching slightly, and then relaxed back into the recliner. She peered at her visitor. She didn't like his bushy mustache or his slick blond hair, but wondered what it would feel like to rest her head on his wide shoulders. "I'm sorry, Chief —I don't know what I was thinking. Can I offer you something to drink?"

"I could go for some water before hitting the road."

"Of course."

He followed her inside. In the kitchen, she poured two glasses of water from the sink and offered him one.

"Thanks," he said and put his hat down on a chair.

Tara sipped her water. "You want to know why I sit out front?"

"Sure," the Chief says. "If you want to tell me."

Tara is aware of his eyes on her body. "I've been kind of lonely since my husband left. I hardly see my oldest anymore, and my youngest is always with friends. Seeing the cars go by makes me feel like I'm a little bit connected to the town. I'm not trying to draw any attention to myself." She could tell he knew she was lying, but he did his best to pretend he didn't, and she appreciated that.

"Of course," he said. "How long has it been? A year?"

"A little over, actually." It had been more than three.

"Give it a bit more time and you'll find something to occupy your mind. I promise." She was more concerned about her body than her mind at the moment, but the Chief was being sweet.

She wiped the moisture from her neck. "I hope you're right."

He slid his fingers along his glass. "You should get involved in some community activities."

"Can you picture me bowling, Chief?"

"Actually," he looked her up and down. "I can."

She laughed. "Thank you. But I guess I'm not much of a joiner."

"I get that. You prefer people come to you."

She had never thought of it that way. "You're very perceptive."

"That's why I'm the Chief of Police."

Suddenly, they ran out of banter. Tara drank her water quickly. "Do you want to sit?" She moved into the living room, leaving him behind. "It's cooler in here."

He stomped in awkwardly.

"Come closer."

Without hesitating, Tim moved to the couch, still holding his glass.

"Let me have that," she said. She put it on the floor and then tucked her legs under her.

The sweat was drying on his face now, leaving dry, salty patches. "You ever think about running away?"

"You sound like my husband now."

"Oh. Sorry. I don't mean to."

"No, it's okay. It's nice."

"Is it?"

"Yeah."

A breathless moment passed.

"Tara Blythe," he said. "Your husband was crazy to leave you."

"Thanks." And she let it happen.

# AUGUST 2014

## WHERE DISNEY WORLD IS

Janey bends and picks up a discarded pepperoni slice sitting on the sidewalk in front of Town's Pizza. It smells okay, she thinks, but you can never be too careful. She waves it over her head, using the early evening air molecules to clean off the bugs and germs, and then tears off a piece with her twelve or so remaining teeth. She swallows, waits a moment, and when she feels no ill effects, takes another bite. "Glorious," she says.

Nimbly, she crosses the parking lot and rummages through the three garbage receptacles on the strip mall sidewalk: nothing worth eating in the receptacle in front of Samantha's Beauties Hair Salon, nothing in the one in front of Soaks & Folks, and again, no food in the bin in front of Norton's Hardware. Still, she feels grateful; some nights she comes up completely empty.

The sun over Benfield High sinks gracefully. Janey plops onto the sidewalk and dreams again of making her getaway. She has fifty-eight dollars and forty cents already; she needs only another fourteen bucks and she'll have enough to buy a ticket to

Orlando, Florida. She can already see herself on the bus—a window seat with no one next to her. She'll run her fingers through her freshly cut hair, smooth the skirt of her smart new dress, and let the forward motion of the vehicle lull her into a sense of contentment. She'll smile happily and the woman across the aisle will say, "Off on an adventure?" "I'm going to meet my boyfriend at Cinderella's Castle," she'll answer. The woman will look confused, and she'll add, "You know, in Disney World."

A sound from one of the trash bins startles her. She lifts her creaky body off the pavement and dashes over, hoping the source of the noise is Scrappy, the raccoon she'd named after the cartoon puppy from her childhood. She'd always liked him better than Scooby—he was a little guy with a big personality. And what better name for a forager?

She and Scrappy used to explore the trash bins together, but he'd stopped showing up sometime last winter and she's been wondering where he is. Maybe he found a better place to scavenge. Maybe he died. Or maybe he's waiting for her some-where. Some days she goes to the woods where she imagines him living with his family. She only goes to the edge, though; the woods are uncharted except for a few walking paths, like the one that runs from Rogers Elementary to Cranberry Street. They are dark and daunting. They expand for miles and she doesn't want to get lost.

The sound isn't Scrappy. It's a scrawny pigeon pecking away at a pizza crust. Janey turns around and walks in the other direction. The grass island that runs down the center of Wood-side Boulevard is illuminated by a row of streetlamps the town installed last year. She feels safer walking here than anywhere else. A half-moon appears overhead and makes the pine trees in the woods look like plastic models from a child's game.

The town center, where the homeless shelter sits hidden in

an alley past the *Benfield Weekly* newspaper offices, seems empty tonight. Too bad because she's in the mood for people; she hasn't washed her hair in a while, but she's pulled it back into a bun and she's wearing a recent find, a sweater not ravaged with tears and holes. She'd like to get lost in a crowd of people and feel just like everybody else.

Sticky and hot, she crosses Main Street, shuffles through the parking lot of Center Bar and Grill, and ambles across Courthouse Road. The Benfield Local is showing one of those stupid superhero movies. She feels sorry for kids today; in her day, there were funny movies. Real movies. But what does it matter? She can't afford a ticket. She can, however, take advantage of the lobby's air conditioning. She walks inside and does her best to look engrossed in the posters for coming attractions. After a few minutes, her stomach starts to rumble; maybe, she thinks, she can find some abandoned food at the concessions counter. She's done this before.

In the lobby there are ten or twenty people in line waiting to get into the show; she strolls past them and then along the red rope that separates the lobby from the ramp that leads to the theater. As casually and quickly as she can, she lifts herself over the barrier. The pimply kid taking tickets has his head down and the manager is helping a woman find the restroom. As she turns, Janey notices a new girl working concessions. The girl's face is sallow, her hair is long and thin, her shoulders are curved. Janey had just read a horrible story about a girl like that in the *Benfield Weekly*. Her parents had been murdered. That makes Janey upset. She watches the girl at the concession stand.

"The poor thing," Janey murmurs to herself.

Overhearing this, a boy sweeping the floor turns. "What's that?"

Janey is startled. "It's just that...it must be hard. She looks so sad."

"Who?"

Janey looks back to the counter.

"Oh," the boy says. "Yeah. Working here sucks."

"Children should have parents who take care of them. They shouldn't have to work so hard."

"Tell me about it."

"How will she get by without a mother?"

"What?"

"I should help her."

She walks away from the boy and begins pacing, thinking about what to do. She's not in a position to care for a child, but the girl's parents have been *murdered*. Any mother figure would be better than none.

It's getting late and she must get to the shelter before they set up the cots; she needs to make sure that none of the so-called "volunteers" plant any of their listening devices in her mattress. Janey makes a decision: She'll leave now and return earlier the next day. It feels good to have a purpose other than Orlando. This is immediate.

The temperature drops that night, and the shelter, unheated in late summer, is cold. Janey sits on her cot clapping her hands together: one, two, three. One, two, three. One, two, three. Doing this brings her luck. She wraps herself in a scratchy blanket, holds the can with that day's money in it tightly to her chest, and lies down, still thinking about the girl at the movie theater.

She and Roy never got the chance to have a baby together; she'd had a miscarriage. She remembers weird things from that day: the shape of the clouds, the sound of airplanes flying overhead. If the baby had lived, she would be in her early twenties now, older than the girl, but would look a lot like her, blonde with freckled cheeks.

The next day begins like all the rest. She checks to make sure none of her things have been stolen. Sneakers. Check. Duffel bag. Check. And of course, the money is still there. After eating a banana and oatmeal in the shelter's cafeteria, she crosses the alley and enters the *Benfield Weekly* offices through the rear entrance. The quiet sound of a clacking keyboard comes from the other side of the room and she's pleased to see that Carol is the only person in the office at 7:30 a.m. Janey's notice that newspaper people are a lazy lot, straggling in at all hours. Except for Carol. She volunteers at the shelter on weekends and holidays and Janey has known her for years—she wishes she could remember exactly how many. Carol once interviewed Janey before a town council vote on the budget, something to do with cutting money for the shelter. It quickly became normal for them to see each other; Carol even helped Janey set up a savings account.

Carol stands and approaches so Janey doesn't have to come all the way into the office; in case someone else comes in, she can make a quick escape.

"You want half a bagel?" Carol holds it up. "There are bacon bits in the cream cheese."

Janey tries a bite. "That's really good." She wants to devour the rest immediately; it's much better than the food they serve at the shelter, but maintaining a sense of etiquette in front of Carol is important to her.

Carol pulls out a chair. "Take a load off for a few minutes."

Janey's knee crackles when she sits. At forty-six, her body isn't what it used to be. "Thanks."

"Go ahead and eat. Don't mind me. I got myself a plain bagel too."

Janey takes another nibble. It's too good to eat slowly and she allows herself to take bigger bites. "This is outstanding," she says. "Roy loves bacon bits in his bagel."

"Everyone does. Except for those loopy vegans."

Janey admires the way Carol has stayed in shape all these years. Her hair is gray and she has lines around her eyes, but her body offers no clues to her age. She imagines Roy just as chiseled as he had been years ago, before he left. He's probably one of those men who has grown more dignified with age.

"Do you have any cash to deposit today?" the editor asks.

Janey pulls out her money and hands it to Carol. "Only ten dollars and fifty-five cents."

"That's okay," Carol says. "There are good days and bad days; you know how it goes. The fact that you're saving up is all that matters."

Janey nods, but she's uneasy. Before, all the money was for her trip, but now she has the girl to think about.

The editor pours the money out onto a desk, counts it, and puts it into her pocket. Later that day she'll put it into Janey's account.

"Thanks for the bagel." Janey stands. "I'm going now."

"So soon?"

"I have important things to do today."

Back outside, an August drizzle wets her hair, and she pulls up her hood, bracing herself for the trek to the train station. The platform is empty. Finding a bench, she sits and closes her eyes, hoping today won't be like other days it rains; people are always in a rush in bad weather and pass her by as if she's invisible. She pulls out her Campbell's soup can. She has peeled off the label because she thinks it's better to be simple and clear with people about what she's asking for. She spits in the can eleven times, for luck. As she reaches into it with a rag to begin wiping it clean, she makes a vow to herself: all the money she earns from now on will be to help the girl from the movie theater. The money in her savings account too. Her reunion with Roy can wait; there are more important problems in the world than hers, after all.

The commuters arrive in a rush.

"Please help me," she says, measuring her voice; sounding honest is the key to connecting with people. Besides, most of them see her every day and they'd avoid her if she put on a big song and dance. A few drop coins into the can, but most rush past her. The tracks begin to quiver and the train arrives, shuddering to a stop. She pockets the money as the commuters board and she sits back down on the bench to wait for the next train. She spits in the can eleven times.

Later, she counts her money; it's not even eight dollars. She'd like to spend some of it on a turkey sandwich, but saving money for the girl is more important. She decides to see if she might find a few stray slices of pizza at the strip mall. Maybe she'll get lucky like she did the day before. Everything already seems better as the rain slows, then stops, and the clouds start burning off. As she begins her trek, a seagull lands on a telephone pole overhead, and Janey wonders what it would be like to float on air. She's sure she was a sea turtle in an earlier life, calm and majestic, and sometimes at night she can hear the sound of whales calling to each other through the chasm of the ocean.

The sun bakes the street. Janey takes a breather, rests her head against a shady oak tree, and tries to take a nap, but frightened thoughts won't let her rest: The girl is in trouble. She's lost her family. Poor thing. How will she recover? Go to college? Get a good job? How can Janey help?

Arriving at the strip mall in the late afternoon, Janey goes straight to the garbage bins and pulls out a pizza box. She gobbles down a few leftover crusts, not even bothering to wave them over her head, and then continues to dig. She finds two more boxes full of discarded crusts. Why do people waste food? When she and Roy lived together in her early twenties, she'd stored any morsels they didn't eat for dinner in Tupperware containers and ate the leftovers for lunch the following day. She can picture him caressing her round baby-paunch and congratulating her on another excellent meal. They were poor, but happy. Now she was alone.

There's a long line of people waiting to get into the movie. Janey's plan is to walk past them into the ladies' room and, as casually as possible, pass the counter where the girl works. The closer she can get, the better. Before she can take a step, though, she notices that the girl is now staring at her with an intense gaze that scares Janey. Maybe she's going to call the police. That's what most people do when she goes where she isn't supposed to. Janey prepares to walk back over the rope so she can run away, but then suddenly the girl's lips curl into a smile, and she raises her thumb as if to say, *good job*. Janey is confused, but then realizes the girl thinks she's sneaking over the rope to see the movie. She returns the girl's thumbs up.

This is definitely a sign. The girl needs her. Janey approaches the snack counter.

"Pretty nimble maneuver," the girl whispers. "But don't worry. People sneak in here all the time."

Janey lets her eyes fall on a small bag of popcorn but doesn't snatch it like she usually would. She's here on a mission. The girl, however, follows her gaze and immediately fills a fresh bag with popcorn. After looking around to make sure no one is watching, she slides it across the counter. Janey is touched. What a sweet girl. "Thanks," she says softly.

"No problem."

She looks around, thinking what to say next and then, suddenly, it seems obvious. "What's your favorite movie?"

"My favorite? Probably *The Little Mermaid*."

Janey is pleased because she's heard of this film. It's a Disney cartoon. "I'm going there to see my boyfriend."

"Going where?" the girl asks. Then, looking amused, "You have a boyfriend?"

"Yes." Janey beams. When she'd heard where Roy was living now, she knew it meant they would be together again. "He lives in Orlando."

"That's where Disney World is."

"That's right."

The girl nods as if she's impressed. "That's great. The park is awesome."

"Roy lives there. He doesn't work at the park."

"But you can go anytime you want. Right?"

Janey had always wanted to visit Disney World, although she dreaded the crowds; the thought of waiting in a long line for a ride made her feel like an ant, small and insignificant. But she could picture herself holding hands with Roy, smiling, eating ice cream; that made her feel big and important. "I'm sure we'll go to the park a bunch of times."

"That's really great," the girl says again.

"Yes, it is." Janey's hands are shaking, spilling popcorn onto the sticky carpet; it's now or never. She blurts out, "I understand about loss."

"Loss?"

"I can help, you know."

The girl furrows her brow and a guttural sound, as if something has just occurred to her, emanates from her lips. "Um," she says. "Your movie is starting." She points. "You don't want to miss it."

Janey looks over her shoulder and then back. "Yes. Thank you." She turns. It would look odd if she suddenly walked outside so she goes inside the theater, feeling excited; she has talked to the girl. She is one step closer to saving her. The movie itself is full of explosions, chases, and men and women wearing tight-fitting superhero costumes. It's all silly, but Janey cries when the credits roll. Being in a movie theater, sitting on velvet seats, surrounded by happy people makes her feel like she is part of something. Stepping back into the lobby, her mouth feels raw from too much popcorn. She returns to the counter, but the girl has already left.

The next morning in the *Benfield Weekly* office, she wants to tell Carol about the girl and how Janey has become like a mother to her, but thinks better of it. Carol would just ask a lot of questions and say cynical things, like, *Who do you think you are, her fairy godmother?* She settles for telling her about the movie.

Carol taps a pencil against her cheek. "How was it?"

Janey considers telling Carol about her moment of sad elation when the lights came up, but she doesn't think the editor would understand. "Not very good."

"Ah, well," Carol says. "They don't make them like they used to." Carol stops tapping the pencil; she does this when she's going to say something important, Janey's noticed. "That's the way things are," the editor says. "Things change and there's not much we can do about it."

Janey can tell Carol is trying to communicate some lesson

to her. *Move on. Get help. Accept the past.* She's said these exact words before. She thinks for a second. "But we *can* do something. We can make things better. We can help people."

Carol points the pencil at Janey. "Are you talking about any particular person you're helping?"

Janey feels defensive. "No. Why?"

"No reason," Carol says.

Janey thinks about the girl. "Do you think working at the movie theater is fun? Is it a good job?"

Carol points the pencil at Janey again. "Are you thinking of applying? I could help you."

"No. I was just wondering."

"Are you sure this isn't about someone there?"

Janey fidgets; she feels trapped. "I just wondered what it's like to work there," she says. "To be so close to movies every day. To see those giant superheroes. How they save people." Janey chokes up.

"Are you okay?" Carol asks gently. "You don't seem like yourself today."

The door in the front office opens. A moment later, one of the reporters enters the newsroom and then stops. "Sorry, I didn't know you were with someone."

Janey says quickly, "That's okay, I should be going." Before she leaves, she furtively hands Carol the money for her savings, making sure the reporter doesn't see.


That night, the movie theater is nearly empty; the girl at the counter leans her chin on both hands and blinks slowly, like a koala bear. A shiny rectangle of sweat glistens on the ridge above her upper lip. Janey steps over the red rope barrier; the usher sees her this time and rushes over.

"What do you think you're doing?" He's thin all over, but especially his nose.

Before Janey can answer, the girl pipes up. "It's okay. That's my mom."

"This is your mom?" His voice cracks.

"Yep."

"Fine." He looks at Janey doltishly. "You can visit with Bailey a minute, but then you have to go."

"Thank you."

The girl taps the top of Janey's hand when she arrives at the counter. "That was clever, wasn't it?"

Janey isn't sure what she means; her mind is on a new bit of information she's discovered. "Your name is Bailey?"

"Yes. That's me."

"It's a pretty name. I'm Janey."

"You don't hear that name too often anymore."

Janey's mother picked the name because it reminded her of a Boston singer she liked. "I guess you're right." Her hands shake; this is the moment. She's the only one who can help this girl. "Would you like to go for a walk with me after work?" she asks.

The girl straightens up. "Really? Why?"

Janey had not expected resistance. "I don't know." She tries to think of a good reason to go on a walk. All she comes up with is, "I like you."

The girl smiles. "I like you too." She puts popcorn in a small container and hands it to her. "You should probably get going, though. I don't want to get into trouble."

Janey takes the popcorn. "Okay," she says. "Thank you."


Smoke from a backyard barbecue settles around Janey as she sits on the sidewalk outside the theater waiting for Bailey. The smell reminds her of the ribs she cooked for Roy every Sunday afternoon so he could lie back in his recliner and watch football. She remembers the sound of pads crashing into pads, Roy's dazed eyes; his snoring. After the game he would nap and then they'd take a walk around the neighborhood. He'd point to a boy falling off his bike and say, "Hopefully our kids will have your sense and my balance." She'd grip his hand tightly.

Bailey smells like butter and salt when she exits the theater. Her gait is long and awkward, which Janey finds endearing. She lights a cigarette.

"You shouldn't smoke, dear."

Bailey turns, startled. "You're still here?"

"Of course. The walk. Do you mind?"

Bailey takes a puff of her cigarette. "It's fine. You scared me, that's all." She takes another puff. Her hand trembles a bit—a tiny tremor that most people wouldn't notice, but Janey notices everything when it pertains to young women. They both have shaky hands. This pleases her. Janey squeezes her fists together five times fast, for luck, and says, "If Roy and I had a kid, she'd be about your age now."

"Oh yeah? That's real interesting." Bailey sucks on her cigarette and doesn't look at Janey.

"I guess she'd actually be ten years older than you are. Isn't it funny how fast time goes? You probably haven't noticed that yet, but you will. It's like when you take off on an airplane. It starts on the runway moving slow, but then it gets going faster and faster and when you're in the air you hardly notice how fast you're moving."

"You've flown on a plane?"

"Not yet." She watches as the girl throws her still-lit cigarette into the road. "You ever been on a plane?" she asks.

"No."

"You should, you know. You should fly all over the world."

The girl glances at her. "Whatever you say, Mom."

Janey likes when Bailey calls her mom. "I shouldn't have said that. I shouldn't tell you what to do."

"It's okay." She pauses a moment. "I've heard California's nice, although that kinda seems like the place everyone wants to go. You ever watch that TV show about Portland?"

Janey shakes her head. She hasn't watched television, except in glimpses, for years. "Tell me about it. What do you like about Portland?"

"I don't know." She grins. "It's weird."

"You like that it's weird?"

"That's apparently what's good about it. It's weirdness."

"That's weird."

"Yes," she says triumphantly. "You get what I'm talking about." She stops walking and faces Janey. "Listen." Bailey reaches into her jeans pocket and takes out a wad of cash. "I want you to take this."

This is wrong. Janey panics. "No, no. I don't want *your* money."

"Are you sure? It's not much."

"I'm sure." She rests her fingers lightly on the girl's forearm. "I'm here to help *you*."

The girl looks confused. "Help me what?"

"Help you do anything you want to do with your life."

"That's really sweet, but—" Bailey waves the small wad of bills in front of Janey's face. "Just take the money, will you? Go visit Roy or whatever."

Bailey really is a special girl, Janey thinks. "I can't take it."

"Are you sure?" She tries to force the money into Janey's hand.

"No, no, no!" She can tell she's screaming by the look on the girl's face, but inside her own mind her voice sounds normal. The first time she remembers this happening was just after her miscarriage, a little while before Roy left. She had been in the dentist's waiting room when a little boy asked to borrow a pen for a coloring book. *I'm sorry, I can't help you.* The boy started crying, and his mother looked up from her book. *What's wrong with you?*

"It's okay," Bailey says, backing away. "You don't have to take it." Bailey shoves the money back in her jeans. "I should get home."

Janey catches her breath. "You're going now?"

"My mom will worry if I don't get home right away."

Janey freezes. "But your mother is dead, dear," she says.

The girl seems stunned; she takes another shuffling step away. "My mother isn't dead."

"Your parents were murdered."

"No they—what's wrong with you?"

"That boy. He killed them. You need someone to take care of you."

The girl's face turns as white as the moon. "I'm trying to be nice to you, but—"

"I could help you with money until you go to college. I could be there for you."

"Please stop talking like that."

"Let me help you." Instinctively, she reaches for the girl. In a flash, she sees that her bony hand looks like a claw and the girl retreats.

"*You're* the one who needs fucking help."

"Let me—"

"You shouldn't come to the theater anymore." Janey tries to absorb this. The girl continues. "Just don't, okay. I felt bad for you, I talked to you because—leave me alone."

"This is important."

"If you do, I'll call the police. I don't want to, but I will."

"No." Janey feels her legs weaken.

They stare at each other. The girl looks thin; she's shivering. Janey opens her arms to hug her, but the girl shoves Janey backwards.

"Leave me alone!"

Janey watches her getting smaller and smaller as she runs away.


On the walk back to Main Street, Janey tries to think about her life, but she can't focus. Her head hurts. She sits on the sidewalk. Where are all the people? It's so empty tonight.

A half hour later she wanders into the back of the newsroom; Carol is busy putting the latest issue together, but when she sees Janey, she comes over. "What are you doing here?"

"I wanted to leave my money today."

"Sure." She takes what little there is and says, "We got a call a few minutes ago from Chief Earley. He said you were harassing a girl down at the theater."

"I wasn't harassing her."

"She called the police, Janey."

"Her parents are dead. She needs someone to take care of her."

Carol bites her bottom lip. "No, honey. That's a different girl. Actually, it's two women. And they're older."

"Are you sure?"

The young reporter rushes past them on the way out the door. "Got that Selectman meeting to attend," he yells as he passes.

"That's fine, Matt."

Carol promises to put the money in the bank. "I have to put the paper to bed, but why don't you wait here and we'll talk more later. How does that sound?"

"That sounds excellent."

For a few minutes Janey, feeling sad, watches Carol dashing around the newsroom. Then she takes a pen and a piece of paper, jots down a note, and leaves it on Carol's desk.

Normally she'd retreat to the shelter, but it's been a long night. There's no way she'll get back before they set up the cots. Anyway, she feels restless. She needs a friend. Someone she can talk to who won't contradict her.

Briskly, she walks back toward the strip mall. The air is cold now; another fall and winter will be unbearable. Once she arrives, she goes to each bin, hoping Scrappy will be there, but finds only rotting garbage. Finally, she walks slowly toward the edge of the parking lot where shrubs and tall trees form a dense woods. It's pitch black beyond the tree line, like outer space.

Janey imagines Carol reading the note back in the news-room. "Give my money to Bailey. I want it to go to good use."

She hesitates.

Then, determined to find the raccoon, Janey steps into the darkness.

# DECEMBER 23, 1998

P ete stood in the doorway. It was as if no time had passed, except there were a few more lines creasing his forehead.

"I didn't think you'd show up," Tara said.

"I almost didn't."

"What made you?"

"I guess I wanted to see you. Can I come in?"

Tara took his heavy coat and led him into the living room. It was odd to lead her estranged husband into a room he had helped decorate. For Pete, it felt awkward to be treated like a stranger in what was once his house.

She held up a bowl of hard candy. "You want one?"

"Not right now."

"More for me." Tara popped a Starlight mint into her mouth.

Pete sat on the couch and closed his eyes. He let his body sink deep into the cushions. "No tree this year?"

"I haven't bothered since you left."

"Ah."

Tara put her hands on her hips to give herself confidence. "Where's Brenda?"

"There's no more Brenda," Pete said.

"What does that mean?"

"It means that me and the cashier are no longer banking on a future together." He smiled as if he'd made a great joke.

"She left you?"

"It was a mutual decision." He let his eyes jog twice around the room. "The place looks good," he said. "You kept everything the same."

"I changed a few things."

"That lamp?" He pointed to it. The base looked like a candle holder; the bulb threw off a dim yellow light.

"Yeah, that's new."

"When'd you get it?"

"Last year. I thought it was beautiful." She looked around the room at all the baubles she'd collected. "I like to have beautiful things around."

"I know what you mean." He winked at her. "I do too."

She rolled her eyes. "Can I get you something to drink?"

"Water'd be fine."

She went into the kitchen and ran the faucet until the water was cool enough to serve. Pete tried not to think while she was gone.

"Here you go."

He drank the water. "Like I remembered it."

"You're very funny."

"That's what I tell everyone."

Suddenly nervous, Tara asked, "Have you talked to the kids?"

"I tried a couple of times. Neither one will answer my calls." He watched her, wishing he could offer comfort like he used to. "What about you?"

"Sam stops by sometimes."

"That's good."

"And I see Shelby at the library, but she doesn't really say much."

"She's stubborn."

"Like her father."

"Like her mother."

Pete sipped his water. "I used to be a pretty shitty human being."

Tara caught a glimpse of herself in the mirror that sat on a shelf mostly hidden by a television. "And now you've changed?"

"I've been thinking about what I could have done differently."

Tara raised an eyebrow. "Thinking about changing is great, but it's not the same thing as doing the work."

Pete fiddled with his wristwatch. "Does the fact that I want to change count?" He stuck his hands in his pockets. "I'm trying therapy."

"Wow." She caught his eye, and her face softened. "I am too. I've figured out that I was a doormat, but that it wasn't all your fault." She composed herself. "Now I know I can never let myself be that way again. I take responsibility for my life. My happiness."

"That's fantastic, Tara." He flashed a playful grin. "I'm still working through my anger at my fucking dad, but you gotta start somewhere, right?"

"That you do." Tara smiled. "So, what else have you been up to?"

"I did some traveling."

Tara sized him up, her mood shifting. "I guess you finally got your wish."

"What do you mean?"

"Your holy grail. Your fountain of youth—backpacking

around the country with a twenty-five-year-old." Her voice tightened. "Remember we were gonna do that?"

Pete looked down. "She's actually thirty. Brenda, I mean."

"Twenty-five. Thirty. What does it matter?" Tara turned away and busied her hands with tidying the coffee table. "Those years when everything seems possible." She spoke quietly. "I had dreams too, you know. But getting pregnant at twenty wasn't one of them."

Pete took a breath. "You know, these past years weren't everything I expected. Brenda was a pain in the ass and it turns out she's pretty..."

Tara looked up at him. "Stupid?"

"I guess that's the word I was looking for," Pete said. "All she did was shop and watch TV. I thought it would be different."

Tara gave up on the coffee table. "Yeah. The problem with dreams is that you wake up."

"And you realize that you slept through a lot of your life," Pete said. "I should have been better to the kids." He tried to think of the right words. "I missed out on being a dad."

Tara laughed bitterly. "You're apologizing for ignoring the kids? What about being there for me? I needed you."

"If you'd just let me finish, I was about to say that I also missed my chance with you." Pete was about to say more but wanted to avoid falling back into their old pattern of bickering. He studied his reflection in the mirror; a crack in the glass radiated from the center and formed a spider web that stretched in every direction. "What happened to the mirror? Did you do that?"

"Technically, a shoe did it. All I did was throw it."

"Was there a reason?"

"There's never a good reason for that sort of thing."

"*That must have been some throw.*" Pete thought for a minute. "*You always had more strength than I did.*"

Tara sniffed. "*I'm sure you could have broken the mirror, too.*"

"*You know that's not what I meant.*"

"*Do I?*" Tara swept a strand of hair out of her eyes. "*I spent my whole life being weak, and you spent your whole life making decisions.*"

"*I never felt like I was making decisions—I felt trapped.*" He sighed deeply. "*Maybe that's why I busted up my life.*"

"*We were both pretty good at breaking things, weren't we?*"

"*We were young. Stupid.*"

Tara pictured how they looked when they first met: a perfect couple sitting side by side at the diner, their whole lives in front of them. "*I hate those kids,*" she said. "*I wish I could get in a time machine and punch them both right in the face.*"

"*I thought you weren't doing that sort of thing anymore.*"

"*So.*" Tara adjusted her flowered dress and turned to face Pete. "*Where do we go from here?*"

# SEPTEMBER 2014

## CONCH

E velyn, a retired marketing manager for a large textbook company, is leaning over the balcony watching the waves lap against the side of the ship when there's a light knock on the door. She moves quickly back inside to answer it.

The man standing at the door is at least a foot taller than she is, with brown, neatly combed hair and an exceptionally symmetrical face. "Hello, Ms., my name is Paulwyn." Evelyn is warmed by the contrast of his formal posture with his lilting Indian accent. He's like an exotic butler, at her service. "I will be your cabin steward on this cruise. If you have any inquiries, I will be happy to answer them."

A gust of wind disturbs the curtain and again she looks back; this time he notices. "It is starting to get cold in New York City," he says. "But the Bahamas will be warm and sunny."

"I don't mind the cold." What does she care what the weather is in New York City? She wouldn't be returning. "My name is Evelyn." Paulwyn blinks; he already knows her name, of course.

She plans to lock herself in her cabin, eating room service and waiting for what would be a return trip for everyone else. She is done with the cold. She is done adjusting her medication. She is done going on benumbing dates with men in their 70s. She is done thinking about Tara and Pete, her closest friends in Benfield, murdered last December. She is done. She pictures herself plunging into the warm water and then vanishing beneath the sea; she has given more thought to that final destination than to the trip itself.

It is her first cruise. In fact, it's the only vacation she's taken in thirty years. She and William had talked about hiking around Acadia National Park for their honeymoon, but somehow they never got around to planning it. And after their amicable divorce twenty-five years ago, she settled in Benfield; after that, she was always too busy with work to take a trip anywhere.

"What kind of inquiries do people usually have?" she asks, careful to use his word. Paulwyn wears a light blue coat with a brass nametag.

"People ask many different questions," he says.

It has been three months since she's had a conversation with anyone who wasn't a store clerk. Before the murders, she used to meet Tara at the gym a few times a week and gossip. She misses that. She even misses having dinner with both Tara and her husband. Pete could be overbearing, but Evelyn had enjoyed listening to him recount stories from his troubled childhood growing up in New Haven. It used to make her think she'd been lucky to live in a small town her whole life—but that was when she still thought nothing terrible happened in places like that. "What do people do for fun on these things?"

"Many things. We have both comedy and nightclubs, five different music acts that you can see around the various bars.

There is a gambling casino that will open as soon as we are in international waters, about two hours from now. There are twenty-eight dining options, three Broadway shows, a full spa and fitness center, a pool, sauna, and water slide." Paulwyn rubs his chin. "I am not sure the water slide would be something you would enjoy."

"You're right about that," she says.

"Can I help you with any more inquiries this afternoon?"

She actually has one important question, and she feels too embarrassed to call desk services about it. Paulwyn's gentleness is reassuring. "Can you show me how to flush the toilet?" She has attempted it three times, but the plastic button above the toilet makes an ineffectual click without actually flushing the water.

"I will be happy to do this," he says, and steps past her and then into the narrow bathroom. It feels dangerous to be so close to a stranger attempting to flush her pee.

"You simply press this button two or three times quickly." He pushes the button and it does not respond. "Ah, I see," he says. "They are clearing the lines now. It will work soon."

"You're sure about that?"

"Yes, they are clearing the lines. You can try again in an hour." She likes the way he toys with his name tag, as if it needs perpetual straightening.

He steps past her again, and this time she can smell his sweat.

"Are there any more inquiries that you have?"

She tries to think of one, but her mind is blank. "I'm good for now. Thank you, Paulwyn."

He nods and smiles before walking away. Evelyn closes the door and turns back to the balcony just as the ship lurches to the port side. She lands on the bed. Sitting up, she peels a plastic, rectangular information card away from her face. It reads, "Welcome to your home away from home."

"This is called a sea cucumber," Hernan says.

The twenty-eight-year-old tour guide stands knee deep in clear water; his muscular arms hold the small creature. Evelyn hadn't planned to go on any of the tours, but her encounter with Paulwyn changed her mind. There is no reason to isolate herself during her last week of life. The cruise ship company actually owns the tiny island on which they docked that morning, so the only other people around are tourists like her, lumbering over the sand, sunning themselves, or lining up like cattle to eat the sumptuous meals prepared by the staff. Evelyn thinks she has more in common with the workers than with the other passengers.

Hernan holds up a starfish. "There are hundreds of tiny tube feet here. I will pass it around. If it grips your finger, slowly pull free. It won't hurt you."

"I'm not touching that thing," a retired accountant says, and her husband guffaws. They are both tall and lean with dark skin; Evelyn likes the way they constantly tease each other. "You don't touch anything good anymore," her husband says. That gets a good laugh from the group of about twenty on the tour. The accountant laughs too, a one-note "Ha" like a bell ringing.

Hernan reaches into the water and holds up a conch. "If you relax, you will see that he comes out of his shell." The guide holds the animal still for several seconds and, as if trained, the creature pokes its brown body out. "This part here is what it uses to move. It's like a fingernail, and if you hold out your hand he'll try to pull."

It does.

"See?"

Oohs and ahhs.

"These are a delicacy here and at one time it was thought the starfish were eating too many of them. To combat this, people began hunting the starfish and cutting them in half and throwing them back in the water. Can you guess what happened? You see, starfish regenerate, so cutting them only made the problem worse. Now we have controlled the ecology better."

The conch has retreated inside its shell by the time it reaches Evelyn. "Say hello to this lady," Hernan says. His teeth are white. Evelyn is surprised by her sudden desire to carry the man off to a secluded section of the beach. She blushes, but it is indistinguishable from the sunburn already brightening her face.

"That's okay," she says. "I'd crawl in there and take a load off myself if I could."

"I thought he is supposed to tell the jokes," Hernan says, pointing to the husband of the retired accountant.

"Everybody's a comedian," a rotund, pale-skinned woman says. "Isn't that what they say?"

Hernan dips his hand into the water and pulls out another shell, this one much larger than the one they are already passing around. "You may find these empty shells all around the island," he says. "Please remember that you are not permitted to take them back on your ship. Organisms may still be living in these."

Evelyn, shading her eyes with one hand, studies the empty shell when it's her turn. She wants to impress Hernan with her wit again, but can only think of marketing jokes. *How many marketers does it take to screw in a light bulb? None. They've automated it.* So she passes the conch onto the next tourist.

"Isn't it a beautiful day?" Hernan asks. Everyone agrees that it is.

Paulwyn is explaining how the room service system works. "It is quite simple," he says. "To notify me that you need your cabin cleaned, simply click this metallic button here next to your door. When you are out, I will be happy to do it." She has already figured out how the system works, of course—he's cleaned her room when she was out all three days so far—but has feigned ignorance so that she might have the chance to talk with him again.

"I won't forget," she says.

Paulwyn looks at the sky beyond the open sliding door. The sun is setting over the water. He points. "You see what I meant about the weather? The Bahamas are beautiful this time of year."

"Yes," she says. "You were right."

"Did you have a good day today?" His eyes are the darkest brown she can imagine.

"Yes," she says. And she prepared in advance to say, "This is the most fun I've had since I was forced to retire."

She hopes admitting this will open up a conversation between them, but he says, "Forced retirement, very good," and scratches his chin. Evelyn wonders if Paulwyn has picked up this habit from watching television; the gesture seems somehow contrived. "Do you have any further inquiries for me today?" he asks.

"No. Not today."

"Very good then," he says and nods before stepping away.

Evelyn steps into the hallway but freezes once there. She watches with a pang of sorrow as his square shoulders recede down the hall. She wishes she'd clutched his hand. With her eyes closed, she imagines his fingers feeling firm and warm.

"Don't you want to know why I was forced to retire?" she could have said.

She pictures his long arms relaxed by his side. "Yes, Ms., I would like to know more about you."

"The company isn't doing so hot," she imagines saying. "No one reads anymore, even textbooks. It's all gotta be interactive. The big salaries go first, not that I made that much money. It's only, I'd been there thirty-nine years. I can't even remember what it was like when I first started. Well, I remember certain things, like, we used typewriters back then. I mean, *typewriters!* There is one secretary, I wish I could remember her name, who insisted on using a manual Olivetti Valentine—even the name sounds romantic, doesn't it? That clacking sound is precious, it classed the place up, it said, 'important things are being communicated.' Now all you hear are those quiet clicking keyboards. It's like everyone is whispering into a howling wind. Can you imagine working one place thirty-nine years, Paulwyn? I liked my job, don't misunderstand me. I wish I were still doing it. But things change. That's the one true thing about life. Things change."

Paulwyn's professional demeanor would have cracked. He would have understood.

Outside, the sun is nearly down and the water, the sky—everything—turns aquamarine. Evelyn leans over the railing. With her eyes closed, she imagines her body sailing over the side and her fingers feeling stiff and cold as she sinks.

Thirteen decks is a long way down.

A dolphin named Sally leaps fifteen feet in the air, crashes back into the water, and then retreats to the pen where it receives a small fish from its trainer.

"These are Atlantic spotted dolphins," Andy says. "It's a relatively small species. Listen, now. They emit a range of sounds, and many believe they have a language of their own." Andy signals to Sally, and she begins making a series of clicking sounds.

Andy is a lean Bahamian wearing a white visor and a red T-shirt that says, "Blue Lagoon Island." His sunglasses make him seem a little insincere, Evelyn thinks, though he does seem to genuinely enjoy it when the dolphins screech and make the tourists giggle nervously.

"These animals are safe, but it is a myth that all dolphins are passivists. Bottlenose dolphins have been known to kill for fun! But do not worry. Sally only wants fish!" This elicits a few more nervous giggles.

Evelyn prefers Nassau to the tiny cruise-ship owned island they visited the prior day. It is a busy city with cars flying around curved roads and Bahamians enticing tourists with hair-braiding or taxi tours or restaurants. The sun seems a brighter yellow here than in Benfield, as if it has been colored by Van Gogh himself.

She stands waist-deep in water surrounded by a dozen or so fellow tourists. This is a thinner, younger breed than those who'd braved the beach tour the previous day. The sand massages her toes as she watches each tourist take his or her turn holding the dolphin's fins and posing for a picture. When it is her turn, she holds out her hands uneasily.

The dolphin's fins feel more pliable than she'd expected, more human. Just then, the dolphin emits its characteristic high-pitched squeal.

"She likes you," Andy says. "She is asking, are you free later for a few hands of gin-rummy?"

"I am!" she answers, and a few tourists applaud. Evelyn beams. Funny how the decision to end her life has somehow lightened everything; she's been smiling a lot lately.

In the afternoon, she wanders around the beach. The water in this inlet is shallow—at its deepest two feet, but mostly less than that—so kids and adults alike float on rafts or wade; few swim.

She reflects on the cruise. She'd spent the days before they arrived at the islands wandering around the decks, in and out of jewelry and electronics stores, sitting at bars listening to cover bands, taking a tango lesson. She enjoyed watching middle-aged couples, relieved of the burden of their children, shuttling frivolously from event to event like kids at a day camp. They seemed happy. And they probably were. This is the small escape they believed they deserved from their mundane jobs. This is America: a relentless grind and then a too-short release from all the suffering. The young couples, of course, appear mostly at meals but otherwise stay in their cabins. She wishes she and William had taken a tour like this when they'd first met; perhaps it would have sparked greater romance in their relationship. But they'd skipped the romance and gone straight to the routine of married life because they both wanted to get on with the proper business of doing what people did. He had since remarried to a make-up artist, a woman who wore shimmering dresses, played piano, and croaked old musical numbers. They had two children.

She is about to wander over to the lunch tent before the lines get too long, but a piercing howl makes her look up. A boy is holding his foot; when he surmises that some damage has actually been done to it, he produces another panicked yelp and then begins sobbing, pausing only to get enough air into his surprisingly powerful lungs. Evelyn rushes toward him, thinking he must have stepped on a sea urchin or been stung by a jellyfish and would need medical attention.

"Are you okay?" She kneels beside him. He puffs his cheeks, trying to contain his tears. "It's okay to cry if it hurts," she says. "I do it all the time." And she smiles so he can see she's a friend.

"I stepped on a shell," he says.

"Let me have a look."

Blood oozes from a nasty slice on the bottom of his foot. "You're gonna be fine," she says.

"It hurts."

"I know, dear." She picks him up. The boy feels lighter than she expects; it has been a long time since she held a child. She visited William and the make-up artist a few times when they had their first, but the visits had felt forced and awkward, and she stopped responding to their invitations.

"You're doing great," she says to the boy. "I'm going to take you to the medical tent."

"Okay." He is warming to her.

"Do you have a name?"

"It's Brian."

"You're doing great, Brian." She can feel his breathing slowing down as he relaxes. He wipes his nose with his forearm. He seems heavier now that she is moving.

"I cut my feet all the time," Evelyn says. "I live near a pretty pond and people leave all kinds of things on the beach. It makes your feet tougher. Don't you want tough feet?" He clutches his arm tightly around her neck.

"Hey!" A man's voice calls out from behind her. "Hey!"

She stops.

"He cut his foot," she says. "I'm taking him to get medical attention."

The boy's father is tall, dark-haired, and has a thick, round belly. "I can take it from here."

"Really, it's no trouble." The words feel wrong on her tongue. Before the boy's father can respond, Evelyn corrects course. "What am I thinking! Here you go!"

He takes Brian from her arms.

"I stepped on a shell." The boy shows his father his bleeding foot.

"You're all right," the father says. "You're all right." Evelyn watches the father carry the boy to the medical shed. She can still feel the weight in her arms, and his wet face against hers.

After lunch—Cobb salad, iced tea, and a big piece of cake—she goes back to the beach and searches for the shell that caused the boy's injury. The tide has gone out, leaving the red-streaked spiral perched on a mound of wet sand. She's proud to recognize it as a conch. She plans to give it to the boy as a souvenir so he can remember how brave he was, but she can't find either father or son anywhere along the stretch of beach where the other cruise ship tourists are lounging. Evelyn walks to the gift shop, purchases a couple of metallic trays that display the name of the dolphin retreat, and then hides the conch between them in her bag. When she passes through the x-ray machine as she boards the ship, it does not detect the contraband. She feels like a smuggler.


The following day, Evelyn experiences an aching nostalgia for the islands and the sun even though the ship hasn't yet left port. She's promised herself that she'll jump tonight.

She takes a stroll before dinner, searching for the boy and his father. She even stops by the medical center on deck five to see if they've been there. The nurse, a serious, thick-shouldered man from Sweden, says, "It's been quiet all day. No one's come in, even with a scratch."

"Isn't that funny," Evelyn says.

"Not at all. People feel well when they're on vacation. They don't worry about every single bump and bruise."

She walks through the upstairs buffet hall, figuring this is the place a couple with a child is most likely to eat. Not that it isn't possible they'd bring the boy to one of the upscale restaurants, but it is easier to grab a slice of pizza and some ice cream here without having to worry about a child misbehaving. The sheer number of people—the scale of the boat and its population—suddenly seems overwhelming. How can so many people be floating together on a ship? How many tons of chicken, lettuce, ketchup, cake, alcohol is the vessel transporting? Every face is a fresh universe, too: there are passengers from every corner of the world.

She continues her search in the Atrium, where many of the social events are held during the cruise. Not seeing them, she tries the guest services lobby and, finally, even childcare. The young attendant there shrugs when she asks about the boy and says, "We have lots of kids here."

Maybe it's time to give up her hunt. Her feet are beginning to ache and it's getting dark. It seems odd that the sun goes down so early—she associates warm weather with long days— and she has promised herself she will witness one final sunset.

From her balcony she can see the entire island as the ball of fire extinguishes itself over the horizon. Evelyn thinks of the boy and his father; she's engulfed by the sadness that has been drowning her all year. The water begins to churn below, meaning the rotors are stirring and the ship will be moving in a moment and it will be time. As she nears the end, her mind keeps returning to Tara and Pete; she flashes back to a time they all went bowling together.

Even there, they seemed refined and elegant. Pete was teasing his wife about something, and she was laughing. Evelyn had been standing off to the side. She was always standing just out of the picture. With a sigh, Evelyn realizes something: Pete and Tara were central players in her story, like William Powell and Myrna Loy in the old *Thin Man* movies; they were the stars around which the rest of the plot revolved. But she'd been an extra. Any actor could have played her part. She should have done better for herself.

There is a light knock on her door.

"I would like to discuss an important matter with you." Paulwyn is twisting his nametag with more vigor than usual.

"Come in." She steps aside to make room for him. The cabin steward hesitates before accepting her invitation. She wonders what it would be like to kiss him.

"I will say it quickly. You left your suitcase open this morning, and when I cleaned, I discovered the shell."

Evelyn looks at her open suitcase and the conch is sitting on top. It was careless, but she isn't thinking about what is right or wrong anymore.

"We are not allowed to bring any plant or animal life on board," he says.

"It's empty," Evelyn says. "And it's not even for me. It's for a little boy. He cut his foot on it yesterday, and I was going to give it to him."

"This does not matter, Ms."

"Maybe you could help me find him." She winks.

"This is not a good idea. We would both get into trouble."

"Kids care about these things." Evelyn picks up the conch and studies it. It is average in weight and height and worn, but the design is wonderful. The ship pitches forward and begins making its way out of the harbor. Evelyn continues, "I wish I'd had children. Not with William, my husband. We fought too much. But I could have gotten around to it with someone else and I guess I never did."

"Ms., please," Paulwyn says.

"Do you have any children?"

He seems to resign himself to this extended conversation. "Yes, Ms. I have two, a boy and a girl."

"The perfect set-up!" Evelyn says.

"It is precisely what we were hoping for."

"Do you think you're a lucky man, Paulwyn?"

He scratches at his chin, but doesn't answer. Evelyn steps onto the balcony and peers down.

"Come out here," Evelyn says. "Onto the balcony with me."

"What about the conch, Ms.?"

"Just for a moment." He hesitates. "Please, I want you to join me out here. Come out here and tell me more about your children."

"I cannot do that, Ms."

"Then just come out here." His eyes are sad; she hadn't noticed that before. "Please, Paulwyn."

Something gives way inside him, and he steps onto the balcony with her. He looks awkward, a cabin steward out of his element.

"I really love the ocean," Evelyn says.

"Everyone loves the ocean, Ms."

"Why do you think that is?"

More chin scratching. "I don't know," he says finally.

The waves swell beneath them. Evelyn takes his elbow.

"Ms., please."

"It's okay," she says.

They stand that way for several minutes. Once he tugs at her arm gently to pull free, but she tightens her grip.

She holds the shiny conch shell out so they can both inspect it in the fading light.

"It is very beautiful," he says.

"Yes," she says. "Even this way. Empty."

She extends the conch as far as it will go over the railing. A light wind pulses as the ship picks up speed. Before Paulwyn can object, she opens her hand and they stand together in the moonlight as the shell makes a small, silent splash and vanishes beneath the waves.

## SEPTEMBER 7, 2002

T he dogs at the adoption facility were well behaved, as if they knew this was their chance to win over a future owner. Tails wagged. Big eyes looked around. Paws were freely given. Tara and Pete stood side by side looking down at one particular mutt. She was yellow with some white on her under-belly. Possibly a Golden Retriever mix, though the facility's owner wasn't sure.

Pete knelt next to the animal and held out his hand; the dog sniffed, then offered her head for scratching. Tara rubbed the dog's head. Smiling, Pete sat cross-legged on the hard ground and Tara crouched next to him. The dog rolled over onto its side, its tongue lolling out. Fluorescent bulbs cast a cold gray light around the facility, making the cages, the desks, and the hard wooden chairs look bleak. Young families stood around pointing, nervous and happy, petting the animals. Pete and Tara wondered why they'd never gotten a pet when the kids were young. But between the raucous antics of the children and the noise of their own arguments, it just would have been too much.

Now, living together again after all this time, the house seemed too quiet.

A slightly smaller dog, brown with streaks of white, was lying in a corner, alone, looking pensively at the human intruders. When Tara noticed it, she felt a tug and, without looking away, stood and approached the animal. Pete followed silently.

The creature growled and went from lying to sitting, drawing its muzzle toward its chest. Tara, bending forward, moved cautiously. It growled again, this time baring its teeth. The cacophony of children playing suddenly grew louder as a family of six entered the facility. Tara, careful not to make eye contact with the dog, held a closed fist a safe distance away from its nose. The dog stopped growling but turned its head away from the human hand. Pete, also crouching, took a step. With a whimper, the dog tried to flatten itself along the wall and move past the couple, but there was no path, and so it stopped, ducked its head, and lay down on the floor, still whimpering.

Drawing a deep breath, Tara let her palm rest on the dog's back. When it was clear the dog wasn't going to snap, Tara massaged its neck. Pete scratched the top of its head. The dog let loose a low, guttural moan that dragged on for several seconds, but then it yawned, exposing its pink tongue and white teeth. Tara and Pete sat on the ground next to the animal, each taking turns petting it. They sat that way for more than fifteen minutes without speaking, but occasionally making eye contact. Without warning, the dog turned over on its back, stretched its front paws straight up in the air, and exposed its stomach.

Tara reached back and took Pete's hand. Then Pete gestured toward the woman with a clipboard. "We want this one," he said.

# OCTOBER 2014

## IT HURTS OUR HEARTS

Adam peers through the narrow window that runs vertically along the right side of his sixth-grade classroom door. He can't tell what Mr. Quigley is saying to his parents, but it's probably some variation of what he's heard a hundred times: *Adam is smart and talented. Adam could be anything he wants in the world. Adam doesn't try hard enough.* His parents are nodding gravely, like Quigs, his homeroom teacher, is telling them their son only has three months to live. Adam flops against the beige metallic lockers and lets himself slide down like he's been shot in the heart. He pulls his phone from the front of his jeans pocket and messages Louis Pearson. "At parent teacher meeting. FML."

After a couple of seconds, Louis sends a GIF of a fiery explosion.

"Not seeing sunshine 'til college," Adam writes.

"LMAO. We just gotta make it through high school."

Adam imagines going to a college some place exotic, like Los Angeles, with the ocean, Hollywood stars, palm trees, and the kind of girls he only sees in underwear ads—and no tutors, no baseball coaches, and no parents.

Louis writes, "Can you hear what they're saying?" Like a cat burglar, Adam steals a glance through the window into the classroom. His father is leaning forward, his sports jacket taut against his narrow back. His mother is slumped over, head in hands. Adam doesn't understand what the fuss is about. If he gets Bs without trying, what's the point of trying?

Adam's phone beeps again and he steps away just as his father is turning his head around toward the door. Louis writes, "Thinking Salt Man should kill Brown Lettuce." Salt Man is their comic book creation. He looks like an ordinary kid, except he's able to dissolve himself in water and then take any shape he wants. Louis came up with one episode where Salt Man saves the day in a diner, becoming a fork to help the local police stop a giant hamburger named Brendan who is planning to kill Mr. Miner, the principal of the high school. And another where their hero becomes a horse and wins the Kentucky Derby, all while foiling an angry horde of French fries who have kidnapped a magnificent mare. They're about to get away with it when Salt Man, as a horse, eats the French fries up and gets the girl. His arch enemy is Oatmeal Man, or "the OM." He can ooze into any crevice, fissure, or cranny he wants and vanish without a trace; the OM has an evil plan to turn all food into tasteless gruel. In his quest to save our taste buds, Salt Man battles his enemy even though he risks being absorbed.

Louis texts, "I have an idea for another story…" The door to the classroom opens as his parents are saying, *Thank you so much, we really appreciate it,* and *we'll be in touch soon.* Adam texts "Code 9" and shoves his phone in his pocket.

His parents are silent for the first five minutes of the drive home. He hates this. When they talk to him in their sternest voices it means they're going to be very clear about what they want from him. He can then pretend he's going to make an effort to give them whatever that is—studying harder, working on his swing in the batting cage—until the next time he lets them down. Their silence freaks him out. The full moon hovers over the distant woods; the outline of pine trees cut out by the light passes over his parents' faces. It's kind of creepy.

His dad isn't that much taller than he is and still speaks with a slight Chinese accent. "I love you, Adam," he says finally.

"We both do." His mom is plump and always looks like she's smiling, even when she's angry.

"We only want what's best for you." Adam can't stand the clicking sound his dad makes when he's cleaning something out of his teeth. You'd think a dentist would know the best way to keep food from getting stuck in his molars.

His mother looks back at him. "It really hurts us when your teacher says you could be doing so much better than you are."

"It hurts our hearts," his father says.

The windshield wipers squeak against the glass.

"Do you have anything to say for yourself?" his mother asks. "Anything at all?"

"I'm sorry." Adam rests his fingers on the portion of the front car seat between his parents. "I'll try harder." He almost believes it.

His mother takes his hand and kisses it. "You always say that."

"I really will this time," Adams says a bit louder.

"I don't know what to do with you, son." Adam knows what his father is going to say next. "You make me worry so much."

"I will be better." He makes eye contact with his father in the rearview mirror and looks away.

In his room, under the covers, he plays with his stuffed animals. The black and white goat, now hornless after years of wear and tear, often plays the role of Captain America in Adam's fantasies, beating up the bad guys, like his stuffed, armless clown—his oldest toy, ragged and eyeless.

Adam meets Louis on the blacktop playground the next morning before school, and they walk in together, side by side. Adam is glad they're in the same homeroom for sixth grade; it makes life easier.

"Dog shit," Louis says. "In case you were wondering what that smell was." He's snapping his fingers to no particular beat.

Adam knows the smell isn't dog shit. His friend wears unwashed brown corduroy pants that don't quite make it past his ankles, a dark green, torn winter parka, and a plain red knit hat that he claimed from lost and found a year ago even though it wasn't his. His shoelaces are tied in perfect bows. It's the same outfit he's worn every day for a week. Adam says, "It was probably the Bronson's dog. They never clean up his shit."

"Yeah, probably," Louis says.

They walk in silence until Adam says, "If you could smell like anything, what would you smell like?"

"Good question. Let me think about that." He pretends he's deeply considering the question. "I've thought about it. I'd smell like pizza."

"I'd smell like mown grass."

"A burning fireplace."

"Gasoline."

Louis holds out his hand. "Then we agree. No dog shit." They slap hands.

Adam enters the classroom ahead of his friend so he's the first to see Louis's overturned desk, its contents spilled out on the floor like torn open guts: a couple of stale, opened packs of gum; an old cell phone; a glass jar containing a variety of dead insects soaking in alcohol; a pair of gym socks; and piles of paper covered with cartoons. Louis enters next, freezes for a moment, and then walks to his desk and begins picking up the mess. Adam rushes over to help. When the desk is righted and they've put everything back inside it, Adam glares at pudgy Richard Kowalski.

"You're a riot," he says. The other twenty students stop chattering and look at Adam.

"What?" Richard says, and smirks. "It wasn't me."

"We know it was you."

Richard stands. "I said it wasn't."

Louis tugs at Adam's sleeve. "It's okay," he says. "Let it go."

Adam, without budging, says to Richard, "You want to finish this after school?"

"Sure."

Mr. Quigley enters a moment later and senses something is wrong. "Whatever's going on here, stop it." He moves slowly through the classroom, eyeing the students like a police detective. "Now take out your pens. I've prepared a pop spelling quiz for your enjoyment."

The students groan, clear their desks, and take out their pens.

In the ratty gym at recess, Louis paces back and forth. Adam sits on the bleachers, leaning back, airing out his armpits. "Adam, don't fight that a-hole."

"If I don't, he'll keep doing stuff like that."

"Who cares?"

Adam says, "You can't let people walk all over you."

Louis stares down at the freshly painted white lines on the gym floor. "You sound like my father. He gets into fights all the time and comes home banged up and bruised. And then he starts in with my mom." Louis folds his arms across his chest. He does this when he's made up his mind. "I'm tired of people fighting." He looks up so Adam can see how serious he is.

"I won't fight him."

"You promise?"

"I promise."

After recess, Adam fakes being sick. The nurse calls his mother, who picks him up.

"You're going to have to make up anything you missed," she says. In bed, under the covers, his ragged goat metes out justice, beating the evil clown and carting him off to jail.

The next morning, Adam leaves early for school and jogs most of the way there. He waits inside the main entrance and runs outside when he sees Richard get off the bus.

Richard drops his book bag, ready to fight, but Adam picks up the books, clutches Richard by the wrist, and tugs him toward the empty loading dock behind the school.

"Where were you yesterday?" Richard looks smaller standing outside than he does in the classroom. "I decided I'm not going to fight you."

"Well, yeah. I figured that out."

"I want you to leave Louis alone."

Richard snorts. "I'll do what I want."

Adam rushes Richard and slams him against the concrete wall. Richard's eyes bug out. He lunges, but Adam easily dodges the assault and slaps the side of his face. Richard lunges again and again, but Adam evades the attack. "I can do this all day."

"You're such a fucking wimp."

"I'm smart enough to know if you catch me, you'll sit your fat ass on my chest and I'll be finished. This way I can keep—"

Richard interrupts by charging at Adam's waist. Adam hops aside, punches Richard, and then pushes him down.

Richard clutches the side of his head. "I'm gonna kill you." He's breathing hard, trying not to cry.

"You can't catch me. I told you."

Richard sits up, still holding his cheek. A rosy bruise is blossoming there.

"The next time I get Louis alone, I'm going to beat the shit out of him."

"No, you won't."

"Why not?"

Adam surprises himself by saying, "Because you're not a bad person."

Richard thinks about this. "You're an idiot." He gathers his books. "Dumb dumb dumb."

Louis isn't at school that day, and when Adam texts his friend he gets no reply. At recess, while other kids shoot baskets or play tag, he runs from one end of the gym to the other. After ten sprints he's exhausted and leans against the padded wall, eyes closed, his forehead wet. A tap on his shoulder draws his attention. It's Richard. Steven Banberry and Sal Rodriguez stand behind him. They're all wearing knee-length blue shorts and white T-shirts.

"I'm going to be waiting for you after school."

"Leave me alone, Richie."

"No way." Steven and Sal snicker.

For the rest of the day Adam feels a warm bubble inside his chest; it's exciting and scary and he wants to hold onto it. Mr. Quigley gives them a math lesson and a few kids start to doze off, mouths hanging open, eyelids drooping.

When school ends, he walks down to the entrance and peers outside. He texts Louis. "Richard is waiting to kick my ass. Can you believe it?"

Adam steps outside, turns left on the sidewalk, and walks briskly past the side of the school toward the blacktop playground. Richard and his friends follow. When he gets close to the narrow dirt path that leads through the woods, he sprints. But his foot catches on a tree root, and he stumbles to the ground. Before he can get up, Steven and Sal grab him and tug him to his feet.

Richard punches Adam in the stomach. He doubles over and begins to yank and tug against the two boys holding him. Richard punches the side of his head and stars explode behind his eyes. He gnashes his teeth, yells, and tries to pull away. He gets one arm free and pushes Sal to the dirt. Steven still has a grip on his other hand and, using Adam's arm as a rope, they begin a tug of war while Richard tries to land more punches. Adam yanks his arm free and careens backwards onto the ground. Tears run down his face, pulling dirt into his mouth.

"I told you," Richard says.

Adam charges, but Steven stops him, and Sal pushes Adam back down. He rolls over, gets himself to his feet, and runs. He glances over his shoulder just in time to see a rock arcing toward his head. He dives into the brush and the rock just misses him. He waits there, panting. When he looks back, they're gone. Hands on knees, he pulls out his phone. His mother has called three times. Did he forget an appointment? A new tutor?

When he reaches Cranberry Street, he spits onto the sleeve of his winter coat and cleans off his face. He walks the rest of the way home feeling the adrenaline tingling in his arms and legs, his fingers and toes.

His parents are waiting for him on the couch in the living room.

"We have to talk to you about something important." His father has his hands folded on his knees. His skin looks pale.

Blue and white flowered wallpaper covers the high walls; blue shag carpeting cushions his feet; a small chandelier dangles in the center of the room. The family parakeet, Bert, chirps from the kitchen to his right. Adam looks down at his grass-stained knees and bruised arms. How could he explain? Of course, his parents will think the fight was his fault.

"Please sit," his mother says. When he doesn't move, she takes him gently by the hand and pulls him down into a hug. Her chest smells like a mixture of mint and perfume. She clutches the top of his head with both hands. Her quavering shoulders, her wet face—she's never like this, especially when she's about to punish him. This is something else.

"Listen, son," his father says. His mother's body heaves. Adam looks up and sees that tears are flowing down his father's face too.

His parents let him stay out of school the rest of the week; he feels sick anyway, like something dangerous is growing inside him. At the funeral service on Saturday, Louis's features in the coffin look white and unnatural. His real smile was mischievous; he never looked placid like he does now. Adam pats his friend's hand and then gently tucks his copy of *The Adventures of Tom Sawyer* into the coffin. He wonders what his friend's chest looks like and how the bullet ended up there. *Ripped to shreds*—that was the description he had read in the *Benfield Weekly*, where they called it a "tragic accident." Adam closes his eyes and pictures Louis taking the gun out of the shoebox and holding it. Studying it. Thinking about what to do with it. When he opens his eyes, he spots Louis's mother sitting alone on a church pew. She looks like a pillar of salt: stiff, white, dead.

Tim Pearson, Louis's father, doesn't attend the funeral. He's a coward, Adam decides.

In the days that follow, Adam hears adults whispering everywhere he goes. The whole town seems to think Tim

Pearson never should have gotten paroled way back when—they blame him for the accident. He also hears them saying things like, "The world is getting angrier," "His mother never paid him any attention," and "Guns are everywhere nowadays, and they're bound to go off." Put together, these explanations for what happened are like pieces of a puzzle, but they don't create any kind of picture that could make sense of what happened.

Adam takes a few more days off from school and spends most of his time in his bedroom. He opens his math book and stares at the numbers, not really absorbing anything. He falls asleep reading *Harry Potter and the Order of the Phoenix*. Some relatives he hasn't seen in years stop by and wish him well. Parents of other kids—some he's never met before—have dinner with his folks and talk about how terrible it is. What a great boy Louis was. What a waste of potential. All he had going for him.

Mr. Quigley calls and suggests Adam come back. "Rip the Band-aid off quick," he says.

The kids are spread out on the floor making Halloween decorations when he enters the class. The few who notice avoid making eye contact. He deposits his books in his desk and sits on the floor, alone.

After a few moments, Violet Perkins whispers, "How's it going?"

"Good."

Robyn Berman says, "You want some paper?"

"Sure."

Franklin Sandorini brings him a few colored pens and a pair of scissors. "Do you want a glass of water?" Sarah Washington asks. Robyn shares her peanut butter sandwich with him.

Adam notices a collage of condolence cards from people all over the state on the bulletin board across the room and walks over to read a few. *I'm sorry for your loss*, one says. Another says, *Everything happens for a reason.*

The kids cover the walls with orange and black construction paper cut into skeletons and ghosts. Everyone is nice to Adam. But at lunch he sits alone at one of the long tables in the cafeteria, staring up at the high windows into a cloudless sky. The new school principal, Zachary Rivers, comes by and pats him on the shoulder. "Don't worry about making up any work. There will be plenty of time for that. Just enjoy being back."

Adam shrugs. In spite of all their parent-teacher conferences, his own teacher doesn't know what his parents are really like. There's no *way* this new school principal gets it; his parents won't let him get away with leaving a lick of schoolwork unfinished. "I will."

The principal sits down opposite Adam and leans forward. "Do you want to talk about what happened?"

"I don't know."

Mr. Rivers rambles for a few minutes about how awful it was, how much he liked Louis, how rare it is to have such a creative student in his school. He lets that sink in before saying, "I want you to do me a favor." Mr. Rivers pulls out a notebook he'd tucked under his arm and hands it to Adam. "I want you to keep a journal. It will help you through this. You can show it to me every week and we'll discuss your thoughts. How does that sound?"

Adam opens the notebook and thumbs through the empty pages. He doesn't have any idea what his thoughts are. "Um, okay."

Mr. Rivers stands. "I'm glad you're back. You're a great kid, Adam."

After school that afternoon he follows Richard along the wooded path. His nemesis stares down at the ground when he walks, as if a hand might reach up and grab him. When Adam is certain no one else is around he catches up to Richard.

"Hey," Adam says.

Richard clutches his book bag. "I don't want to fight you."

Adam remembers Louis begging him not to fight. "I don't want to either."

"What are we gonna do, then?"

"I don't know."

Richard coughs into the cold air. "Do you want to walk to my house?"

Adam thinks about it. This is confusing. "Okay," Adam says. "Let's do that."

Richard Kowalski's house on Mullins Circle is set back from the street. The lawn is brown and muddy, but the white siding looks new. Branches from a yellow birch tree cover the face of the house in bobbing shadows. Inside, a sparse living room leads to a kitchen cluttered with cooking equipment.

"My mother bakes a ton," Richard says. "Sometimes for parties and stuff, but mostly because she likes it."

Adam resists saying, *Well, that explains your weight*, and instead walks to the metallic door of the refrigerator and pulls it open. Cupcakes decorated in light shades of pink, blue, and yellow fill an entire shelf.

"Go ahead and have one." Richard takes a cupcake and bites into it. "They're really good."

Adam tries one with blue frosting. He's never tasted anything like it. "I wish my mom made cupcakes all the time. We only get cake on special occasions, like birthdays."

"Your mom is hot."

He's heard this from a few kids before. "Shut up."

"I was only saying."

Adam takes another bite of the cupcake. "What else does she make?"

"Lots of stuff. Casseroles and things like that. Pierogis."

"What's a pierogi?"

"It's meat or spinach or whatever cooked inside dough."

"That sounds really good."

"It's okay." Richard closes the refrigerator. "You want to come upstairs?"

Painted model airplanes fill an entire shelf in Richard's room. On the shelf below that, a row of textbooks lean up against a large tome called *American Military History, Volume I: The United States Army*. A blue and white quilt is tucked tightly around a twin bed that's pushed against a wall. Adam can barely see the leg of a much-used stuffed animal sticking up from beneath the pillow.

"Your father was in the army?"

"He saved three men when their truck exploded."

"Wow." Adam takes down a picture of Richard next to his dad wearing a tidy military uniform. His jaw is rounded and soft and he's missing his left leg. "What happened to him?"

"I told you. There was an explosion."

Adam can't imagine how a legless man saved three others and wonders if the story is made up. Either way, Richard believes it. "What's he do now?"

"I don't know. Computer stuff. And he gets disability money or something."

"He's home a lot, then?"

Richard's face turns red. "Why are you asking me questions about my dad?"

"Just curious."

"I have PlayStation." He pulls the game controllers out of a wooden drawer and turns on a large, flat-screen television.

An hour or so later—Adam happily loses track of time—he's standing in the doorway on his way out. "That was fun."

"Sure," Richard says, and together they acknowledge that something important has happened today.

"I'll see you in school tomorrow."

"Yeah. See you."

Adam pauses. He feels like he's betrayed Louis by being nice to Richard. But this is probably more of what his friend would have wanted anyway; somehow, no matter how mean Richard had been, Louis had never written him off as a bully. Adam remembers the stuffed animal under the pillow. Maybe they're more alike than he'd thought. He works up the courage and asks, "We're friends now, right?"

Richard leans against the doorframe. "Yeah, we're friends now."

That night Adam sits at the kitchen table staring at the blank notebook. The wind presses against the window above the sink. He decides to write what he thinks Mr. Rivers wants to read. "I am sad that Louis is dead," he writes in his journal. "I hope I will understand why this happened someday. I will always remember Louis, even when I'm old." He fills out two more pages to impress the new principal.

Mr. Rivers pulls Adam out of class to discuss his journal one afternoon. "You're a born writer, Adam."

Adam shrugs. He's used to drawing. Louis had been the real writer.

Adam catches up on everything he missed in school, gets A's on all his make-up quizzes, and then begins to read ahead. He finishes his history textbook and insists his parents take him to the library. He reads *The President Has Been Shot!*, a book about the ten presidential assassination attempts in the United States, and *Japan in the Days of the Samurai*. He gets both the seventh and eighth grade math books and does problem sets in bed when he's supposed to be sleeping. Every day after school, his mother takes him to the batting cages for thirty minutes. When he swings too fast and hits a ball off the end of his bat, the vibration that runs through his hands and up his arms obliterates his thoughts. Some nights he just goes out into the family backyard and walks the perimeter of the fence.

Mr. Rivers promises to read more of his journal pages but never gets around to it. Eventually, Adam stops writing altogether. One morning he wakes up with the idea of throwing it away, but when he reaches the trash barrel in the garage, he decides that just getting rid of the journal isn't enough. He gathers all of the cartoons he worked on with Louis and shoves them deep down into the garbage container.

Adam arrives at school on time now and stays late to ask Mr. Quigley questions. One night he studies until dawn. He's glassy-eyed the next day, and his mother insists he stay home from school.

"You'll make yourself sick, honey."

"I feel fine."

Going without sleep actually makes him giddy; he thinks about a time when he and Louis went to Sweet Edge, the best place for ice cream anywhere in the world. They had walked the whole way—a full hour down Colt Avenue. He can't remember what they talked about, and he doesn't know why this day stands out to him, but he can feel the spring sun on his face, smell the cut grass, taste the butterscotch ice cream.

"There's such a thing as working too hard," his mother says. Her arms tighten around him. He allows himself to feel his mother's warmth for a moment, but then pulls free.

"I don't want to be late for school." He races out the door hoping he hasn't missed the bus.

# NOVEMBER 27, 2014

P ete bent down, making sure not to wrench his back, and pulled open the oven. He leaned in and checked the meat thermometer. "It's ready," he said enthusiastically. "I'm taking it out."

Tara sat at the kitchen table in jeans and her favorite sweater reading a crime novel. "Sounds like a plan, hon."

Pete placed the turkey on the cutting board. "It looks great this year."

"I really does." Tara turned the page of her book. "But it's an awful lot of turkey."

"You can never have enough turkey." Pete chuckled.

"It's an awful lot of everything."

Pete waved his hand grandly. "Don't worry. The kids will take some home."

Tara raised an eyebrow. "We've invited them every year since you moved back in, and they've never come."

"What can I say? I'm an optimist."

Tenderly, Tara said, "I just don't want you to get disappointed when they don't show up."

"*I won't be disappointed.*"

"*Uh huh.*

"*I promise.*"

"*If you say so.*" Tara surveyed the pies covered in foil, the casserole, the plates of cheese. "*If they don't come, all this food is going straight to my thighs.*"

Pete approached his wife, bent, and squeezed her leg. "*You know I like my thighs juicy.*"

Tara laughed and Pete kissed her on the forehead.

"*Let's run the checklist,*" Pete said.

"*Again?*"

"*The man of the house insists.*"

Tara rolled her eyes.

"*I am the man of the house, right?*"

Tara caressed his arm. "*You sure are.*"

"*Okay, then. Here we go,*" Pete said. "*Mashed potatoes.*"

"*Check.*

"*Candied yams.*"

"*Check.*"

"*Green bean casserole.*"

"*Check.*"

"*Cranberry sauce.*"

"*Check.*"

"*Cherry pie.*"

"*Are you doing the pies separately?*"

"*Cherry pie!*"

"*Check.*"

"*Blueberry pie.*"

"*Check.*"

"*Banana cream pie.*"

"*Christ. How much food do we have?*"

Pete looked around their kitchen. "*Yeah.*" He winked. "*We may have overdone it this year.*"

Just then, Penny hopped up and nuzzled into Pete's arm. "Good girl." Pete scratched the old dog's head. "You're such a good girl."

Pete looked at Tara. "What do you want to do if they don't come over?"

"I don't know." Their usual routine was a comfort to both: morning walks, afternoon chores, after dinner talk, and then the inevitable. "TV?" Tara said.

"There's never anything on."

"There's got to be a Law & Order marathon on some channel."

Pete clicked his tongue. "I guess that'll have to do."

Tara took her husband's hand and squeezed it. She re-opened her novel and began reading, still holding his hand.

Pete listened as a light rain began tapping against the windows; it sounded like a song without lyrics. "I hope Shelby comes. And Sam. I hope they both...It'll be like old times. Well, better than old times because...you know what I mean. Remember how we were before?"

Tara closed her book and looked at her husband. Their years together passed between them like a silent movie.

"Do you think we should start eating?" Pete asked finally.

"No." Tara smiled warmly at her husband. "Let's wait a little while longer."

# NOVEMBER 2014

## EVERY HAND REVEALED

Barry Epstein is driving a beat-up Camaro on Interstate 95 in Massachusetts with a heavy wind swirling dead leaves into the air. He spots a turkey vulture hovering above the trees, circling, searching for carnage it can pick over. Janine leans back in the passenger seat, half-dozing, her bare legs lifted onto the dash above the glove compartment. *Grey's Anatomy* sits on her lap, opened to a page depicting the vertical median section of the Encephalon.

Barry swerves to avoid a divot in the road; they're everywhere on this stretch of highway. The car bucks to one side and Janine smacks her forehead against the side window. "Jesus! Watch where you're driving."

He hadn't done it on purpose, but she's had a bug up her ass about this entire trip. "I was."

She rubs her head. "Just be careful, okay?"

"Is it my fault this road was paved by Hobbits?"

Exasperated, she says, "I guess not."

"Why don't you close that book and quiz me on poker hands?"

"I'm not in the mood." She crosses her ankles, which turns him on. "Do you think we can stop at the next rest area?" she asks.

He gives her his famous side-eye, then grips the wheel with one hand and caresses her tanned calves with the other. "Hold on, all right? We're almost there." He hits the accelerator and the Camaro flies into the breakdown lane and past a line of traffic. "I'll speed things up a bit."

"My hero." She closes *Grey's Anatomy* and sits up.

"Sarcasm is the lowest form of wit," he says.

"You're the lowest form of wit."

"I can't argue with that." The speedometer needle edges past 100 miles per hour. He tightens his grip on the wheel with both hands until he can feel the car shaking. Billy Lawson had loved pushing the Camaro to its limits. With one hand on the wheel, he'd hold his torso outside the window and howl like a wolf. Now Billy is in prison, and Barry tries not to think about how close he had come to joining him.

He eases off the gas pedal and, with the sun blinking below the horizon, slows down on the exit ramp. Moments later, they pass Rogers Elementary School. The asphalt is cracked, and the basketball hoops are rusting or missing entirely. They drive in silence for ten more minutes. The Camaro shoots tar and rocks into the air as Barry takes a turn onto Fifth Street. The houses are set back from the sidewalk and barely visible through the tall pine trees lining the road.

Janine jams her finger against the window, pointing at nothing in particular. "This place is kind of quaint."

"Home sweet home."

"So many lawns and so many houses."

"It's suburban America. You can find a million other towns just like it."

"Yeah, maybe." Her voice is wistful. "Los Angeles is one giant, fucking strip mall."

"That it is, but we won't be going back."

"Well, I hope that's true."

"I know my brother. He'll give me the money."


About eight months before, his father had booted him out of the house. Barry had barely been able to resist the temptation to kick in his dad's teeth, but he knew what happened to people when they let violence get the best of them—he wasn't going to end up like Billy. "I'll never come back here again," he had said.

His father lit up a cigar. "Well, that's the best news I've heard in a long time." Barry had begun zigzagging across the United States in his Camaro, stopping at the Statue of Liberty and Lake Michigan and in Arizona to marvel at the Grand Canyon. He was hoping to settle in a warm place where he could sell pot, fuck hot women, and live near a beach. But driving across the country wasn't as easy as he thought it would be: The car broke down a lot, he was constantly thirsty, and he felt lonely without even a television for company. He had limped into Los Angeles with a few bucks left in his wallet and some kind of rash on his inner thigh that itched like crazy. He slept on Venice Beach, scavenged for food, and began to see his future like the horizon over the Pacific Ocean, infinitely far away and impossible to reach. How could it be that someone with so much promise had come to this?

One morning, after gnawing the chicken bones left over in a box of KFC that he'd found abandoned on the beach, he got himself cleaned up and marched over to IHOP on Lincoln Boulevard planning to devour the breakfast sampler and bolt when no one was looking. When he sat down in a booth against the window, he changed his mind. The waitress was cute, with a lean, curvy body; Janine had been a cheerleader for four years at Michigan State before moving to L.A. to pursue acting.

"I don't have a cent on me," he confessed. "Do you think you can help me out?"

"I shouldn't..." He watched as she looked him up and down. Barry was used to women checking him out. A mischievous smile crept over her face. She bent closer. "But wait outside."

She brought him some leftover French fries and an untouched pancake in a paper bag. "Don't tell anyone."

He was moved. "I won't."

She had seemed surprised that he was still waiting for her when she got off work that evening, but she flashed a smile, and he quickly saw that she was the type of person who couldn't hide what she was thinking. He hated having to guess what women wanted all the time.

They walked together along the boardwalk, the beach a watercolor painting, all blues and yellows. They traded stories about where they'd grown up, their favorite memories, things they'd done when they were kids. Janine had grinned mischievously and asked, "What's the worst thing you've ever done?" She'd meant it as a fun question—just a little dangerous. The fact that a guy like Barry might have such a shady past probably never crossed her mind. He hesitated. He didn't usually open up, but Janine was easy to talk to. He found himself telling her the whole story: hanging with a bad crowd in high school, planning a robbery with his best friend, and then backing out at the last minute. Billy killing two people.

Janine had taken it all in stride, like that kind of thing could happen to anybody. Her own story was typical. After Michigan State, she'd almost been selected as a Laker Girl. Encouraged, she went on four or five auditions a day for dance gigs, theater, anything, but she never got close to another job again. That first audition had been a mirage and she decided that eighteen months was enough; she wasn't going to be one of those women who spent their lives pursuing a typical kind of Los Angeles fantasy. She despised those eager, hopeless girls at auditions, mumbling their lines under their breath, so she started saving up for medical school.

He kissed her as the sun descended; she tasted like salt and chocolate.

She nuzzled against his shoulder. "I don't know why I'm doing this."

"Some men are irresistible."

"Yeah, that must be it."

She helped him get a job as a busboy at IHOP, but he quickly grew frustrated with the tedious work. He deserved better. One night they were sitting in McCoy's—a bar across from their tiny one-bedroom—when the World Series of Poker came on television one evening and a spark ignited in his gut. Here was his future, he thought. Life was a gamble, and why shouldn't the cards fall his way for a change? He began to spend his spare time in the kitchen reading poker books like *Every Hand Revealed* and *No Limit Hold 'em Theory and Practice*, or Janine would quiz him on *Poker Odds for Dummies* as he shaved. In the evenings, he played nickel and dime games with waiters and other busboys and learned he could use his charm and good looks as a weapon. It was all an adrenaline rush. And it was practical; Janine cut back her shifts and had time to study, and with his winnings they still made rent every month. But there was a cap on how much he could make in low-stakes games and he was tired of playing it safe. He needed a hefty chunk of change to take his shot in Vegas.

Back in Benfield, there are already four cars jammed into the driveway and two more on the gravel beside the house. Barry cuts across the dirt lawn and parks under an oak tree. An acorn pings off the windshield.

They step out into the frigid air. Janine stretches like a panther, then shivers; she looks good in her skirt and leather jacket. Barry stoops to brush dirt off his boots, but his back is stiff from three days of driving straight from L.A., so he lets it go.

He watches as Janine takes in his parents' yard; it's a sharp contrast to the neatly groomed lawns on either side. "What the hell happened here?" she asks.

"My father stopped giving a shit when I was, like, five. Now we have all this." He opens his arms as if embracing the house and yard. A rusted-out green van sits against a rotting six-foot picket fence, its engine and other spare parts strewn about the dirt. Overgrown tree branches tick against a split-level ranch house. The paint on the siding has mostly worn off, and two of the upstairs windows have holes in them.

"I bet your dad was really popular with the neighborhood association."

"Oh, yeah. They especially loved that he kept raccoons in cages in the back yard."

"Why the hell he'd do that?"

"To protect them."

"From what?"

"People, I guess."

Janine hops up and down, kicking up a cloud of dust. "I really have to go to the bathroom."

"Let's get going then."

Barry rings the bell, and his mother comes to the door wearing a black dress and makeup that fails to cover the bags under her eyes.

"Jesus, you cut things close, Barry. We're leaving for the funeral in twenty minutes."

He holds his breath. Best not to start an argument. "Yeah, sorry about that. There was a lot of traffic." He thinks to himself, *There was traffic because I drove all the way across the fucking country in three days!*

"You should have left earlier, then."

"Next time," he says.

She glares and then looks Janine up and down. "This one's pretty."

"Ma, this is Janine. Janine, this is my mother."

"It's nice to meet you, Mrs. Russell." Janine unleashes her million-dollar smile and somewhere angels sing. Barry is impressed.

Barry's mother opens the door wider. "Come in the house and freshen up. Janine sprints in ahead of him to find the bathroom.

"Down the hall, to the left," Barry calls out, and then he follows his mother into the kitchen.

The Formica countertops sparkle. The chairs around the kitchen table are pushed in and overlook placemats with pictures of pilgrims on them. The whole place smells like fresh lemons. His father must really be gone; the house had always been a chaotic mess when he was alive.

Mark comes into the kitchen. He's wearing a blue suit with a dark blue tie and black shoes. He hugs Barry. "Hey there, brother."

"Hey."

"You drove all the way from California?"

"Uh huh. I really wanted to be here."

Mark seems confused by this reply. "Sure, but why didn't you fly? I mean, driving all that way must have been hard." He still has the regional accent—*haahd*—that Barry has worked to get rid of.

"It wasn't that bad."

"Is this your girlfriend?"

Janine has reappeared by Barry's side. "Yep, this is her."

Janine holds out her hand, but Mark goes in for a hug. This warmth is something new, though Barry suspects it won't last. Once he adjusts to their father being dead—and really, how long will that take?—he'll return to being his aloof self. Still, this is a good sign. He'll be much more likely to fork over the money in this condition. Mark releases Janine. "It's so good to meet you."

"You too. I've heard so much about you." Barry can detect a twinkle in Janine's eyes that's meant for him. It says, *This guy is such a tool.* Barry's brother is just over six feet, but he has put on some weight. Mark looks doughy now, like he swallowed a couple of pillows and topped it off with whipped cream. His chin is softer now too. His linebacker days are over.

Mark squeezes Janine's hand. "You must be tired after driving all that way." He probably wishes his wife had Janine's angles and curves; if she's eating from the same trough as Mark, she's probably a regular Porky Pig.

"I'm okay," Janine says. "You're the one who has it rough today. I'm so sorry for your loss." Barry is impressed. Maybe he should shut up and let Janine ask Mark for a share of the inheritance.

"Thank you for saying that. Today is really sad, but we're hanging in there." He looks to Barry to back him up on this.

"Oh yeah. So sad." He can't mask his sarcasm, even when he's trying to sound sincere. Barry watches his brother process this response and then decide not to say anything about it.

To Janine, Mark says, "Can I get you two something to

drink?" Without waiting for a reply, he pours three glasses of whiskey and holds his up for a toast. "To Dad."

"Definitely. To Dad." Barry swallows his drink in one gulp. Janine swirls hers in her glass, then pours it down the sink when Mark isn't looking. She wrinkles her nose as if to say, *Cheap shit.*

Mark's wife, Vanessa, enters and gives her husband a disapproving glare. To Barry's surprise, she actually looks none the worse for wear. Her thick dark hair is pulled back into a ponytail, her skin is porcelain, and she looks thin beneath her black dress.

After greetings and introductions and a discussion about traffic, Mark takes Janine out into the back yard to show her where their father had kept the raccoons. When they're gone, Vanessa pours herself a whiskey.

Barry points to the glass. "I thought you disapproved."

"No," she says, drinks the entire shot, and pours another. "I just don't want Mark to overdo it."

"You take good care of my big brother."

"I guess so." She drinks the second shot.

He senses some kind of tension but decides this isn't the right time to probe. Better change the subject. "You look good." Barry imagines what she looks like naked, something he's done many times before; she was a senior at Benfield High when he was hitting puberty. Mark had entered the picture later; he and Vanessa connected at UMass Mark's last year there and, against the odds, it stuck.

"Yeah? Thanks. You look good too." She checks him out. "Good job with the growing up and becoming a man."

"Thanks." He kisses his bicep. "It was hard work."

She rolls her eyes. "I bet."

"So..." He breaks eye contact. "Will I be an uncle this time next year?"

Vanessa purses her lips. "Oh. You don't know?"

"What?"

"There's no baby any time soon."

Barry puts down his glass. "I thought you two were determined to get a family started. The last I heard—"

"It's not as easy as you think." She laughs ruefully. "At least that's what the doctors keep telling us."

He feels bad. "Shit. I'm sorry." Even in high school she'd talked about having children.

"Thanks."

Barry wasn't sure what to say next. "I guess Mark and I haven't been in touch."

"It's okay."

She's always been kind to him. He has a sudden desire to kiss her. Instead, he moves closer and puts his hand on her arm. "It must be really difficult for you."

"It's difficult for both of us." A beat passes. "It's really hard on Mark."

Barry takes this last bit to mean that the problem is his brother—just like him to have a low sperm count. "I'm sure it's not your fault," he says. Mark hates when he can't control every aspect of his life. He's making decent money now teaching in some band program in Texas, but Barry imagines his students are all miserable. Mark is a dick when the people around him aren't perfect.

"We're doing as well as can be expected." Vanessa rolls her arm under his hand so he's touching the soft skin of her forearm.

He draws small circles with his fingertips. "You'll let me know if there's anything I can do, right?"

"I will." She lets him hold her arm for what seems like a long time before she gently pulls free.

Dry, crisp leaves cover the cemetery grass. It's a small gathering of fifteen or so, but more than his father deserves. There are a few familiar faces—people Barry knew from his childhood when they'd still gone to temple regularly—but not many. His father's life hadn't exactly been full.

A mound of dirt sits next to a gaping hole. Barry peers in as the rabbi rambles about his father finding his place in heaven. Utter bullshit. The hole is dark and deep, and the coffin sits at the bottom, squeezed tightly against the sides. Ain't that too bad, he thinks, since his father was claustrophobic. Sometimes his dad would even vanish into the woods for days at a time to camp and get away from everyone who made him feel hemmed in by life. What was he escaping from, exactly? He didn't have any responsibilities except remembering to wake up and breathe every morning. He'd been a mailman but had smashed his ankle in a car accident and spent the last decade of his life living off disability. Instead of being grateful, he'd acted like he'd earned the money. If you suggested he get off his ass, God forbid, and get back to work, he would start in on a rendition of his favorite aria: *This town owes me!*

Janine squeezes his hand. She's crying. Her tears look legit, too. Which is strange because she never met his father and whatever stories he told her about him wouldn't exactly inspire Niagara Falls. But if she's faking, it's a remarkable performance; her cheeks are drenched. He's surprised; she's a pragmatist about everything, even death, and that's why he's been so sure she'll have the stomach to be a doctor. But this makes him wonder if she's not as pragmatic as he thought. Maybe he can even convince her to forget this medical school nonsense; instead, they could take his Vegas winnings and buy a big house with a swimming pool.

When the rabbi invites the brothers to throw a pile of soil into the grave, Mark goes first. The dirt lands with a thud and then slides off the sides of the coffin. He releases a mournful groan and then hands the spade to Barry. The wooden handle is ice cold and stings when he lifts a shovelful of dirt, balances it a moment, and then tosses it into the air: another thud, another flurry of dirt. There's something final-sounding about that thud —like a man's last heartbeat—that the cascading dirt undermines.

Life always looks for a punchline, Barry thinks, even at the end. He scoops up another shovelful of dirt and waits for some warm memory of a time he spent with his old man to come to mind, but instead he feels a strange sort of frustration; it's how he gets when Janine beats him in a hand of poker. She lords it over him, like her college degree makes her better than him. He flips the dirt into the air. "For luck," he shouts giddily, and turns back to find Janine scolding him with her eyes. *Don't do anything that will piss off your brother!*

On the drive back to the house, Barry and Janine sit without speaking. The sound of the Camaro's engine competes with a stiff breeze that whistles through a gap in the driver's side window. She's stewing, a custom that often leads to a vicious cycle of worrying that she can never quite kick. He wants to say something, but there's no pulling her back from the abyss once she starts falling.

After another few minutes of silence, she says, "Do you ever wonder why you didn't go into that house with Billy Lawson that night?"

She'd never asked him this question before, which was fine because he didn't know the answer. Sometimes he wished he *had* gone in; maybe he could have kept Billy safe. Barry thinks about that sometimes while he's driving alone on the highway at night, but when he tries to picture Billy inside that house, he can't; instead, an image of his friend just hanging out in their spot behind Benfield Commons pops to mind. He sees Billy screwing up his face to look like some celebrity or making a joke about how fucked up their lives are. He can't imagine him pulling out a gun and killing two people in their sleep.

Barry takes out a stick of gum and shoves it into his mouth. "Sometimes you draw a pair of aces," he says. "And sometimes you draw a pair of twos."

"What the hell does that mean?"

"It means, who can say why we do the things we do?"

"That's the dumbest thing I've ever heard." Then she says, "I don't think we should go to Las Vegas with your father's money."

If the car weren't still in sight of his family, he'd slam the brakes and pull over. "What the hell are you talking about?"

"If we lose it all, we'll be—"

"If we lose it, we're back where we started. Exactly." He can hear her taking short, cowardly breaths. He spits hot air. "Why are you changing your mind all of a sudden?"

More stewing. He hates this. She says, "Do you know what you want to do with your life, Barry?"

So this is where the conversation is going. "I'm thinking hired assassin."

"I'm being serious."

"Or the pope."

"Please."

"Or a financial planner."

"Nevermind," she says. "Forget I said anything."

His life would be a lot easier if she weren't like this. "You're looking at things all wrong," he says. "Try to picture what it will mean if we win. Fill your head with images of the two of us cashing in for a quarter million dollars. You could go to medical school without it costing you a dime of real money." He puts his hand on her thigh. "And I can get you a diamond engagement ring."

"We probably *won't* win, though."

Warm air from the car's heater curls up under his jacket, suffocating him. "You don't know that. Why shouldn't I catch a break for once?" He sees himself winning at blackjack, beating his chest.

"I don't think it works that way."

"You don't know how *it* works.

"I got myself into college, and it was really—"

"You don't know shit. You're a waitress."

"Barry." He feels her turn to face him.

Trying to force himself to be calm—there's still business to attend to—he says, "I shouldn't have said that."

She grips the dashboard with both hands.

The sound of the wind whistling through the window stops for a moment, then starts again.

Later, in the kitchen, Barry chews a salty meatball and tries to avoid looking his mother in the eye. Janine is holding a glass of Three Wishes Chardonnay, a cheap wine they picked up at the gas station before returning to the house.

"It was a good service." His mother is eating meat on a stick. "Rabbi Kaufman is wonderful. I think I'm going to start going to temple again."

Kaufman seemed arrogant to Barry. He could see it in his eyes when they shook hands after the service. "That's a good idea, Ma," he says. "A little spirituality in life goes a long way. Don't you think, honey?"

Janine takes a sip of her wine. After a beat she says, "What do I care? Remember, I'm just a waitress." And walks out of the room.

So the fight isn't over. Great. "She's on her period, Ma. You know what that's like."

His mother bursts out laughing. Then she puts her glass down and, to Barry's surprise, embraces him. He hesitates, but then wraps his arms around her. He wants to squeeze tighter and make the last five or so years evaporate.

"Please leave first thing tomorrow," she whispers. "Out of respect for your father."

He pulls free. "Sure, Ma. Whatever you want." He holds up his glass. "Love you too."

But she's already ambling toward the other side of the room to talk to one of her friends.


Mark is sitting at the dining table, thumbing through a photo album. Pictures of him from little league, high school graduation, and college make the walls of the room a shrine.

Barry pulls up a chair. "Hey, brother. How are you?"

Mark's skin looks blotchy and his breath reeks of coffee. "I've been better."

"I hear you."

"I was thinking of what dad was like when we were really young. Do you remember any of that?"

He recalls a baggy mailman's uniform coming in the door at night and watching television, but nothing else. "Sure. Lots of great memories."

Barry can't tell if Mark has heard him or not; he seems lost in his reverie. "There was this time he took us down to Nelson's Pond to teach us to swim," Mark says. "I was eleven and you were five. It was April or May, I think, and the water was so cold. He stripped down to his underwear and said, 'The only way to do this is to dive right in.' I think he was trying to teach us a lesson. He took a running start and *pow*. He came out cursing like a sailor. *Shit. Fuck. Shit!* We were giggling, and he wrapped a towel around himself and then started rolling around on the ground. *To hell with this*, he said and took us for ice cream."

Barry can't remember that day, but he does remember that Mark was the one who got the grades, who looked good in cleats, who took the pretty girl to the prom; his brother was the one who inherited the money to pay for his grad school loans. "Dad was okay," he says.

"He did his best."

Barry edges next to his brother. "What are you looking at there?"

"My Bar Mitzvah pics."

"Oh yeah? Lemme see."

"Dad was drunk. Look at this one."

It's his father leaning back in a folding chair, glassy-eyed. "Can't say I'm surprised."

Mark puts his finger on one of the photos. "There you are."

"I look very tiny in that suit."

"You always were the cute one."

"I *was* adorable."

"You still are." Mark looks up and studies Barry carefully. "I mean, your eyes are bloodshot and you're a little worse for wear, but you still have something."

Is his brother lecturing him about drinking? If that continues, he'll lose it. "I know. I'm planning to take better care of myself."

"Oh yeah?"

"I'm gonna try."

"That's great," he says without enthusiasm. "Good for you."

Barry decides it's time for his pitch. Get in quick, get out; he doesn't need to see these people ever again. "I'm thinking of making a lot of changes in my life. Janine has really helped me with all of that."

"She seems great."

"The thing is, I want to go to college and there's this technical program at UCLA that would be perfect for me." This is plausible; Barry was always good at math. It was the one subject he excelled in more than his brother.

"Great. Go for it."

Barry tries to affect a hangdog look. "Well, you know. It's difficult, though."

"What's difficult? Get your college education. Make something of yourself." He sounds like the man of the family already.

"You don't make college money working as a busboy."

"Get a better job, then."

"That's exactly why I want to go back to school." Barry steadies his pulse. "Mom told me Dad left you some money."

Mark delicately closes the photo album. "Yeah, he did."

"Maybe you could split it with me. Or make it a loan. I mean—"

"No, man. That's not gonna happen."

From the wary look on Mark's face, Barry understands his brother is unlikely to bend. But Barry is pot committed at this point. He's all in. "I know you have every reason to doubt me, but you said yourself that you wanted me to finish college. Please, I'm asking you for help."

Mark rubs his hand over the cover of the photo album. "You're something, you know that?"

"What do you mean? I'm asking for a little favor."

"Do you think Dad would want you to have that money?"

He knows the answer but says, "If he saw that I was honestly trying to change."

"Uh huh. Sure."

"You don't know."

"Dad and I understood each other. We had a special bond."

"Yes, but we—"

"And you don't take responsibility for a damn thing."

Barry becomes aware of the tiny hairs on the back of his forearms standing straight up. He remembers these arguments with Mark; it feels good to be back in the rhythm of one. He stands and again takes in all the photos of his brother. "Vanessa told me about your little problem," he says, smirking.

Mark blinks. "What?"

"Yeah. She told me. That must be tough."

Mark takes a deep breath; his whole body expands as he rises from his chair. "You can mock me about anything you want, but not about that."

"Is that right?"

"If you say another word, I'll fucking kill you."

Barry holds as still as he can as rage bubbles toward the surface of his chest. As he cracks open his lips to make another snide comment, Mark punches him. A screaming metallic pain shoots through his skull. And then he blacks out.


An hour later, Barry is sitting by himself in the dining room icing his jaw when Janine enters. Her nose is pink and chafed, but her eyes are clear. She crosses her arms. "I've had enough of this."

"What do you mean? There's still lox and bagels."

"Barry, I'm not in the mood for your—"

"Mark sucker punched me."

"I'm sorry. I heard." She shakes her head. She looks sadder than he's ever seen her.

He clenches his fist. "You found out there's not going to be money, right?"

"Barry."

"What?"

She heaves a sigh. "I called a car. It's taking me to the train station."

He stands and she retreats two steps toward the hall, but then stops; they make eye contact. He realizes that if she goes, he'll be back to square one, alone and broke. Small. He needs her, even if it means he has to hand her his balls. He takes short, quick breaths and, trying to sound reassuring, says, "I said some things, you said some things. But you don't have to leave." He offers his hand. "Don't go," he says quietly.

She hesitates, but then says, "It was a mistake coming here with you. All of this has been a mistake."

He moves toward her. She throws her hands up to protect herself. He sees that she's actually afraid of him. But he would never hurt her; people assume he's a bad guy because of what happened a year ago. In a flickering instant, he knows the reason he didn't go into the house that night: Billy had a crazy look in his eyes. He'd actually said, *I'm dying to feel alive, man.* Billy was always saying things like that just before he did something terrible. Barry wouldn't have been able to stop him that night no matter what, so he'd done the smart thing—run. Why couldn't people see that he wasn't Billy?

"I'm sorry," he says. For once, he means it.

She unclenches. "Thanks for that." Then she turns and, with her back to him, says, "Have a nice life."

He hears the front door creak open, then gradually close.

He's setting up his sleeping bag and a pillow on the basement floor just before midnight. The room is cluttered with boxes of papers and other paraphernalia from his father's working days. The bulkhead door rattles as the wind tries to bust through. He settles down on his back; the floor is icy, and he shudders.

There are footsteps on the stairs. Maybe Mark's had a

change of heart; blood is thicker than water and all that. He laughs to himself because it's a ridiculous thought.

"Knock knock." Vanessa flicks on the lights. She's wearing baggy shorts and a Taylor Swift T-shirt. She wraps her arms around herself to keep warm. "It's drafty down here."

"I know. I'll probably catch my death."

"Do you have enough blankets?"

"Yeah. I'm fine."

A tense silence fills the room.

Barry points. "Are you going to stand there looking cold or are you coming in?"

There's a folding metal chair pushed against the wall. A plume of dust shoots into the air as she drags it closer and sits. "Mark told me what happened."

"What can you do? I'll be fine."

"I tried to convince him to give you a little something, I wanted you to know that. It's only fair."

He takes this in. "You're always nice to me."

"I'm sorry Mark is so stubborn."

"He's like my father."

"Hmm." The wind thumps willfully against the bulkhead door, like ghosts are trying to break in. "I always thought you were the one more like your dad."

Barry considers this, but then decides she's wrong. "No. We hated each other. He loved Mark."

He sees her struggling to find the right words. "There's no point in arguing about all that now."

Barry sits up. "Did you come down here to cheer me up? Is that what this is?"

"I'm sorry about Janine too."

"It's okay."

She smiles; it doesn't even look like she feels sorry for him.

"We're getting an early start in the morning, so I wanted to say goodbye."

He suddenly feels stupid in his sleeping bag, like a child at a sleepover. He says, "Eager to get back to Texas?"

"It's kind of lousy, to be honest." Vanessa is picking at one of her fingernails and seems distracted. She's got something on her mind besides goodbyes.

He decides to cut through the bull. "Are you really happy with my brother?"

"I love Mark," she says. "He's reliable and caring."

"Sounds like some real passion there."

She bristles. "Stop it, will you?"

He plays with the zipper on the sleeping bag, down then up then down again. "I'm sorry."

"That's okay." She slides off the chair and sits at his feet. He retracts his legs to give her room. "You could make it up to me...God that sounds cheesy."

"What are you talking about?"

She slides closer. "You know what I want."

"Do I?"

"Don't be like this. Come on."

He hesitates. This is a chance to fuck his brother's wife and get some retribution, but if he does this won't he always be the kind of person his family thinks he is?

His jacket is sitting on the couch near his sleeping bag. He reaches into the pocket, pulls out a deck of cards, and puts them down in front of Vanessa.

She tilts her head to the side, curious. "What are these for?"

"I'll tell you what." He taps the deck. "If you cut a red card, I'll have sex with you. But if it's a black card, you head back upstairs, and we'll never mention this to anyone. What do you think?"

She looks at the playing cards for a moment and then up at

him. "I don't like to leave my fate to chance." She looks vulnerable. "I want to be a mother."

"Jesus," Barry says.

Another gust of wind bangs against the bulkhead door; it's nearly winter. Soon the earth will freeze over, trapping his father's bones underground. The door shudders and flies open, and a single red leaf flutters into the room, then quickly settles down on the floor. Nothing ever works the way it's supposed to. He flips backwards out of the sleeping bag and picks up the leaf to toss it outside. He pauses and studies the delicate veins and the worn, jagged edges; it disintegrates as he tries to enclose it in his hand. He shuts the door and jams one of his father's old boxes against it to keep it from opening again.

When he returns to his sleeping bag, Vanessa has already cut the cards.

# DECEMBER 3, 2013

**B**illy ran as fast as he could, but the bag he'd filled at the Blythe's house slowed him down. He collided with a barren willow tree, fell backwards, and landed on his ass. He checked his forehead—no blood—and got himself to his feet. Woozy still, he stumbled forward. The ground was hard and slippery. Above him, an owl hooted. Running again, Billy blinked, trying to see in the dark. Images from the Blythe's home ran like a movie in his mind; maybe he should bang into a few more trees and knock the pictures out of his head.

He slipped, this time landing on all fours, and when he looked up he saw that he was at the edge of the narrow stretch of beach at the south end of Nelson's Pond. Still breathless, he brushed himself off and took a hesitant step onto the sand. There was a rowboat bobbing on the wooden dock even though it was December; he imagined jumping into it and escaping across the water. Then, with his hands on his knees, he realized he'd just end up on the other side of the pond. Still in Benfield. It wasn't Mexico over there—a land where he could disappear into another life. He rubbed his neck and clenched his eyes shut.

*Maybe he could fall asleep right here and never wake up. That would be the perfect solution; he could evaporate into a puffy dream and float up into the atmosphere. They would think he'd escaped and would be upset at how unfair it was. And it would be unfair, but what did fairness have to do with anything? When, for example, had he ever caught a break? His fantasy was interrupted by the sound of a gun being fired and a dog barking, and his eyes opened wide and he looked around. The sounds had come from inside his head. He put his fists against his skull and let loose a high-pitched scream. Still, he staggered forward again. Maybe he should come up with a plan. Yes, clear his head and think what to do before the sun rises over the trees.*

*By now he was standing ankle deep in the pond. There were chunks of ice floating near the shore, but it had been an unusually warm winter so far and most of the pond hadn't yet frozen over. He remembered learning about gaseous and liquid states in Mr. Nasisse's ninth grade class. His chemistry teacher, a thin man who smoked too much, somehow saw potential in Billy. He said to him once, "You have a real knack for analyzing things. That can take you far in the world if you let it." That was before Billy's life had changed.*

*His feet were getting numb, but he didn't move. He was tired. Then, feeling his shoulders slump, he gave up.*

*They'll find me and see that I'm remorseful, he thought. They'll see that I didn't mean it.*

*And so he stared out at the water and waited.*

*It's so small, this pond—he'd never realized how small until today. A person could sprint across the ice during a normal winter and not even get tired. A shaft of light cut through the trees as the moon began to vanish back over the horizon, illuminating a cereal box that sat on the shore, ripped, wet. Shivering chickadees hopped in and out of it. Billy dropped his flashlight into the pond. It flickered and went out before vanishing. The* water lapped gently. A shadow crept overhead—it is a god, he thought, moving over the water, snuffing out the moonlight, coming for him. A breeze kicked up a prayer and he strained to make out the words.

Please, he thought. Please.

Then the sun crept over the trees, and Billy knew his life was over.

# DECEMBER 2014

## THE BLUES INSIDE

Sam stops at the Sunoco halfway across town to fill her tank. The ancient Toyota Corolla is still three-quarters full, but she wants to take a moment to gather her thoughts before driving on to Amanda's house. Just past five o'clock, it's already frigid and pitch black. As Sam pumps gas, she notices a middle-aged woman bundled in a heavy, black winter parka staring at her from inside the convenience store attached to the station. It's not uncommon for strangers to recognize her; most have seen her picture in the local newspapers or online over the last year. There's an urgency to the way the woman walks toward her, and Sam knows she'll want to talk about the murders.

"I'm sorry to bother you." Her hair is tucked into the hood of her parka. Thick eyeliner and red lipstick make her look slightly clownish under the glaring pump lights. "You're Samantha Blythe, right?

"Yes."

"Ah, I thought so. Do you remember me? I was in your shop

about a month ago." Sam owns and operates Samantha's Beauties Hair Salon in Benfield Commons.

"Sorry, no."

"The young girl did my hair. The pretty one." She means Amanda.

The woman pulls her hood down, as if revealing her curly hair will magically spark some recognition in Sam. But it's hopeless. Each day has become a replay of the last, like a television program with only one episode: dressing in the morning, driving to work, cutting hair, eating lunch, cutting more hair, driving home, dinner, watching television, sleeping. She's become a robot version of herself, efficient and mindless.

"Ah, of course, yes." Lies usually make these conversations easier. "I remember now. I'm sorry, it's been really difficult to concentrate lately."

"It must be, you poor dear. That was such a terrible thing that happened to your parents."

These people don't care about Sam, she's learned that much; all they want is to prod her for salacious details. "I'm fine, actually, I really am."

"Just be careful you don't imagine you're better off than you are. Recovery can take a long time. My mother passed two years ago, and I still think about her all the time."

"That's awful."

"You're lucky to own that little shop of yours. Customers coming and going. People are a comfort in times like these." Sam wants to change the subject and since Amanda was the stylist who cut the woman's hair, Sam asks if she's seen her lately.

"No, I haven't." She flutters her lashes with concern. "Is she okay?"

"She hasn't shown up at work for a few days." It's actually

been a week. "But I'm sure everything is fine. You know how young people are."

"Yes, I do." The woman wipes her nose. "My daughter's a sophomore at Tufts, and if she doesn't call me every week, I start to think about bringing in the National Guard. You gotta take the good with the bad." She exhales a joyful puff of cold air. "That's what it's all about."

Sam finds this kind of parental banter difficult; it reminds her that, at age thirty-seven, she doesn't have a child of her own. Over the past few years, she and Carlton had finally been having serious discussions about starting a family; her parents' murder had changed all that. She couldn't imagine bringing a child into the world. Her separation last February has made having a child seem even less likely.

Still, she imagines saying to the woman, *My own daughter, Amanda, is going through a difficult phase. She's dating some angry kid with a motorcycle and a scar and she just can't seem to land on a career. Don't get me wrong, I love that I have her all to myself at the salon. She's a delight and she's funny, smart and considerate. I hope I can get through to her. You know how it is; the last person they want to hear from is their own mother.* Instead, she says, "I'm sure you're right about all that." She pulls the pump out of the gas tank and replaces the cap. "It was great to talk to you, but I really should get going."

"Oh, of course." The woman pulls her hood back over her head. "I'm sorry I interrupted you. I just wanted to wish you the best."

Melancholy seeps like a heavy syrup into Sam's chest. If only she could get a decent night's sleep. "Thank you."


Amanda's house is not what Sam expects. A loose board hangs from an upper window and occasionally clatters against the side of the house; the gray-green paint is chipped and peeling; many of the asphalt roof shingles are missing or twisted awkwardly. Amanda had talked about her home as if she lived in a tiny mansion. *Sometimes I hide from my parents in the attic and they have no clue where I am.* She'd claimed both of her parents were doctors who cared more about their careers than their only offspring. This is not the house of a doctor, let alone two.

Sam tries the doorbell; it's the sound of a hammer striking a gong and it's surprisingly loud. When she doesn't hear anyone stirring inside, she knocks. The wood clatters and feels hollow against her fist. After a moment, she knocks again. There's a rough shuffling behind the door and then, finally, it opens. A tall, lanky man wearing a loose-fitting flannel shirt, wrinkled jeans, and a beat-up Bruins hat appears. A bony tabby cat curls between his feet.

"I'm sorry to bother you. I'm Sam Blythe. Amanda's boss down at the salon?" He blinks a few times and Sam expects a reply, but even the half-smoked cigarette dangling from his thin lower lip doesn't wobble. "I was wondering if I could talk to your daughter."

He clears what can only be a hockey puck out of his throat, then removes the cigarette from his lips and flicks it over Sam's shoulder. "She hasn't been home in a while." He can't quite hide his worn-out teeth when he speaks, but his voice sounds surprisingly refined, like he's the family butler.

Sam digs her fingers into her palm. "So she's just missing?"

"I guess you could put it that way."

"Has she disappeared like this before?"

"She comes and goes as she likes." He rubs his hands together, fending off the cold. "She's got a good head on her shoulders, so I don't worry much." No wonder Amanda made up stories. If Sam had paid better attention—if her mind had been clearer—would the lies have been obvious? Sam knew what it meant to have unstable, self-absorbed parents. It got so bad once that her older sister, Shelby, had nearly dropped out of high school to run away with a drug-addled drummer named Phil. Their plan was to roam the country like a couple of coyotes, with no particular purpose in mind. Sam isn't sure what exactly prevented Shelby from taking that plunge, but she does remember a conversation she'd had with her sister. Sam had said, "Don't do anything you think Mom and Dad would do." Even at eight years old, Sam had played mother to her older sister; it had made her proud at the time.

"Do you know any places Amanda likes to hang out?" Sam asked.

"No."

"Any friends she might be staying with?"

"Nope."

Sam takes a long breath. "Any chance I can talk to your wife for a second?"

With shaky hands, he pulls a fresh cigarette out of his jeans' pocket and tosses it between his lips. "I haven't seen that woman in two years."

Sam's stomach clutches. Poor Amanda. "I'm really sorry to hear that."

"Good riddance and good luck to her. You know what I mean?"

"Well..." Sam nods. "If your daughter calls, please tell her to get in touch with me. Her job is still there if she wants it."

She turns to leave, but he clears his throat again. "Amanda's got a mind of her own." He bends to pick up the cat. It meows a protest as he folds it into his chest. "If she wants to get in touch with you, she will."

Sam stands in the cold as he slams the creaky door.

That night, as she sips a glass of white wine, Sam browses through photos of Amanda on her phone. The girl's dark, thick hair swirls halfway down her back; it's the envy of every woman who comes into the shop. Sam looks closely at one picture that she'd taken at a work party a few months back. In it, Amanda stares absently out the window, her face in profile, still and yet deeply troubled. Sam should have seen. She should have asked more questions. She should have prompted her to talk to her friends: *My boss said I should think about college. My boss said I should get out of Benfield.*

In another picture, Amanda is sticking her tongue out at the camera and winking; it was one of the girl's favorite poses. To hell with Amanda's father, Sam thinks. There's love in these photos, Sam's sure of it. The girl would be happy to hear from her old boss.

She carries her wine into the living room and puts it down on the side table next to the leather couch. Gently, she pulls a cardboard box of photos off the wood-stained corner shelf and plops them on the floor. The cardboard is soft from age and gives off an acrid smell. She pulls it open; black and white photos, Polaroids, and color snapshots are stacked in haphazard piles. She hasn't looked at any of them since retrieving the box from her parents' house back in January.

There's a Polaroid of her parents in their early twenties. Her father has his arm around her mother and they're both beaming; they're gorgeous lovers, like Hollywood stars posing on the red carpet. The next photo is a snapshot taken at an amusement park. Sam and her parents are waiting in line for the Ferris wheel, carefree smiles lighting up their faces. Sam feels a twinge of nostalgia, then remembers that the picture had been taken the day after her older sister's final knock-down drag-out with her parents; Shelby had left home that night. The amusement park had been her parents' way of making Sam feel like everything was still normal. Now, for the life of her, Sam can't remember what the fight had been about. Sam closes the box. The voice of Amanda's father echoes in her ear: *If she wants to get in touch with you, she* will. Maybe it just doesn't take that much for a girl to walk away from her family. Defeated, Sam puts the box back on the shelf.

In the morning, as she's dressing for work, Sam happens to glance through the living room window and sees a boy bundled up against the cold, pacing around the perimeter of his back yard. He and his family had moved in a few years back and Sam still hadn't met them. The boy moves slowly along the wire fence, turning left when he hits each corner and then continuing. The hood of his coat is pulled tightly around his head, hiding his face, but she can see his breath puffing into the air like a train engine as he plods around the yard. She's seen him doing this before and wonders for the first time what he's up to.

When she's finished putting on her makeup, Sam peers through the window to check on the boy's progress. The back yard is empty now.

At work later that day, in the middle of coloring Sheila Kobliska's hair, Sam sees Amanda's Ford Mustang cruise by. She rushes outside in time to see the car turn onto Old Pond Road and then vanish. Sam texts Amanda, "I think I just saw you!" Amanda doesn't reply, and suddenly Sam isn't sure if the car was even the right shade of blue. Confused, she reenters her shop. Colleen, busy giving a rare male client a quick trim, asks if everything is okay.

"I thought I saw Amanda's car." Sam adjusts her blouse. "Maybe I was dreaming."

Colleen snips the man's silver-brown hair. "Maybe you were." She smiles sympathetically.

Sam returns to Mrs. Kobliska. She works diligently but can't stop thinking about Amanda.

Colleen, her longest tenured employee, can read her mind. "You really shouldn't worry about that girl."

"And why's that?" She knows the answer; they've had this conversation several times already in the last few days.

"People come and go in the world, young lady." She is only two years older than Sam, but insists on this term of affection. She snaps her scissors three times quickly. "We can't control them, though. We can only control ourselves. Am I right, Todd?"

Todd, her client, looks up at her in the mirror, surprised. "Ah...Absolutely," he says.

Colleen isn't finished. "If you spend too much time trying to fix other people, you'll end up losing track of the only person you can really help."

Sam chit-chats with clients to gossip about the town or the latest TV show, but Colleen has fashioned herself into an armchair therapist. The clients love her for it; Sam, however, finds her prescriptions simplistic. "Maybe you should take your own advice and let me do my own worrying."

Colleen takes this reprimand as playful banter and says, "I would if you weren't such a lost little puppy."

Sam's spirit animal, to the extent she buys into such nonsense, has always been a lioness. Protective. Powerful. A hunter with piercing eyes and razor teeth. Colleen's assessment hurts her. "What makes you say that?"

"Well..." She stops cutting Todd's hair to consider the question. "You have the blues inside you." She says it like sadness is a disease. "That's a terrible thing for anyone."

Sam squeezes her fingers into her palm again; this time it feels like she'll rip a hole right through her hand. "Don't worry,

I'm not going to kill myself if I can't find Amanda." Sam makes eye contact with Colleen in the mirror: enough is enough.

Colleen quickly looks away. "Well, good for you. I'm glad to hear it."

Sam takes a deep breath and gets Mrs. Kobliska's attention. "I'm going into the back room. You'll be ready for your rinse in thirty minutes."

Mrs. Kobliska turns the page of her magazine. "No problem."

Sam retreats to her office, plops down on her creaky office chair, and looks at the pictures of Amanda on her phone again. In one, Amanda has her arm wrapped around a stringy-haired girl about the same age. This other girl is wearing a CVS uniform—a red top and khakis—and a nametag. Looking closely, Sam can just make out the name: *Tanya*. Sam recalls the girl coming in during her lunch break now and again and palling around with Amanda. Inspired, Sam throws on her parka and runs back into the salon.

"I'll be back in twenty minutes," she says to Colleen. "Don't burn the place down."

"I'll do my best," Colleen says.


The CVS parking lot, about a mile up the street, is half-full. From inside her car, Sam stares at the store entrance and wonders if Colleen is right—should she mind her own business? Is she being obsessive? But no, she thinks, this is important. It's a chance to help a girl who obviously needs it. She wishes there had been someone to mentor her when she was in her twenties. Maybe she would have finished college; she'd had an interest in the law back then.

The air inside the CVS is damp, the carpeting at the entrance is wet and muddy, and the fluorescent lights flicker too brightly. Remembering little about Tanya except that she seemed skittish around adults, Sam decides that running into her will have to seem coincidental or else she'll scare the girl away. She hurries down the oral hygiene aisle and pretends she's trying to pick out the ideal toothpaste. She holds up one package. What's better for sensitive teeth, generic or brand-name? Feeling ridiculous, she puts the toothpaste back on the shelf and begins strolling through the aisles one by one. She only has a few minutes before she has to get back to the salon and contend with Mrs. Kobliska's hair. A pair of twenty-something boys, leaning against a hand truck stacked with peanut brittle, chat in the snack aisle. Sam resists the urge to ask if Tanya is working today; they'll certainly let Tanya know later on that Sam was asking for her, which might scare her off.

In the last aisle there's a girl sitting on a crate putting allergy medicine on the shelf; her hair is mostly covered with a flower-print bandana. She looks vulnerable and pretty.

Sam picks up a bottle of aspirin and begins reading the packaging. Then, as casually as she can, she approaches. "Tanya?"

The girl looks up. "Yeah?"

"You're Amanda's friend, right?"

Her eyes narrow defensively. "Yeah?"

This isn't going to be easy. "You remember me from the salon?" Tanya shrugs. Aren't they supposed to grow out of teen angst? "Funny to run into you here."

"Yeah. It's truly hilarious."

Sam pauses; she can't bullshit this girl. "All right, you got me. I was looking for you. Amanda hasn't shown up for work in a week, and I'm trying to find her."

"Why, exactly, are you doing that?"

Sam isn't sure she has an adequate answer. "Just to, you know...Make sure everything is okay."

There's a lightning bolt of red in the girl's dark eyes that makes Sam think she knows something. "She doesn't need help."

"You know where she is?" Sam kneels.

Tanya defiantly juts her jaw. "No. I don't."

The girl is painfully thin. "I'll buy you dinner if you'll have a quick talk with me."

Tanya bites her lower lip, and Sam thinks she's found a soft spot. But the girl says, "If you want to buy me some food, that's your problem. But I won't be able to help you."

"Great." It's progress. She can worry about beating down the girl's defenses later. "Meet me at the Benfield Diner tonight at seven." She waits for a reply. "Does that sound okay?"

"I said *fine*."

Sam's aware that Tanya had not, in fact, said anything resembling "fine," but stiffens her own expression to make sure she doesn't look annoyed. "Great. I can't wait."

In the car, Sam closes her eyes to stop herself from tearing up; Tanya reminds her of her sister. Almost ten years older, Shelby had borne the brunt of their parents' selfishness over the years and it had turned her angry and self-destructive. After the funeral, Sam had promised to call Shelby every week to check in on her, but never did; she didn't have it in her to sit and listen to Shelby's inevitable rants about the murderer, their parents, or the horrors of dating. Sam no longer felt proud she could mother her sister and resented feeling like their roles in the family had always been reversed. Wasn't the older sister supposed to watch out for the younger one?

At the diner, she finds a booth near the window. The restaurant is crowded and a little overwhelming. Taking a deep breath, she runs her fingertips over the surface of the table. It's smooth but sticky in places. She surveys the glass cases across the room filled with desserts: Boston cream and lemon meringue pies, chocolate pudding, carrot cake. She hasn't eaten anything that sweet since she'd wolfed down a box of Oreos an hour before her parents' funeral. Closing her eyes, she takes in the smells: something greasy frying on the grill, a whiff of ammonia. The sounds: a blur of voices interrupted by bursts of laughter, the low hum of the television over the counter, the light footsteps of the wait staff.

"Sam?"

She hears someone approaching and opens her eyes, expecting it to be Tanya, but it's only the waitress—an older woman wearing a blue Benfield diner uniform with thin white stripes. It takes Sam a moment to realize she knows the woman. It's Evelyn, her parents' closest friend. She'd visited on all their birthdays, opened presents with the family on Christmas morning. Sam had never been close to her but understood why her parents had liked her so much: The Blythe house had always been loud and chaotic, while Evelyn radiated a sense of calm. She'd simply absorbed the children's tantrums, the couple's arguments, Pete's rages, Tara's crying jags, their affairs, threatened break-ups, and over-the-top reconciliations.

"Hi, Evelyn, how are you?"

Evelyn pushes a pencil behind her ear. "I'm okay, Sam. But how are you?"

Sam's heard this question a million times, but Evelyn is the first person who really seems to want an answer. "You know how it is. I'm hanging in there."

"Yeah, me too. I miss them."

"I do too." The truth is, her relationship with her parents feels unresolved. She'd visited them for Thanksgiving dinner a few weeks before the murder and the conversation had been awkward and strained—enemies tiptoeing through a minefield

—but she's glad she'd accepted their invitation. It had seemed like a new kind of relationship would be possible. But now they were gone, killed because some kid thought they were rich. If he'd known the way they squandered money on shiny cars and expensive clothes, they would still be alive.

"I didn't know you were working here," she says. "It's great to see you." She's embarrassed to realize she can't recall what Evelyn used to do. Something to do with books? "Did you leave your other job?"

"I retired, yes. But I just got restless being at home all the time."

"You should do some traveling." Sam can't imagine mustering the energy to get on an airplane and spend her days walking around unfamiliar streets or ancient ruins but remembers that this is what people are supposed to suggest during this sort of conversation. "You really should see the world."

Evelyn hesitates. "Travel isn't for me, I'm afraid. I tried a little bit of wandering but, after a while, I figured out that Benfield is home."

To Sam, Benfield has been more like a gravitational force that has held her in place her entire life. She nervously drums her fingers on the table. "I'm never leaving either."

"I'm glad," Evelyn says.

Sam forces herself to smile in response. She can't see her own face, but she imagines it must look terribly strained. She wonders how people don't burst out laughing when they see the way she contorts her facial muscles in an effort to appear pleasant. An awkward break in the conversation follows until Sam realizes what Evelyn is waiting for.

"Can I just get a coffee for now? I'm expecting a friend."

Evelyn wipes her hand on her apron and turns her head to look out the window; it seems like she is about to say something but changes her mind. Most likely she wants to tell Sam that she's too young to give up on life, or some other bit of trite advice like that—the kind of advice she had been getting from her clients. Sam hopes she'll just leave her alone. Finally, Evelyn says, "Wonderful. Friends are a blessing." She pockets her notepad. "One coffee coming up."

A few minutes pass. Sam does her best not to think about Amanda. Where she might be. If she's okay. But the moment Evelyn drops off the coffee, Sam checks her phone. Nothing from Tanya. Sam presses her face against the window. Outside, snowflakes, looking like moths in summer, flicker past the parking lot lights.

"You went through that pretty fast." It's Evelyn again. Sam looks at her empty cup. She doesn't even remember drinking the stuff, but she feels the caffeine beginning to crawl through her bloodstream. Evelyn holds up the coffee pot. "Do you want another?"

"Sure."

Evelyn pours. "Looks like snow."

"Just flurries, though."

"It's so pretty."

Sam imagines a snowflake landing on her face. "It is." She feels the imprint on her cheek as Evelyn walks away. The last time they'd seen each other was at the funeral. Evelyn had given a short, moving eulogy, calling Sam's parents the "strongest people anyone has ever known." Sam wondered what she meant by that, but she liked that Evelyn hadn't called them "glamorous" or some variation of that word as so many others had when offering condolences. Sam remembers one line. "I hate that they were deprived of their final act, because I think it was going to be magnificent."

When Sam's nearly done with the next cup, she checks the time on her phone. She's been waiting for Tanya for over an hour. Exhaling, she accepts that the girl isn't coming. She finishes her coffee and leans back in the booth. She feels heavy; it's as though she's wearing thirty winter parkas.

"You want another refill?" Evelyn is standing over her yet again.

"If I drink another drop I won't sleep at all tonight." She tries a playful grin.

"Can I get you anything else then?"

"No. I think that'll cover it. I'll take the check."

Evelyn smiles sweetly. "I'm sorry your friend didn't show up."

"That's okay," Sam says. "These things happen." She hopes that will put an end to their conversation.

Evelyn taps her pencil against her pad. "How's Shelby?" she asks. "Is she doing all right?"

Sam tenses. "I'm not really sure."

"I hope she's doing okay," Evelyn says. "That girl deserves good things in her life."

Sam lets her hand rest lightly on the table. She feels ashamed again that she hasn't called her sister in...how many months? But the truth was, they lived in the same town and hadn't shared more than a cup of coffee and a few minutes of small talk in over a decade. Had they ever been close?

"I'll find out and report back," Sam says.

"That would be great." She tears the check out of her pad and puts it down on the table.


The flurries have become a snowstorm and the roads are slippery. The wipers squeak. It's been a strange day, Sam thinks, and as she pulls onto Alderwood Drive, there's something heartening about seeing her home through the haze of snow and trees. She eases the Corolla into the driveway. The sound of snow crunching tires, the car engine whirring and then sputtering, the wind. After heating up some leftover chicken stew, she sits in the living room listening to the wind fling ice against the window. The television, which usually acts as an analgesic, doesn't tempt her. She checks her phone and sees a text from Carlton. "Want to meet for coffee?" She has to give him credit for this much: He's persistent. But he'll want to talk about getting back together, healing old wounds, having children. How can she move forward when she can't even talk to her own sister about the murders? She puts the phone in a drawer.

As she turns, thinking she might just go to bed and put the whole day behind her, Sam remembers the boy and rushes to the window. He's there again, alone, marching along the perimeter of his yard, lighting his way with a dim flashlight. For some reason Sam yearns to join him and, without thinking, puts on her coat and dashes outside. Cold air bites at her cheeks as she struggles against the wind to get around to the side of the house. Leaning against the chain-link fence that separates her property from her neighbor's, she watches him. He walks steadily, never breaking stride. He's worn away the snow and even much of the grass, leaving in its place a mud track. When he turns at the back of the yard and heads toward Sam, he stops.

"I'm your neighbor." She offers a weak wave. "I'm Samantha." She feels ridiculous; he's probably scared of her.

He turns the beam of his flashlight toward her. After a moment, he approaches and she can see his face for the first time. He's an Asian boy of about eleven or twelve; he has red, thick lips and a dark mole next to his nose.

"I'm Adam," he says, and extends his gloved hand. She offers hers and they shake, mitten to glove.

"Whatcha doing out here?"

"Walking."

"I can see that. Any particular reason?"

There's something too serious about the way he considers her question. "I don't know."

She looks past him to the beat-up yard. "You've done quite a job on your lawn."

"Yeah." He looks over his shoulder. "I guess I fucked up the grass pretty good." He puts his hand over his mouth and his eyes get wide.

"It's okay," Sam says. "You can swear. I don't mind." He's a good kid, she thinks. He wants to please her.

He looks relieved. "Sorry about that."

A plump woman appears in the back doorway of the house. "Adam?" Sam hears the tension in her voice and can picture what this looks like from her perspective—a strange woman talking to her twelve-year-old kid on a snowy, gloomy night.

"It's okay, Mom." The boy claps his hands together and blows into them. "She's our neighbor."

Sam waves, trying to seem nonchalant. "Hello there!"

"Oh, hello," the woman says. She has a slight accent. "Is everything okay, though?"

Adam smiles. He's patient with his mother. "Everything is great, Mom. Don't worry."

"Okay, good." She shivers. "But maybe you should come inside."

"I'll be right there." He turns back to Sam. "Yesterday," he whispers conspiratorially, "was my birthday."

"Happy birthday," Sam says.

"We have leftover chocolate cake. There's ice cream too." Sam sees where this is headed, but she's not in the mood to invade her neighbor's home. Before she can politely decline the invitation, however, the boy calls out to his mother. "She's coming in for some cake!"

"Oh, good," the boy's mother says, her voice sounding warm. "Yes, come inside already."

Sam begins to stumble through an excuse for why she can't go with him, but Adam insists. "Just come." He talks like someone who understands life already.

Sam can't resist him. "I do like cake."

"Who doesn't like cake?"

"Crazy people."

"Stupid people," he says.

She walks through the gate that separates their yards and follows Adam into the house.

Adam's father is thin and friendly. "I'm Kevin," he says. Sam introduces herself and looks around. The kitchen is bright and warm: yellow paint with beige, flowered curtains. Sam approaches a small shelf filled with tiny glass animals.

"That's Daisy's collection," the father says.

"I can't stop myself," the boy's mother says, cutting the cake.

Sam looks closely at the collection; they are all unicorns. "They're so beautiful."

"You can touch them," the boy's mother says. Did the father say her name was Daisy? Sam gets a mental picture of a flower sticking up out of the snow.

"I'd better not," Sam says. "I'm pretty clumsy."

Adam picks one up. "It's okay." He rests it in Sam's open palm. The figurine feels fragile in her hands. She looks more closely and notices how it reflects the light coming from the yellow bulb on the nearby shelf. She wants to swallow it; rays of light would shoot out from every pore in her body and she'd finally feel warm again.

"Cake is served," the mother says. Sam carefully places the glass unicorn back on the shelf.

Daisy puts a large helping of cake on Sam's plate.

Sam takes a bite. "Mmmm."

Daisy beams. "It's homemade!" She cuts a piece for the boy and then for the father.

The boy takes a bite of his. "This kicks ass."

Daisy stops cutting and waves the cake knife at her son. "Adam!"

"Sorry, mom. It slipped out."

She exhales. "No more of that, okay?"

"I promise. No more."

Sam watches Daisy cut a large piece of cake for herself and then, for a moment, there is nothing but the sound of chewing.

Sam remembers one of her birthday parties and her own mother cutting cake; theirs had been store-bought and a little stale, but no one complained. After the party, her father had gone out, leaving the rest of the family to clean up the mess. Back then, Sam's mother had been full of life—energetic, hopeful, angry, and in love. Now Sam, caught up in the blizzard that has been raging inside her since her parents were killed, longs for the warmth she felt every time her mother entered a room.

She decides to ask her sister if she feels that longing too.

# APRIL 2, 1965

He sidled up to her at the counter, ordered a coffee, and didn't say a word for ten minutes; he listened to her light breathing, felt the heat of her dazzling skin and hair. The Benfield Diner bustled with noise. "Daydream" was playing overhead.

She felt the heat too. She had on the low-cut dress her mother forbade her from wearing; it accentuated her curves and offset her dark brown hair.

"I'm Pete," he said finally.

"I'm Tara." She nodded at him and then shifted her focus back to her mug.

"You're a coffee drinker?" Pete asked.

"Sometimes."

Pete looked around. When he was sure no one was watching, he poured something from a silver flask into his coffee and then into hers. "Try that." He winked.

She took a sip; it burned her throat, but she swallowed it anyway so he wouldn't see that she didn't like it. "Thanks."

"You're welcome." He gripped his own mug. "What brings you in here?"

"I'm waiting for my friend, Evelyn."

Pete liked the way she talked; her words were round, and the cadence of her voice was melodic.

"What are you doing here?" Tara asked. She eyed his clothes; he wore a leather jacket and tight jeans.

"I like diners. This place seemed worth a visit."

"You're not from Benfield, are you?"

He shook his head. "I'm from New Haven. Just passing through."

"You're this close to Boston and you stop off at some diner in Benfield?"

He leaned closer. "People think diners are the same every-where, but they're not. Each one teaches you something about the people in the town."

"What does this one teach you?" She looked up at him.

His eyes sparkled. "I'm still figuring that out."

"No really. I mean it."

He swiveled on his stool to take in the restaurant. Everything looked new: red and silver stools, faux-leather booths. Even the linoleum floor shone, reflecting the overhead lights.

"See that guy over there?" He pointed to a large man alone in a booth sipping coffee. "He's on a business trip. And he's lonely."

"But hopeful," Tara added.

"If you say so."

"What else do you see?"

"That couple there. They've been married too long. Notice how they're not talking."

Tara watched them a moment. "Maybe they're just hungry," she said.

Pete swiveled back around to face Tara. "You have a funny way of seeing things."

Feeling overwhelmed, she looked away. He was more self-assured than any man she'd ever met.

He sipped his coffee as casually as he could manage; he didn't want her to see how nervous he felt. "So, what are you and this Evelyn getting up to tonight?"

"Nothing very exciting, I guess. We're going to see The Sound of Music."

"I heard that's good," Pete said.

Tara perked up. "You like movies?"

Pete hesitated. He really hadn't seen many. "I happen to think real life is more interesting."

Tara took a sip of coffee.

"Don't get me wrong," Pete continued. "There's nothing wrong with people who like movies."

"No, no. I understand." She thought about it for a moment. He was absolutely right. "Why watch life when you can live it. When I graduate from high school next year, I'm moving far away from Benfield."

"You're not going to move to New Haven, that's for sure. It would be too much for someone who looks like a princess."

She blushed. "Hey. I'm tough."

"There's lots of crime there."

"Really?"

"Yeah. This buddy of mine joined a gang when he was eighteen. Three years later, no one knows where he is."

"Oh my God." It was easy to picture Pete hanging with his friends on street corners, afraid of nothing.

"It's not so bad as long as you have eyes in the back of your head."

She leaned back so Pete could get a good look at her. "It's so boring here."

He opened his flask and poured another shot into Tara's mug. "Seems exciting to me."

She resisted a sudden desire to put her hand on his sleeve.

"I think it's important to treat life like an adventure," Pete said, his voice low. "Otherwise you feel dead inside."

"I think that too." She sipped her drink while she thought of something else to say. "What kind of adventures do you think you'll have in the future?"

He held his coffee mug from the edges with his fingertips, lifted it, and took a sip. "I want to travel across the United States and meet people. I'll work odd jobs, make enough to survive. Just live."

"That sounds wonderful." Tara pushed a strand of hair out of her eyes.

Pete leaned closer. "You're beautiful."

Just then, a ceiling light flickered and went out; both of their faces were covered in shadow. Tara looked around uneasily.

Pete held her hand. "Are you afraid of the dark?"

"Not at all." His hand on hers felt warm.

He handed her the flask and she drank straight from it. He took it back and did the same. The lights flickered back on just as he was tucking it back into his jacket pocket. They smiled conspiratorially. After a moment, they looked up and admired themselves in the mirror behind the counter—a young, attractive couple.

He shook his head. "If my friends ever saw me with you, they'd die."

"Really?" she said.

"They'd drop dead."

"Come on." She smiled without showing her teeth.

"I only speak the truth."

"I'm glad to hear that." She sipped her coffee and then

looked out the window into the parking lot. "I wonder where Evelyn is."

"You in a rush to get going?"

She turned; his eyes were the color of the sky at dusk. "I guess I don't mind sitting here for a while."

# ACKNOWLEDGMENTS

Claire Van Winkle, caring, generous, creative, and insisting on Oxford commas. Because love. Thank you for (gently) guiding me. For (always) believing I could get to the end. And for (sometimes) telling me my ideas were dumb. Also, thanks for knowing so much about grammar (and preventing me from using too many parentheses); my parents, Steven and Allene, for a lifetime of unconditional love and for convincing me that most things are possible with hard work; my sister Robin, who taught me most of what I know about will power.

Lisa Kastner, because starting a press to help people fulfill their dreams is generous, fearless, and bold. My editor, Benjamin White, supportive, steady, and clear-headed, who somehow notices that the thing on page 47 doesn't really work with the thing on page 138. Thank you both.

My writing teachers, Alice Elliot Dark, who gave me the tools, and the late Fred Hudson, who gave me the courage. My professors at the Queens College MFA program: Richard Schotter, Nicole Cooley, Wayne Moreland, Maaza Mengiste, Rhoda Sirlin, Kimiko Hahn, and Jeffrey Cassvan.

Anne Mironchik, my best friend. Thanks for everything.

My writing students. I learn from them every week while we have a load of laughs: Carmen Antreasian, Haran Peckney, and my close friend, Sarah Doudna.

Friends and colleagues: Felipe Ossa, who read an early

draft and gave me invaluable advice, Mark Goldblatt, Jacques Duvoisin, Jacob Appel, Sean O'Connor, and Charles Salzberg, the most generous writer in New York.

You. Because I'm absent-minded and forgot to mention you while I was putting this list together.

Running Wild Press publishes stories that cross genres with great stories and writing. RIZE publishes great genre stories written by people of color and by authors who identify with other marginalized groups. Our team consists of:

Lisa Diane Kastner, Founder and Executive Editor
Cody Sisco, Acquisitions Editor, RIZE
Benjamin White, Acquisition Editor, Running Wild
Peter A. Wright, Acquisition Editor, Running Wild
Resa Alboher, Editor
Angela Andrews, Editor
Sandra Bush, Editor
Ashley Crantas, Editor
Rebecca Dimyan, Editor
Abigail Efird, Editor
Aimee Hardy, Editor
Henry L. Herz, Editor
Cecilia Kennedy, Editor
Barbara Lockwood, Editor
Scott Schultz, Editor

Evangeline Estropia, Product Manager
Kimberly Ligutan, Product Manager
Lara Macaione, Marketing Director
Joelle Mitchell, Licensing and Strategy Lead
Pulp Art Studios, Cover Design
Standout Books, Interior Design
Polgarus Studios, Interior Design

Learn more about us and our stories at www.runningwild-press.com.

Loved this story and want more? Follow us at www.runningwildpress.com, www.facebook.com/runningwild press, on Twitter @lisadkastner @RunWildBooks